THE GLIMPSE

LIS BENSLEY

Matador
9 Priory Business Park,
Wistow Road, Kibworth Beauchamp,
Leicestershire. LE8 0RX
Tel: 0116 279 2299
Email: books@troubador.co.uk
Web: www.troubador.co.uk/matador
Twitter: @matadorbooks

ISBN 978 1800462 95 3

British Library Cataloguing in Publication Data.
A catalogue record for this book is available from the British Library.

Printed and bound in Great Britain by 4edge Limited
Typeset in 11pt Baskerville by Troubador Publishing Ltd, Leicester, UK

Matador is an imprint of Troubador Publishing Ltd

THE GLIMPSE

For David

The world of art is firmly established as an independent object; this makes it a picture.
Outside of it is the outer world.
Inside of it, the world of the artist.

- Hans Hofmann

ONE

Liza

(1951)

It seemed so simple, dark against light.

From the back of the studio, Liza Baker only had to tilt her head to look out the window and see the comings and goings on the street below—West 8th Street. The sky was thick and snow fell like a wash of white, turning the figures into shadowy forms trying to break into definition. Any dabs of color that might highlight the street, a yellow umbrella or a green overcoat, even the pink of frozen noses, were obliterated by the snow flailing against the backdrop of buildings. Liza paused, transfixed by pedestrians moving in and out of visibility, pushing through the cold, the wind, the shroud of whiteness. So easy to decipher; the drama, the struggle. Certainly more obvious than the still life set up in the center of the room for her painting class. A red ball, a rusted bicycle wheel, a handful of pigeon feathers, a drapery of cellophane, all mottled by the overhead light.

Suddenly she could feel a presence behind her. She turned. Her teacher, Hans Hofmann, stood motionless, staring at her drawing, his brow tight, his lips pulled in at the edges. He was a big man and Liza could feel the weight of his criticism gathering like a storm. She looked at the piece of paper tacked to her easel, a maze of gray forms protruding off the white surface. *Protruding, Protruding.*

The word pounded inside her head, reprimanding her even before her teacher could speak. *The picture plane is flat. Yet your form protrudes. You have lost the picture plane!* They were his words amplified by her frustration. Could no one else hear? Liza sensed the other students nearby. Though she did not look up, she could feel pity in their silence.

Finally, Hofmann moved. Without a word, he reached his arm toward her, took the charcoal from her hand and drew three thick lines across her work. "Now this is tension," he announced, his strong German accent filling the room like an echo. Then he walked away.

There were other criticisms, other students' failed work, she could be sure of that, yet Liza had stopped registering the comments. She removed Hofmann's altered drawing and tacked up a fresh sheet of paper. Then, without thought, without reference to anything save the agitation shooting up and down her spine, she drew three lines and let it go at that.

After class, she hurried to wrap her scarf into the collar of her coat and tucked the legs of her corduroy pants into old work boots, cracked and beginning to leak. Several students were considering how to navigate their large portfolios through the snow.

A hand grabbed her shoulder.

"Hey, Liza, you coming for a drink?" It was Hank, a promising young student from Philadelphia. Bold in his work. Outspoken too. His bravado had attracted her soon after they met.

"No. Not today."

"C'mon, Liza, baby." He spun her around to look at her face. "What, you're not upset, are you?" She shook her head, tried to break her shoulder free.

"You are, aren't you?" He was smirking at her with his unbearable self-confidence.

"Stop it, Hank." Liza wiggled free and pulled a pair of gloves from her pocket.

"Look, he marks on everyone's work. We're just students, after all. Here to learn." Liza shot back a perfunctory smile, then turned to leave.

"One drink?" Hank asked, stepping after her.

"Got to go."

She darted around easels, out the door and down the three flights of stairs, surprised at her agility under layers of clothes. The shock of cold air and snowflakes against her face startled her as she leapt onto the sidewalk, joining the few human forms moving through the storm. The wind yanked the flakes sideways, upward, sideways again like erratic marionettes, until they paused mid-air and settled on the ground, a thick, lumpy carpet that clung to Liza's boots as she plodded through. She crossed her arms over her chest, made her way to Fifth Avenue and turned toward the park.

Why was she here? Not here in New York. That was obvious. She had come with her childhood friend Tess the previous fall to study painting. But the National Academy, which suited Tess, only bored Liza with its rigid traditions. She was looking for something less formal and stilted. But what?

"You should look into Hans Hofmann's school," another student mentioned one day.

"Who?"

"The modernist from Europe. If you like that sort of thing."

Yes, yes! Liza could feel her blood pick up speed. A miracle, the vision of Cézanne, Soutine, Picasso, Kandinsky, the modern painters whose work she studied for hours in the museums in New York. Paintings that tore everything apart—form, perspective, space, even color. How this new work coming out of Europe calmed her with its passion, courage and honesty, ripping tradition to shreds, stripping the surface to expose the turbulent energies within. Standing in front of this new work, Liza felt awake. Alive! More than that, she realized she had finally found her community. Those who dared to ask questions, who craved truth above all else, no matter how shattering or alienating. This is what is real. Not the cool exterior of her placid father, the good doctor, a man beloved in their small town by the lake in New Hampshire that attracted people escaping cities for the summer, families like Tess's. Not the rules, the niceties, the freshly painted houses and neat interiors, the life as usual that was ground into her as a child. The flat surface that drove her crazy. If only one could scratch it, mess it up, rip it open, look! What creatures would be set free and fly away. What darkness and despair. And the hard-crusted, bruising scales of fear. But also hope. Really, if people only let themselves *look*. There is such purpose, such beauty here.

If she liked this sort of thing. Ha, she countered, this work was her salvation.

That Hofmann had accepted her, too, was a miracle. As he studied her work for what seemed an interminable time, she struggled to sit still, feeling like a helpless child instead of a capable, twenty-four-year-old woman. Finally—when she thought she could not bear another moment—he had said, "Yes." It was at that moment that Liza was sure her life had begun. Hearing that *yes* as he closed her portfolio. That affirmation of her potential. Or was it Tess's good perfume she had sprayed on hurriedly as she left? Maybe it was just the perfume.

Liza had reached Washington Square Park and stopped under the arch to hold her gloved hands out to the snow. How she loved this city, the trees that strained to grow out from cement, the odd mix of buildings, of people, the ever-changing smells. A palpable energy coming off the streets, from around the sharp edges of buildings, that could nearly pick her up and twirl her around just as the wind did the snow. But she felt paralyzed by the weight of Hofmann's criticism and the impossibility of his class.

Smack!

She felt a zing of impact at the back of her head.

Smack! Smack!

Two at her back, a clump of white whistled by her face. Then the laugh, an annoying cackle of victory.

Hank was doubled over, several yards away, folded into his laughter.

"You should see your face."

"Fuck you, Hank."

Hank laughed harder. "Your face is bright red. Look at you dripping, covered with snow. You look like a snowman in hell."

He approached her then, stopped laughing, and began wiping her face with the end of his scarf, dabbing the melted snow that had beaded onto her eyelashes like two waves of tiny jewels.

"Even so, you are still the most beautiful thing."

As she tucked her fingers into the rim of her collar to clean out the cold, Liza made a face. He did look funny, his cheeks glowing red, his brown eyes peeking out from beneath his wool cap, his gaze hopeful. Liza could have said something curt, but when he lifted his arm to wrap it around her shoulders, she decided to let her resistance go.

"You must be frozen. Let me buy you something hot to drink," he said.

Hours later, Liza uncurled herself from his arms. His skin was warm from sex, his bedroom overheated from the radiator that seemed to respond to nothing but 'off' and 'hot'. It had been easy falling into bed with Hank. He was attractive enough with his clean-cut, chiseled features, someone comfortable in a three-piece suit. He reminded Liza of the boys she had dallied with at the boarding school when she was in high school, teased really. A challenge coming from these boys of privilege, oozing superiority. How badly they treated the girls at the local public school, the ones who longed for nothing more than attachments to eminent families. They could be talked easily into sex, mistaking it for commitment. Silly girls. But not Liza. She too just wanted sex. How it drove the boys crazy that she was done with them afterward. She had other things that mattered more to her and honestly did not care.

Hank did not stir as she eased his hand back on the pillow. It was dark outside. The snow had stopped. She opened the window, stood naked behind the glass to witness the still city, not a movement, barely a noise, covered in sparkling snow, only the buildings as bones of form to define the clean white space in between.

She found some charcoal and Hank's sketchbook on his dresser and began to draw, sliding the charcoal sideways up and down to cover the paper in a layer of black. Then she ground down quick, determined lines. With the ball of an eraser, she worked away the black in between, pulling white space out of the dark. Quick, hard lines up and down against the rubbing in of white.

And then she saw. This was what Hofmann had meant in his lectures, confusing enough in his broken English, overwhelming in concept. The picture plane is a two-dimensional surface. There should be no trickery of perspective. No illusion of depth. It is simply about flatness and the tension of the surface. "Put the spot on the surface and let the surface answer back," he had said during her first class. Color, line, space of the form, the space outside it, and movement, always movement. The ideas had whirled around her brain, colliding in confusion. Create tensions between form, between solid and void, movement and stability. Activate your surface with the creation of forces that push and pull. This was how you bring your surface to life. It was all there, in the push-pull, the energy of tension.

Working now in the darkness, drawing almost without thought, it all made sense. Yes, she thought, pausing a moment to feel a gust of air shiver her skin. This is why I am here.

Despite the cold air blowing in from the open window, she felt warm sitting there, happy and light. There is a world out there to paint. Not what one sees or even names. Snow on asphalt. Darkened buildings. Sorrow. Joy. An empty cup. What are those? Nothing, really, in and of themselves. Just snow, stone or brick, emptiness, wholeness, a curved slab of porcelain. It's the spaces in between that spark life and give it definition. What can be deemed spirit is simply this. Tension.

It was nearly dawn. She was cold now and dressed carefully so she would not wake Hank, who had thrown off the covers in his sleep and lay sprawled across the rumpled bottom sheet. Ripping her drawing off the pad, she rolled it up, stuffed it into her coat pocket and slid out the door.

Tess was asleep when Liza returned to the apartment they shared on 13th Street. Carefully closing the bedroom door, which Tess had left ajar, Liza stripped off her scarf and coat and kicked off her boots, leaving them dripping in the hallway. She had almost skipped her way home in the snow, feeling as alive as she had ever felt. It had to be more than sex with Hank or difficult art concepts finally making sense. Maybe it was everything—New York. Her love of painting, working with the most talked-about art teacher in the city, the promise of it all.

Whatever it was, she wanted to capture it in paint, for she knew such ecstasy was fleeting. If she could lay it down on canvas, make a dance out of color and form, she would have it as a map to find her way back into, so that she could hold this moment forever.

A large canvas was tacked to the wall in the living room where Liza worked. Across the room was a spacious window that looked uptown. The sky had lightened and was coming alive with the colors of dawn: frosty reds and yellows and— Liza looked carefully again at the sky to be sure—hints of green, yes, green. Squeezing out colors onto her palette, she began to paint, letting her body guide her quickly before the sky's brilliance burned itself out, spread and faded into a flat sheet of blue.

Looking back, Liza would remember the painting as an effortless process, something that took minutes to execute. She'd recall the idea, the drama of the sky, the energy that fueled her work. Later, sitting across from the wet canvas on the couch, she studied the painting as though she were looking for the first time at someone else's creation. She closed her eyes to clear her head. She was awed; everything about it was perfect. She did not hear Tess come out the bedroom, didn't realize that she stood in the doorway for several minutes without making a sound, transfixed as well. Finally, Tess found her breath as she moved closer.

"This is incredible," her voice trembling at first. "Exquisite! Is this what you stayed up all night doing?"

Liza smiled and nodded. It had to have taken hours. How else could she explain?

When the painting was dry, Liza rolled it up and brought it to class. It was a day of critiques. She attached the canvas to a wall and waited. Hofmann began with another student's work, speaking loudly much of the time, probably because he could not hear well. Often he reverted to German because his English was poor. "What did he say?" was a common question among students. But they always knew what he felt.

Just as Liza did when he finally approached. Watching him study her painting, she saw his shoulders slack, the ruddy skin of his face soften, and she knew. Even so, she almost fell over when he finally spoke. "This is so good. You wouldn't know it was done by a woman."

*

11

After class, they would meet at a cafeteria around the corner on Sixth Avenue, any one of several students eager to continue chewing the wisdom of Hofmann's instruction, more to try to decipher his lectures, when he would lose his tentative grasp on English and slip into German. How much easier it was under the spell of his presence during class, watching him demonstrate 'push-pull' as he described the various tentacles of tension. Yes, students would nod. Yes, we understand. Later, away from the buttresses of easels and paint, the energy of the man himself, it all seemed elusive—his radical views, this different way of looking, of seeing. But possible, they felt, if they could incorporate it into their lives, into how they looked at other painters' work, at least into their conversations over coffee and pie through the ubiquitous curtain of smoke.

Late afternoon in the middle of March, Liza took a break between classes and headed to the cafeteria. It was a gentle day, the air sweetened by the tentative arrival of spring as buds dotted the branches of wispy trees. A middle-aged shopkeeper rolled up his sleeves, exposing still firm arms as a young child skipped ahead of his mother pushing an empty baby carriage, hurrying to keep up before the street crossing. As Liza approached the cafeteria, she darted in between the two, sensing the mother's urgency, smiling at the child's insouciance as she yanked the door open. By contrast, the air inside the cafeteria was thick with smoke, a discordant symphony of voices and clattering dishes, the smell of grease and old coffee surprisingly inviting. She found her group seated at their usual back booth—Hank, Phil, Jeremy, and a dark-haired woman, Phil's new girlfriend, there as well. Phil was a robust man and took up most of his side of the booth, wedging his girlfriend against the wall. As Liza approached, Jeremy rose to offer his place across the table beside Hank.

"Here. Sit here. I'll get a chair."

Liza put her hand on his shoulder as he was rising, easing him back down.

"It's all right. I'll sit here. There's plenty of room next to fat-boy Phil." He laughed at that, having no apparent guilt about his girth. Besides, she explained, she could not stay long. Just long enough for a cup of coffee. That and she knew Phil had gone to see the show of the Armenian painter Arshile Gorky the day before and she wanted to hear. So many new artists; the names were just beginning to sink in. Baziotes, Motherwell, Still, Rothko, and Gorky, too. Gorky was among those everyone was currently talking about.

She nodded at Hank, then turned quickly to Phil and waited for a lull in the conversation as she signaled to the waitress for coffee. The men were big talkers, volume and content both. Poor dark-haired girl. No wonder she sat silent, snuffing out one cigarette, immediately lighting another. Her hands were tiny and birdlike, her nails beautifully trimmed and colored blood red. They were perfect hands, Liza decided. She looked up, intending to join the conversation. The men had been discussing line from Hofmann's viewpoint, of line originating from the meeting of planes. "The course of a spatially conceived line develops from different positions in a multitude of planes," he had instructed recently. Line to plane to volume to spatial unity. A large napkin lay between them, myriad lines drawn this way and that, grappling, experimenting with simple marks that, for Hofmann, have multiple meanings. Phil wrapped his arm around Liza as if to draw her in.

"Really, there's little point in continuing until you've seen the show."

"He's talking about Gorky," Jeremy explained across the table.

"I've heard the work is quite sensual," Liza said.

"Yes. And sexual too. You'll love the one, *The Liver is the Cock's Comb*."

"Love the title," Hank chuckled, eyeing Liza.

"*Garden in Sochi* and *Pirate*, too. You see the inspiration of Kandinsky. The forms, rich colors over grays. And the rhythm. Kandinsky's influence without question. But you must see the work for his lines. His line does not contain form or color. It directs it. It holds it all together. Looking at this work, it's clear. The vitality of line."

"Refills, anyone?" The waitress interrupted, setting a cup and saucer down in front of Liza, filling it deftly from the pot she also brought. This waitress—Ellen, Gladys, what was her name?—served them often. The afternoon was her shift. One table alone could go through several pots at a sitting. She barely looked at the cup as she poured, yet she knew, every time, when to stop and right the pot with just enough coffee remaining in the air to fill the cup to the brim. Marvelous precision amid the sudden silence around the table. Until they saw Gorky's paintings, really, what more was there to say?

Hank cleared his throat. Ah, yes, Hank. He would fill the silence with some sort of art trivia. He had a mind for that. Setting his arms on the table around his refilled cup, he leaned into the center.

"So, what do you think you're going to do with this?"

Phil smacked his back hard against the booth. "What in hell do you mean by that?"

"Just that. Have you thought of how to make a living with this great new work?"

Hank was being heckled by his father, Liza knew, an insurance man who had little vested in his son's interest in art. Just a hobby, was all. One year, his father had allowed him, a year with this nonsense before he needed to knuckle down and do something serious, law or business school. Something useful.

"Are you kidding? Make a living. You sound like someone's father."

"His father, actually," Liza was quick to inform.

"Why should you give a damn about what he thinks?" Phil retorted.

Hank's face flushed. "I don't. Of course I don't. It's only a consideration. I'm just curious about what you're planning to do. That is, if you can't make a living selling your work."

"One could teach. There's that," Jeremy suggested in his unassuming voice.

"Sure. Sure. High school art. There's a fine thing." Phil swallowed his coffee in one gulp.

"Are you kidding?" Hank almost shouted. "Teaching? Why, even Pollock, who, by the way, Greenberg thinks could be the best American painter of this century, even he can't get a job teaching." Having shifted the focus away from himself, Hank's voice resumed its characteristic insolence. "I heard that he asked Julien Levy from the Art Students League for a job. That's where he studied. But they wouldn't give him anything, because he's so crazy. Then he went to Peter Busa at Cooper Union. Can you imagine Pollock at Cooper Union?"

Hank paused, waiting for a laugh, maybe, at least a nod, at the image of such an avant-garde painter teaching in a traditional school. The image should be funny. "All Busa said was, 'What the hell can you teach here?' What the hell could he teach?"

"Hofmann does a spectacular job." Liza had grown impatient with the talk. It was nearing time to go. "In fact, I have to get back to class."

"Yes, the figure," Hank said. "There's always portrait painting. There's a living in that."

Phil laughed. Jeremy smiled. Liza stood. She was angry at Hank's comment. Not the notion of portrait painting. She had little interest in that. It was his tone, the imperious implication, yes, this is what you can do—all you can do—with this skill. She threw a dime on the table. It rolled and fell just inches from the perfect red nails.

"You know what Hofmann says," she said, her eyes locking on Hank's. But it was Phil's voice that sliced through.

"About what?"

"That women make better artists than men."

"Ah, yes, but finish that thought," Hank answered without looking away. Then offered it himself. "He said women make better artists until they fall in love. After that, it's the man who is better."

"Oooh," Phil whistled.

The dark-haired woman spoke. "So, the moral of the story is never fall in love." The men clapped. Liza liked her immediately. There was camaraderie there. She smiled back, mouthed the word, 'Never', then left.

But she was apoplectic when she hit the street. The spring air smelled stale. Fuck Hank. Fuck him. Portrait painting. Teaching. You can do this, you can't do that. Who does he think he is? But it was not Hank she was addressing. No, it was her father. The beloved doctor, home from the hospital. It was already dark outside and Mrs. Carton, the housekeeper, had Liza washed and ready for bed. But first she wanted to show her papa what she had drawn that day, what beguiling shapes had come out of the sky as she was working. Nothing but clouds, but the forms were the beginnings of something else. Wait, Mrs. Carton held her back. Let your papa wash his hands. Oh, the washing, washing, always washing. Liza hated the smell of soap on his long, clean fingers. She hated the skin that always felt cold and damp. When Mrs. Carton released her, her drawings spilled from the pad and flew across the floor as she threw her arms around him. Mrs. Carton bent down to retrieve them as the good doctor sat down, allowed the wiggly girl to scamper into his lap. At eight years, still small, still hopeful, she could barely sit quietly upon his patient thigh. He took so long looking at each colored drawing. Finally, he said, "They don't really look like anything, Elizabeth. You do so much better when you draw something real."

Though she was late coming into class, and the model had already assumed a pose, a few other students were setting up their easels. Liza would not be noticed slipping into a space left near the front. Unlike the still life class, she preferred seeing the figure up close. From a distance, the objects of the still lifes relinquished their function and the accessibility of their context. At the back of the room, it was easier to see them simply as form. From here, Hofmann's words fell into place: *Every subject has a characteristic basic form. The choice of basic forms is dependent on the artist's feeling for his subject.*

His feeling develops from comparisons. Comparisons provide a perception of oppositions and relationships. Only through relationship and opposition can 'form' be defined in its relative and characteristic proportion.

Liza had chosen to take the figurative class because she longed to draw everything she could in order to absorb as much as she could hold. Even as it felt crammed in and confused—as it often did. One day, it would all become clear.

This evening's model was a large woman. Thin ones are easier to draw, a few students grumbled as they set up to work. If so, this one was selected to challenge. Her breasts hung heavily, halfway down her ribcage, like vessels of liquid about to burst. She had her head turned away from Liza, up toward the overhead light, and the angle of her chin was padded by a chunk of thick skin so that only a slight shadow fell onto her neck. Even the flesh on the backs of her thighs was loose and dappled. This woman couldn't have been more than twenty but already her skin showed the signs of age. What resilience remained was bolstered by fat. Liza tacked up a sheet of paper, selected a piece of charcoal but could not go on from there, her eyes transfixed by the rippled skin of this model. So sad and defeated, this pale-colored flesh. What sadness caused it to let go? Liza could not see the woman's face. Maybe there was a sign of tragedy in her eyes or deep, irrevocable sorrow. Maybe the eyes could tell a story that would explain the indelible despair Liza felt permeating the air, moving into her own skin. Through osmosis, she could feel it. A sadness in her was rising to meet that of the woman whose face was twisted up into the light.

Liza stepped back and drew a breath and into the space of her sudden shift only words moved in. What was her sadness? Well, she had no mother. There was sadness there. Hers had died in childbirth. A ruptured placenta—Liza had come out so fast. Her mother had bled to death as the infant was swaddled in Mrs. Carton's arms. There had been a storm that night, a tempestuous mix of snow and ice. The baby had not been due for another several weeks, so Dr. Baker had gone to work at the hospital. When he received the news that his wife's water had broken and contractions were coming on fast, he ran to his car and drove—too quickly the police later said—over unplowed roads, hitting a patch of ice on one curve and skidding into a ditch. It was well over five miles from home and he passed no other cars as he trudged through the snow, arriving nearly frozen. There at the door to meet him was Mrs. Carton, holding a blanket and all he needed to know in the swollen, red eyes that greeted him. He was too late.

Staring at the blank sheet of paper, Liza shuddered as though she had been the one pulled into the storm and the cold was surging through her. She put on her sweater and picked up a piece of charcoal.

"All right," she muttered to herself, repeating instructions given to her earlier in class. "Let's start at the beginning. Make a line. It doesn't matter if it's long or short or which direction it travels." She drew a thick, diagonal line to approximate the angle of the model's spine. "Now, make another shorter line." She did, reminding herself of what she had been taught. The first line gets its meaning from its relation to the second line. Two lines. Simple enough.

It was a little after ten, and Hank was waiting for her in the hallway outside. Stepping lightly through the doorway, she could recall little of her past irritation and moved, almost without consciousness, toward his welcoming face.

"I hope I didn't offend you earlier," he said, putting an arm around her.

Liza laughed. "You can't possibly offend me, Hank." What a lie, she thought to herself. At times, he did know exactly how to jab under her skin. But at the moment, restored by her sketching, she was feeling too good to remember her earlier disgust. How quickly her feelings could change.

"Well, even if I could, I was only repeating what Hofmann said. Let's go have a drink."

Hank lived on Waverly Place, atop the Waverly Inn, where they could sit at the bar and drink until closing. He chose Scotch, she preferred bourbon, and they had quite a few. The room, paneled in mahogany and dimly lit at this hour, was inviting, and the few other patrons conversed in hushed tones. The effect was lulling. Liza leaned back against her bar stool and caught their reflections in the mirror behind the bar. A young couple out on a date? Dinner? Dancing? Would that be how they were viewed? Liza wondered as the bartender passed them, eyeing their glasses. She grinned. Love seemed much easier than these elusive concepts. What was love after all, compared with the tenets of modernism, the principles they struggled with daily in class that they continued to dissect now?

"What is this really?" Hank considered, holding his empty glass up to catch the reflection of the soft, overhead light, a twinkle in the mirror when he tipped it just so.

"What do you see here?" he repeated as the bartender passed by. The words slurred out.

The bartender grinned. "You want a refill? Is that what you're asking?"

Hank chuckled and held out his glass for more. "See what I mean," he said, turning to Liza. "People don't know. They don't get it."

"They get trapped in the surface. They see only glass, reflection, a container for liquid."

"Precisely."

"They don't read emptiness, the spaces in between, the undercurrents that tug and pull. They just see glass."

"My point. Where is the tension in that?"

Yes, the tension. She could see it gleaming in the glass, seducing her with its turmoil. This palpable energy that was the point of everything. Everything. The excitement made her spin.

Finishing the last of her drink, Liza closed her eyes and sensed the flow of bourbon through her body. This was where it began. The dreams, the hopes, the determination. She would be a great painter. She was on her way. She could see herself in a studio with dealers, in a museum, at openings, traveling abroad. Even meeting Picasso and Matisse. Envisioning herself bathed in the limelight of success, she smiled.

Yet, the volume of liquor was beginning to confuse her thoughts even as Hank continued to talk. Maybe he too felt blurry but that didn't matter. He was there. Now was the time to fuck. Leaning into his shoulder, she thrust her tongue into his ear. The talk stopped.

"Let's go," she whispered.

Hank pulled out his wallet but struggled to separate the bills. At last he found a ten and laid it on the bar. "Keep the change," he tried to say. Who knows what the bartender heard.

They made it into the elevator, down the hall, to his door where he could barely get the key in the lock. He was drunker than Liza and she could not wait.

"Give me that." She opened the door and pulled him in, began to peel off his clothes. Hank tried to kiss her as she did, but she turned her head downward and knelt to slide off his pants as he sat on the bed. Saturated with liquor, his penis could barely take shape. Liza wet it with her tongue, then slid it into her mouth. Hank moaned and lay back on the bed. Cradling it with her tongue, she maneuvered the tip over the roof of her mouth. Rapidly it surged and straightened and just as it did, she reached under her long skirt and ripped off her underpants. Quickly she mounted the supine body, pointing his penis into her moistness and pushing down hard. He groaned, opened his eyes and tried to pull her toward him. But she held him back, sat straight and worked rapidly, up, down, up, down, feeling this foreign rigidity muster her disparate energies like a drill sergeant calling young soldiers to attention. Up, down, up, down, everything building and building, straining hard to come together and release. She caught it just as he began to wither. Too much Scotch, she thought. No matter. Liza rolled over beside him to catch her breath.

Then a jab of sunlight. She opened her eyes. Slats of light beamed into the room. She could hear Hank muffling around the kitchen just around the corner, sorting through the pile of dishes in the rack. Was that toast she smelled? The odor made her queasy or ravenous, she wasn't sure. When was the last time she ate? Yesterday before class. She pushed away the blanket and tried to sit up, but a searing pain in her head pushed her back down.

"You have any aspirin?"

"In the bathroom." Hank stuck his head around the corner. "Want me to get it?"

"Please." Liza lay back and pushed her hand against her brow, attempting to diffuse the pain. She quickly swallowed two small pills Hank brought as well as a glass of water and laid back down to wait for the aspirin to do its work.

"I've got coffee and some toast. If you want more to eat, we'll have to go out."

"Just coffee." She accepted the hot cup and looked around for her smokes. But Hank was one step ahead, pulling a pack out of his shirt pocket, lighting one for her, then for himself. He put a saucer between them for ashes before taking the newspaper and nestling himself back into bed.

Now, the morning's mundaneness seemed like a trap. Order deconstructed, begging to be put back together. Hank sat by her, ignoring the job. Wasn't this her domain, even in his space? Woman's work. Yes, he had made her coffee, fetched her aspirin. She was grateful for that. It was more than most men would have done. But attending to the mess of living, well, he was busy reading the paper. Isn't it always that way? The reason Mrs. Carton insisted she learn to tuck in the bottom sheet, press a shirt, cook a stew. Liza had resented the directives, her gut locked tight as she did what she was told. Not to adequately prepare her for life, as her father would tell her. No, she did it first for his approval, but later for the money he doled out after inspecting the bed, the linens in the closet. Her allowance properly earned.

She could feel his hand on her head now, patting her to show his pleasure. Always this patting on the head. Good girl. Good girl. As she stood straighter, pushing into his hand to try to get closer, feel more of his flesh. Please, just a hug this time. But never that much affection. Only the pat, pat, pat. Good girl.

It was their fathers who had brought them together. Most people assumed it was the art, the novelty of abstraction and Mr. Hofmann's teachings, the long afternoons at the Met studying classic Greek and Roman forms. But really it was their fathers. Liza's meted out silence or polite disapproval. Hank's was downright insulting, calling his interest in paint a sissy's game. They had talked about them only once, the afternoon Hank's father told him he was pulling his allowance. It was time that Hank do something serious with his life.

"Serious!" Hank all but yelled. "What does he know of serious? He makes his fortune off of other peoples' worries and the catastrophes that await if they don't buy his insurance. When it comes down to it, I've never seen him sweat a day in his life. Make a real effort over anything. He just stirs up fear and they jump."

Liza saw immediately through the bluster. She put her hand on his, though in his agitation he knocked it away. Still, she felt a moment of connection in this intractable pain that kept them anchored to their childhoods. Though seldom evident, it was easier to attribute their relationship to the fact that Hank was attractive and smart and a decent painter. But now, in the daylight, Hank's place felt claustrophobic, the disorder of it unsettling. She had to get away.

"Don't go," he implored as she reached for her coat. "You haven't even had breakfast."

"Another time."

She drew fervently that spring, both in class and in the apartment. Though she produced commendable work—and was considered one of the best painters in class—she found it impossible to recreate the success she had experienced with *Sunrise,* the ease and the deeply satisfying harmony of the composition. More and more, it seemed a fluke, as though someone else had been the artist. Even though she studied the work closely and tried to reclaim her emotional state of mind, its genesis eluded her.

"You've hit a plateau," Tess observed one evening after Liza expressed frustration. "Restlessness is just the rumbling of too much information. You need a break. It will all make sense, if you're patient."

"Patience has never been one of my virtues," Liza retorted. She was sprawled on the bed, watching Tess choose among her dresses for a date that night. Tess was standing in front of the mirror holding a turquoise dress against her, clearly aware how the tight-fitting garment showed off her curvy hips and generous breasts. She liked the guy—a young medical student. Though they had only had two previous dates, she admitted to Liza that he might be the one, an uncharacteristically quick decision for Tess. Throwing the dress on her bed, she selected pearls and matching earrings from the top drawer of the bureau.

Liza lit a cigarette and watched her friend. Unflappable Tess. Liza wished she could offer some help, but she had no talent for fashion. Tess was the one with taste. Manners and sophistication too. It seemed only a few years ago that Tess was dressing up Liza like a doll when they were, what? Twelve? Fourteen? Those carefree summer afternoons in her mother's large dressing room in that sprawling white house set overlooking the lake outside Liza's home town, their family's summer retreat. Long, thin windows letting in slices of summer light, illuminating them as they dressed themselves in Tess's mother's finest, prancing across the room in spiked high heels, tripping, laughing, flopping on the floor like fish trapped in sparkly nets, gasping for breath through their laughter. Had it really been so long ago?

Tess glanced over at Liza as she snapped on the last pearl earring. "What are you staring at? Don't I look all right?"

"You look fabulous, as always."

Tess smiled. "You just need to stop thinking so much. Have a drink. You'll feel better."

"Maybe you're right," Liza said as she rose from the bed and went into the kitchen to find the bourbon.

On her way to class the next morning, Hofmann stopped her in the hall and asked her to come into his office. "Sit, sit," he motioned to the free chair in front of his desk as he closed the door behind her. She sat quickly on the edge, curious and nervous. "A group of artists is organizing a large show. There will be those you know, de Kooning, Marca Relli, others, members of the Club. But they are looking at work of many others. I think you should submit your painting. You know the one."

Liza stared at him askance, as though he were speaking completely in German. His words went right through her head. Hofmann scribbled on a scrap of paper, then handed it to her.

"Here is the phone number of Leo Castelli. He is organizing the event. I told him you'd call."

Liza thought she would faint and put one hand on his desk to keep herself from falling. "Thank you," she said quietly, as if it meant nothing at all.

*

The next afternoon, Liza carried her painting, rolled up and hoisted on her hip, to Leo Castelli's storefront on East Ninth Street. The space was empty except for several paintings leaning up against interior walls, but standing outside, she could see it had been cleaned and freshly painted. Inside a short, trim man stood in front of a group of paintings making notes on a pad of paper. The door was open; Liza stepped gingerly onto the threshold.

"Mr. Castelli?"

"Yes?"

I'm Liza Baker, Hans Hofmann's student. I spoke to you yesterday."

"Ah, yes." He placed the pad onto a stool near the wall. So small, thought Liza, barely as tall as she, yet elegant in his carriage as he came to greet her, his stride smooth like a dancer's. "Please come in," he said, offering to take her canvas. She relinquished it and followed as he led her past several partitions that must have been built recently—the smell of newly cut wood lingered in the air—to the back of the gallery, where the floor was clean and he could unroll and view her painting.

He accepted it graciously, telling her how pleased he was to have it in the show. She could return with stretchers the next day when they would begin hanging the work, but first he needed her name, phone number and the title of the piece. He left her for a moment to retrieve his pad.

"This is the list of participants thus far," he said, showing her the names he had written down. "I'm sure you know many of these artists."

She knew the work of de Kooning, Franz Kline, Jackson Pollock, Barnett Newman, Mark Rothko, Robert Motherwell. She had heard the names of others mentioned at the cafeteria or the Cedar, the bar where they often congregated. But many she did not recognize. Castelli told her there would be sixty artists participating, maybe more. "As word gets out, they keep coming by. You know how that happens."

Liza didn't really know, having never experienced anything like this before, but grinned and nodded as though she did. Suddenly they heard footsteps and a big, accented, "Hello? Leo?"

Castelli responded, his voice slightly raised. "We're back here, Bill." Then to Liza, "It's Bill de Kooning. Have you met?"

She shook her head in disbelief. De Kooning! She knew his work—there had been a show recently of his black and white abstractions, work she adored. His reputation, of course—an accomplished draftsman, brilliant painter, everyone's favorite artist despite Pollock's success in the press—and the stories! The handsome expatriate from Rotterdam; his captivating wife, Elaine; generous; enormously talented; she had heard all the talk. But no, she had not yet met the man.

28

The weight of his footsteps echoing through the front room belied the small man who rounded the corner. Small, yes, but what presence emanating into the space, this handsome, blond-haired man with sweet, sad eyes, drawing his lips into a smile as he approached them.

"This is Liza Baker," Castelli said. "She's one of Hans' students and has a marvelous painting for the show."

De Kooning glanced behind them at the canvas lying on the floor and his eyes came to life. "Ah, yes. Terrific work. Leo, these young painters of yours will bring us to shame."

He was only being polite, Liza thought. A bit of a flirt with those sparkling eyes that lit up his face. Good maybe, not bad for a student, but terrific? Not compared to his paintings. *Excavation,* a masterpiece shown at the Venice Biennale. His black and white abstractions that had knocked her over with the strong, sweeping brushwork, so elegantly controlled, every element coming together into an indelible equilibrium. Hofmann's definition of great art.

Castelli laughed. "You needn't worry, Bill."

Liza could not help but laugh. "I doubt that anyone could be a threat to you, Mr. de Kooning."

"Bill, please."

"Bill."

He had come to talk to Castelli about his work, saying he had nothing new to show and was considering a painting he did two years ago, which he wanted to discuss. It seemed an appropriate moment for Liza to leave. As she interrupted to say her goodbyes, Bill put a hand on her shoulder.

"Why don't you come by the studio? Bring me some drawings. It's always good to see what students are up to.

Come tomorrow if you like. Around eleven. It's on Fourth Avenue, number 85. We'll have coffee."

Liza could barely contain herself as she left the gallery. Outside, in the flash of sunlight and busy streets, she wanted to scream out her ecstasy. Yell at the top of her lungs, "YES!" Instead, she began to sprint, running the whole way home.

It was hot the following day by mid-morning, and Liza's shirt was damp by the time she climbed the stairs to de Kooning's studio. She could not believe her luck, everything happening so quickly. She didn't dare stop for fear that if she stepped outside this current, even for sleep, things would change.

De Kooning's door was open and she found him seated on a chair halfway across the room, facing the large canvas he was working on, a wrenching composition of orange and red as forms struggled to define themselves amid harsh black lines and blocks of white. Was he painting already? Maybe she should go. But she lingered at the door, marveling at his face in three-quarter profile, the edge of his jaw working hard, clenching his cheek taut like a canvas, then releasing and letting the flesh go. He sat and stared, smoking half a cigarette without moving off the chair, and Liza did not dare shift from the door even though the bundle of drawings and paintings she held under her arm grew heavy.

Finally, he got up, took a large scraper off the table lined with bowls of paint, approached the canvas and with one quick motion, scraped the left side of the painting clean of wet paint. Stepping backward, he turned enough to see her out of the corner of his eye.

"You're working. I'll come back another time," Liza said once their eyes met.

De Kooning put down his tool and wiped his hands with an old rag. "No, come in. She is getting away from me today."

"She?"

"This woman I am painting," he explained, tilting his head toward the canvas. "I cannot get hold of her. Let's see if you've had any better luck."

He took her work and put it on the only table in the large studio.

"Sit, please," he told her, taking his chair from the middle of the room and placing it near the table. "One of these days, I will buy furniture. Did you bring any cigarettes? I seem to have finished mine."

Liza reached into her pocket and pulled out a fresh pack. "You can have it."

"Ah," he laughed. "Now I can use my nickel for some coffee."

De Kooning smoked as he studied her work. He was unshaven and his strong body odor was tinged with the sweetness of safflower oil, which he must use to thin his paints, Liza realized. She could see a can sitting on a piece of plywood propped up against the windowsill along with his paints. While he went through her drawings and small paintings, Liza stared at his large canvas, trying to decipher the woman there. Two heavy orbs hung in the middle, touching as though caught in a corset. Above them, teeth. How could she have missed that menacing bite? Everything else looked like the colorful unleashing of fury and frantic momentum. She could see how this painting could easily escape him.

There were other paintings of women propped up against the long wall of the studio, semi-abstractions, the figures seated, clothed in tight-fitting bodices and billowy skirts, each one contemplative, the brushwork calmer, more controlled. Wistful work compared to the turbulence of this.

"Liza." She turned. He was holding a drawing she had made with colored oil pastels. A green-tinged sphere, three subtle lines and a brown pear-like shadow, indeterminate objects on the verge of definition. It was an odd composition, something that had just come from the moment, nothing particularly planned. Like *Sunrise* but from a quieter, less consolidated place. At the time, she thought the work decent, nothing particularly special, but it had possibility, maybe a new direction. Certainly something worth showing, she had decided last night when she set it aside with the others.

"This is good," he told her. "The others, you have many Hofmanns there. But with this one, I am beginning to see your attitude."

"My attitude?" Liza squinted at the work cradled in his hand. What *was* her attitude? What did he mean? She hadn't any idea, but obviously Bill could see something of it.

"See this space at the edge of this form," he said, tracing a finger slowly along the outside of the green circle. "Here, see how you've created space out of movement, speed and stillness?"

Liza nodded, though she hadn't understood it until he defined it for her. She had not intended this detail.

"It is like a door you've left open in the work. A place in the picture plane that will let you in."

"I see," Liza said, intrigued.

"It's important." De Kooning set down the work, then turned to her and continued. "Content is a glimpse of something. The trick is to slip into this and paint it. Not the glimpse, but the emotion of it. That's my interest anyway."

Liza drew in a breath. The glimpse of the emotion. Yes, that made so much sense. Capturing the essence of what sparked the content. The emotion of it. Looking again at the woman de Kooning was wrestling with, Liza felt a chill. The woman seemed to be dancing on the canvas—her big, buxom body swirling in a frenzy of paint. But the glaring gray eyes and the grin locked tight by her teeth made her dance anything but joyful. No, he was holding her down, forcing her onto the canvas, trying to paint her still. The woman's seeming rage made Liza shudder. Maybe all he needed was to set her free.

The glimpse of the emotion. Much there to consider. Liza was titillated by the enormity of his ideas and curiously at a loss for words. Besides, she had to stretch her painting for the show.

"I've distracted you long enough," she said as she gathered her work back into her portfolio. "I should go."

"I trust I'll see you later at the Cedar. I should get back to that woman there before she gets jealous," he answered, tipping his head toward the painting in progress.

"You will. And thanks."

Liza hurried home. She could not wait to tell Tess that de Kooning had approved.

Hank would also be exhibiting in what was being called The Ninth Street Show. Liza and Hank, the two stars of Hofmann's current class. But at Hofmann's invitation to submit a painting, Hank could not make a choice. He needed Liza's discerning eye.

How they had argued over three possible canvases; all she thought were inspired by Hofmann's own work. Hank had been playing with chunks of color amid gestural brushstrokes in bold hues that had yet to satisfy him, though he would never admit this to anyone but Liza.

"Hofmann chose this," Hank said, pointing to the boldest of the work. "But I like this one better."

He had poured them Scotch, which Liza sipped as she considered. "No," she decided. "None of these." She began looking around the studio. "Where's that painting you worked on last week?"

"This?" he said, drawing a smaller canvas from behind a few he had leaning up against the wall. He had been so agitated painting this—a difficult visit home, his father telling him to leave—and the effort had infuriated him that day in class. Blocks of color he could not seem to push through. How quickly he had packed up and stomped off, though she had been touched by his struggle.

"Yes," she beamed. "This feels close to the bone. There's a rawness and vulnerability here. The others are distracting. You're trying to hide something that is trying to come through here. This is the beginning of something strong. Show this one."

"No, this isn't even finished. I can't show this." Hank slammed the canvas back into the pile.

"Suit yourself. But it's your best work yet."

"You're crazy," he was all but yelling, and poured himself another drink. "No. I'm going with Hofmann's choice."

"Fine. Then don't ask me."

"Fuck you, then. I won't."

Hank was his characteristic assured self the next day in class, confidently tackling the new still life and commenting on other students' work.

"We are going to the Cedar to celebrate," he announced to her at the end of the session. "You should come. We'll drink a toast."

"Maybe I will."

"Meet us at ten, then."

If it were only for Hank, Liza might not have bothered. But everyone in the art community came to the Cedar Tavern and she was eager to be seen. Though the bar was packed, she spotted Phil's bright red cap at the back of the room and found Hank and a few other students huddled at a table over a large pitcher of beer. She would start there.

As she approached, she noticed Hank light a cigarette and lean back away from the dim overhead light, the darkness muting his large doe eyes, his full lips. Then, with a quick inhale of smoke and the red glow of embers, his face lit up again. It was a handsome face.

He looked relaxed, but she knew him better. He had already scanned the room, knew who was or wasn't there. He was aware of the gossip, the news, of everyone's work, remembering each detail. Every layer of complexity even when it looked simple. Even something as mundane as turpentine had tension in it, all those mistakes, miscalculated strokes, disappointment, exoneration, another chance, all there in that translucent liquid. He could look past the smell and see it. As could she. She loved that about him.

"Ah, Liza," Phil announced, his voice amplified by beer. Liza noticed the pitcher was nearly empty. "Come," he said, motioning her to the one empty spot beside Hank. "Sit," he blubbered. "Have a beer. Or would you like something stronger?"

"Maybe I should to catch up to you."

"A bourbon, then?" Hank knew her drink of choice.

"Or," Phil leaned into them, Liza now seated next to Hank, "should we be getting a bottle of champagne?"

"Here?" Hank quipped.

Phil emptied the pitcher into Hank's glass. "Then beer it is. Liza?"

"Bourbon."

"Bourbon for the lady. Swill for the clowns."

Randy, a new student of Hoffman's, sat across from her and smiled. "Good work, you two," he said, clearly envious.

"Your turn will come." Hank was diplomatic in his assurance. "Things are going to change with this show. Doors will open. No doubt about that."

Liza looked around. She was suddenly impatient and wished Phil would hurry back with her drink. A few booths over, Bill's wife, Elaine, was holding court over a group of men. So striking, Elaine. Thick red hair and ruby lips, her face animated in conversation. And brilliant about art, too. Liza had read several of her articles in *ArtNews*. One day, Liza hoped, she'd have such poise.

"Here you go." Phil was back, setting glasses of hard liquor on the table for all. "A toast to the next generation."

"Yes, to us." Hank was quick to clink glasses, making sure he caught Liza's eye as his touched hers. Liza sensed provocation in the look he gave her, a tease—or was it a challenge? He knew she disapproved of his choice. She nodded and swallowed her shot in one gulp.

"Look," Randy announced, "here comes Franz Kline and Bill de Kooning."

Liza looked up to see the two artists making their way to the bar, greeting several people along the way. A trim, lovely woman followed close behind Bill, who was holding her hand. As they walked by the booth, he noticed Liza and nodded in her direction, recognition that no one missed.

"What was that? Do you know him?" Phil asked, his voice uncharacteristically muted, in case de Kooning could still hear.

Liza waved him away. "I met him at the gallery and made a studio visit the other day. It's nothing really." But it was and she knew it, and she reached over quickly to pour herself some beer.

Moving close to her shoulder so he could whisper, Hank said, "I'd be careful, if I were you. He loves pretty women, women like you. He has mistresses everywhere, but he's still very much married to Elaine."

Liza bristled at even the idea, coming from Hank especially. So petty and demeaning. That he would even consider that she'd try to sleep her way to success.

"Don't worry," she snapped back, "he only interests me as a painter." Pulling the empty pitcher of beer toward them, she slid it in front of Hank. "How about getting us a refill?"

Standing to let Hank out, Liza eyed the room. She could move up to the bar and talk to de Kooning, but he was surrounded and deep in conversation with the older artists there, his arm anchoring the woman beside him. How long could she stomach the tepid conversation at their table, the banter that now seemed juvenile compared to what was being discussed by real artists? She thought of leaving, but the night had just begun.

Loud, raucous voices filled the air and Phil shot a high-pitched whistle toward a group of young women who had just walked in the door, his girlfriend and several others. Fresh distraction, sorely needed. The girls would be chatty, with any luck, entertaining enough for a few more drinks. As they made their way to the table, Liza slid in beside Randy, asking for one of his smokes. Tall and scruffy, Randy had the ruddy complexion of a Midwesterner, the place he had left to come to New York as an illustrator. Phil, his studio neighbor, had introduced him to Hofmann's class where he quickly found his palette in black and white. He could be loud in his enthusiasm, but affable too, easily impressed by anyone with more experience. His eyes glowed as Liza moved close, making room for the others. He knew de Kooning's work and they were in solid conversation by the time Hank returned. He squeezed himself into the group of girls who had gathered around Phil. Liza could not hear their conversations over the noise, but she could see in Hank's animated face the play of charm and bravado—the superficial courting that might get him laid—his attention glued to one young woman, a new student to their class. She knew this game and could play it too.

Turning back to Randy, Liza tried to focus on the story he was telling about his childhood working on a farm, the cattle, the persnickety bull, but her mind drifted in and out. All the smoke and raucous noise. What time is it anyway?

The clock on the wall was no help at all. It was never right. It was late enough; everyone was sloppy. Hank could barely hold himself upright. Randy was hers if she wanted him. But she was sick of it all and needed some air.

*

The Ninth Street Show opened, finally, amid a flurry of excitement. At the time, Liza thought this night marked the true beginning of her life. Her life as a painter that was about to take off. Liza Baker. A name to remember. Years later, however, she would remember it as the beginning of the end. But not then. Then, that lovely warm night in May, it was everything. So much so that she could barely contain herself. The store that had temporarily been transformed into a gallery was abuzz with conversation, a congestion of bodies, everyone, EVERYONE who was anyone in the New York art world, and everyone else it seemed, pressed together, staring, pointing, gossiping, laughing. The air was a cloud of cigarette smoke, dreamlike, the talk escalating into a symphony of indecipherable words, while large, colorful paintings fenced in the crowd, splashes of color swirling behind heads, around shoulders, highlighting spaces between bodies.

She fingered the pearls Tess had loaned her for the opening, spheres of coolness against her hot neck, and glanced again across the room at her painting on the wall, holding its own amid the works of so many great New York artists. In the momentary lull of conversation, Liza labored to believe she was actually a part of this show, only twenty-four, still an art student; how could this be? But there it was, her painting, its vibrant dance of colors continuing to amaze her. Those twisting, twirling shapes that had spun off her brushes as if by magic. Whenever she lost touch with her skin, her bones, her quick, gasping breath—whenever she was uncertain whether she existed at all—she could anchor herself in her work. *You painted this!* It had to be real. This opening, the people, all of it.

"This is a bit overwhelming, isn't it?" Tess announced as she came through the crowd. "Are you holding up?"

"Of course," she answered, admitting only part of the truth. For it was overwhelming, but marvelous too. "How could I not drink up such attention?"

"Well, you've always been bolder than I could be."

Maybe she was. But Liza still needed Tess. To dress her, for one thing, a fairy godmother to prepare her for this ball. "Here," Tess had instructed after rummaging around the top drawer of her bureau. Liza had been a bundle of nerves all afternoon; dressing for the reception was impossible. She had her new dress and shoes and that was all she could manage. "Try these on." Tess held out a pair of golden disc earrings. "Yes, I think these would look fine with that dress." Liza's simple, tight-fitting black dress. "You need something to accentuate the black and your gorgeous red hair. Something sparkling."

Now Tess was here to smooth a chunk of hair off Liza's shoulders and brush something off her dress.

"I just ran into Tom Hess. You know Tom Hess, from *ArtNews*. Maybe they'll write something about you."

"Maybe they will." Liza shot Tess her most sarcastic look.

"No, I'm serious. He loved the painting. At least he said he did."

"What did he say? Exactly."

"Exactly…? He said brave. That was the word he used. In the movement and all the white space, especially the white space. He said that was brave of you to do."

"Brave!" Liza repeated the word under her breath, rolling it around her tongue. Liza could make a feast of such a word.

"I'm dying of thirst," Tess said, breaking her revelry. "Shall I bring you a drink?"

"Yes, a shot of anything."

"I'll see what I can do." Tess winked. "Relax. The painting's fabulous. Everyone's talking about it."

Liza watched Tess weave her way through the crowd. So many lovely people, even the men, painters she knew from visiting studios and hanging around the Cedar. Typically disheveled; hair all askew; worn, dirty clothes splattered with paint. Look at them now. How clean and neat, they were almost unrecognizable in their sport coats and ties, looking more like bankers than painters, their hair tamed and greased back, collars buttoned, ties perfectly knotted. Even their fingernails were scrubbed and groomed. And the women so elegant in their neatly coiffed hair and stunning dresses, long, beaded necklaces adorning their chests. Thank God Tess had insisted on attaching false eyelashes, loaning Liza her pearls.

"There you are." Two strong arms wrapped around her from behind. It was Phil, looking comical, his bear of a body stuffed into a borrowed jacket, tufts of his thick hair breaking free from hair cream in the most capricious of places. Clown-like, he was a bit of an embarrassment in this sleek, impressive crowd. Liza both welcomed and dreaded his presence.

"Helluva crowd," Phil yelled at her. Whiskey sweetened his breath.

"Yeah, yeah." The response was more cavalier than Liza intended. "Hey, do you have a smoke?"

"Yeah, yeah," he mimicked her as he fished through his pockets. "Just be careful you don't get swallowed up by all these big fishes. Even you, my tiny Irish beauty."

Smiling, she accepted the cigarette graciously, though her stomach winced.

"Helluva painting, though." Now he looked at her with pride. "I gotta say."

Liza's spirits instantly inflated; she was soaring over the crowd. How quickly it all changed. With only a compliment, she was something. How easy, just one or two eulogizing words. She was glad he had come.

"Hey, look who's here. David Smith, over there in the door." As fast as she had risen, she spiraled back into the claustrophobia of the place, the stuffy air, the throng of bodies, so many famous faces that they were canceling each other out. At least to Liza. Phil had no trouble zeroing in on his idol, Smith's signature cap a dead giveaway in this room of well-groomed bodies.

"Excuse me while I go bask in his presence."

Then he was gone. Liza sucked on her cigarette. A blister on her right heel had begun to burn. Damn these new shoes! Where was Tess with that drink? She looked around the room. All these people! Phil's comment had unnerved her. Well, screw him, she thought. She could hold her own in this crowd.

Flicking her ashes on the floor, she perused the room as the chatter enclosed her. The air was stuffy, a bad mix of tobacco with too much perfume. A dry, hot, sickening sweetness. *Damn you, Phil.* She had longed for this opening like a child awaiting Christmas. Now here she was in the thick of it, living her dream. For this was it, wasn't it? Everything she had lived for. Why was the air so suffocatingly sweet?

Ah, here was Tess finally back with a drink. And Hank right behind her. Of course, Hank!

"Look who I found," Tess announced, handing Liza a glass. Hank's painting had been hung in the rear of the store and this was the first time Liza had seen him that night.

"Some party," Hank said. "I can't believe who's here. What a coup for us. Are you getting any good responses?"

Liza took a drink—it was a gin and tonic. Not her favorite, but it was cold and would do. "Of course. But what would people say? That they hate your work?"

Hank smirked. "Well, not to your face anyway. But if you move around, you hear things."

"And what have you heard?"

"Nothing but gossip."

"Ah, the usual stuff."

Suddenly she felt a hand on her shoulder. It was de Kooning and Franz Kline coming to congratulate her.

"Soooo big," Kline proclaimed in a bellowing voice about her painting. "And for such a tiny, beautiful woman." Kline stood close, his breath hot and reeking of old cigars. "Why, Bill, this girl has balls! We poor boys must watch ourselves," he announced with a twinkle in his eyes. "These young painters will be the death of us."

Liza beamed, feeling Kline's words fill the room. "This girl has balls!" Heads turned their way and her cheeks flushed hot, yet her bare arms turned cold. She loved the spotlight but dreaded the weight of it, too, as Kline and de Kooning closed in with their coterie of fans—they were the masters after all—so many eyes upon her. Maybe she should not have chosen such a tight-fitting black dress, her small breasts squeezed into a swell of false cleavage. And those damned eyelashes, shadowing her peripheral vision, getting heavier and heavier as the room closed in around her.

"Why, there's Janis," de Kooning announced, looking over her head, waving toward the back of the room. "He must be blind." De Kooning swung his arm around her waist. "Come with me. I want to introduce you to an important dealer."

Liza glanced at Hank and Tess as she was led away. The look Hank gave her was one she'd never forget: a brown-eyed stab of jealousy and aloofness, judgment that didn't seem fair.

She spoke briefly to Sydney Janis, a dealer Bill was courting at the time. He was a slight man, well dressed and knowledgeable about European artists. Yet his deep-set eyes with their sagacious glare unnerved her. As he and de Kooning fell into an easy banter, she excused herself, went to the bar and got another drink. Downing it quickly, she asked for another, trying to ignore the stinging blister, the hot, stuffy air.

As though spread thin by a giant brush, the crowded bodies in the room began to blur together into a sea of streaking colors, indecipherable noise. Liza strained to steady herself, find a target of focus as she scanned the swirl of bodies until her eyes stopped at the front door. A tall, thin man, elegantly dressed, was slipping into the room through the crowded entrance. Liza's heart stuck in her throat. Her breath froze. Was that him?

How can this be? It was impossible. He had been long gone. Liza blinked again and pinched her thigh, tried to focus through the smoky haze of the room. She could have sworn it was him. Look at that finely pressed suit, the white shirt stiff from the extra starch he always requested to keep himself presentable throughout his long days. His favorite silk handkerchief, a gift from a grateful patient, pale yellow, folded into a perfect triangular peak atop his breast pocket. He paused at the door, perusing the room, his eyes taking in the crowd, then slowly traveling over all the work on the walls, patiently, as was his due, yet this time without judgment or emotional reaction. Until his gaze finally found *Sunrise* and stopped. Liza was transfixed, watching him engage with the work, saw his eyes exhibit something she had longed to see all her life—a sparkle of joy.

Papa, she wanted to cry out. *Papa, look how special I am. Nothing's going to stop me now!*

*

TWO

Rouge

(1966)

It was nearly dawn when the car door slammed. Rouge startled awake as though it were the noise itself that had shaken her. Outside, beneath her window, the grass crunched under tentative footsteps. She heard a deep voice, a man's voice, mumble but could not discern the words. Then a familiar slur, hushed and hurried. It was Liza. Her mother.

"Shut up. My daughter's sleeping right upstairs."

"You have a daughter?" The voice was clearer now. "Oh, yeah. The daughter."

"Shhh! C'mon."

The back door creaked open, then banged shut. "Shhh!" again, followed by muffled laughs. "God," Rouge muttered as she glanced at the clock. *4:35.* Someone banged into the hall table downstairs. It must be the man. Despite herself, Rouge listened to the fumbling up the stairs, the barely contained laughter, her mother slip on the stairs, then giggle herself up. *God damn you, Liza,* she thought. Why don't you finish with your men in the city and come home at a decent hour? Alone. Like other mothers would do.

When Rouge woke again, it was mid-morning. Her room was filled with light. Its seasonal companion, heat—heavy and wet—was holding her down. She peeled herself free from bed, then her nightgown, itself damp and clingy.

Even in irritation, for there was that lingering, she marveled at the orderliness of her room—the furniture, the books, the audience of stuffed animals and old cloth dolls atop her bookshelf, squeezed together at the shoulders to keep them upright, even her laundry folded neatly at the foot of her bed. A girl's possessions suspended in oppressive, wet air, the friendly gargoyles of a teenage room. A cold shower first as she relished the prickling of brisk water against her hot skin, then on to the day.

Her mother's bedroom door was closed, but there was coffee in the air, telling Rouge all she needed to know: Liza would not have slept much, if she did at all. She would have waited until the newfound comrade beside her was asleep then slipped out. Off to the kitchen, to a few cups of coffee, many cigarettes, smoked while she sat on the porch and watched the sun fill the sky. She marveled at the colors of dawn, the complex hues that seemed to explode over the horizon before beginning their crawl toward dissolution. When Rouge was small and slept in her mother's bed, she would often wake to Liza's early morning footsteps as they pattered out of the room, down the stairs, into the kitchen and finally out onto the porch. Once it was quiet, Rouge would wrap herself in her child's blanket and creep over the wooden floor, gingerly picking her route over cracks and around spots known to groan, a game, almost, as she imagined herself her mother's dilatory shadow. If she opened the screen door only so far, it would not announce her presence and she could crawl up beside Liza and lean into her mother's body. The smell of coffee was thick and soothing. The warmth of Liza, the strong odor of coffee, the crisp morning air.

"Watch carefully," Liza would whisper to her those

mornings as the first rays of red spilled over the hills, jolting the dark sky. "See how the light moves like water, with every ounce of itself, as it claims the day. There, how it softens and begins to break up and lose itself until it fades away. Can you see it?" Rouge was never sure she was tracking the change, not as her mother seemed to, but she would nod anyway. They would sit that way together when Rouge was very young, nestled into the back wall of the porch, until the coffee cup was empty, the cigarette snuffed out, the sky pale blue, not an inkling of red left to linger. Then what?

Then it was off to the studio, Rouge trailing behind with her blanket, parking herself on the mattress in the corner—her studio fortress fortified with pillows big and small, building blocks of protection or clouds of softness to cradle her as she lost herself in other worlds while Liza painted. A makeshift bookshelf by the bed offered a myriad of adventures—hunting heffalumps with Pooh, drifting toward a new home with the Borrowers, eating fried pigs' tails somewhere on the prairie. But when her eyes grew tired and her body itched to move, Rouge would slip out the door to find her trusted childhood companions.

"Who are you talking to?" Liza would ask, coming out of the studio for more coffee, spotting Rouge wrapped within brambles, chatting away, a high-pitched voice of excitement.

"Emmeline and Edsel and Pucchi and Willamina," she'd call back as Liza crept up to have a better look. "Can't you see them?"

"What are they? Bugs?"

"Liza!" Rouge hissed back. She never called her Mama anymore, at least not that Liza could remember. "They're not bugs. They're fairies."

"Ah," Liza proclaimed without skipping a beat, "that explains it. Fairies never show themselves to grown-ups."

Pausing now on the porch, over the remnants of Liza's early morning watch, Rouge could only remind herself that the clear sky had once been afire. Dawn's chill, Liza's comforting body, now only memories in this sultry heat, noisy with the chatter of cicadas. The fairies, too. Gone. Though at times Rouge was sure she could feel their presence lurking behind shadows, just out of view.

Rouge stood at the edge of the porch to take in the rich summer day, letting her toes wrap around the coarse wood. The smell of honeysuckle was strong, and the wild roses that had taken over the flowerbeds were as pink as they'd ever get. It's the humidity that swells out their color. When Liza gets in the mood, she will pull it all up, insisting instead on delphiniums and asters and delicate tea roses, but Rouge loved this reckless growth, preferring to let things be.

Suddenly the screen door creaked. Usually she heard most things coming, but not this moan of tired, old wood. She nearly separated from her skin. Then she remembered the man and turned. There he was, hanging just inside, a large hand propping open the door. Not at all good-looking. Heavyset and coarse. And his eyes bulged like a reptile's. Liza must have been really drunk when she found this one.

He seemed to be sizing Rouge up as well. She bent down to gather Liza's empty cup and a plate heaped with cigarette butts, the ashes still warm.

"You're the daughter." It was more a pronouncement than a question, his voice gentle but deep.

Rouge wanted to answer curtly, *No, I'm Cinderella*.

Instead, she pushed through the small space left between him and the doorjamb and hurried toward the kitchen.

She stood at the sink, running the water to let it get hot, tracking the sound of him behind her back as he moved down the hall, into the kitchen to the table in the middle of the room, seating himself quietly.

"Your mother around?"

Rouge turned to lean against the counter. The water still ran.

"She's around." She could steady her gaze on him now. Seated, he seemed less formidable and Rouge found herself slipping into perfunctory manners. "You want some coffee?"

He smiled at her, a lopsided grin. Maybe he was in his late twenties, but smiling he looked young. Rouge smelled what was left in her mother's thermos, though she already knew. Bordering on too strong when Liza first made it, left to fester in its warmth, it never kept beyond the first hour. Rouge poured it out and began to fill the kettle.

"Don't bother. I'll just smoke a cigarette."

"I'm making coffee anyway."

She wanted him gone. She did not like strangers in the house. Liza's students were different. Besides, she relished the mornings she had to herself. In a few hours, she'd be off to her job playing with the two Donoghue boys, enough to tire them out for the requested 9 pm bedtime. It took all her energy to capture six-year-old Willie's attention, to peel him off furniture or precarious ledges, his younger brother, Andy, curious to follow but complacent enough to take orders, backing down when she'd bark out *No!*. At least Andy would listen. How did Mrs. Donoghue manage? It was so much work—but Rouge was paid well. Not many of her friends had the stomach for babysitting the Donoghue boys.

"You old enough to drink coffee?" the man asked. In jest? He had to be kidding. She looked at him. His eyes twinkled back. "You old enough to smoke, too?"

"Liza smokes enough for both of us."

"I see." The man pushed himself up. "Must have left mine somewhere. I'll be back in a minute." The kettle was heating up. Rouge could hear the water begin to rumble. He headed for the back door, then stopped and turned. "Poor manners," he said and took a step toward her, his big arm unfurling and reaching out. "Ben Fuller."

Rouge said nothing. She was considering whether or not to take his hand.

"Yeah, your mother did mention you, now I remember. You've got that great name. That Tennessee Williams name. What's it again?"

"Rouge." She swallowed. Emma, Liza's student who often stayed at the house when Liza went to the city, had introduced Rouge to Williams last spring. A drama course she was taking. Yes, it is a Williams name, isn't it? "It's Rouge," she said more firmly. She decided to shake hands, but it was too late. His was now hanging at his side.

"Yeah. Rouge Baker. Is that French or something?"

"No. It's color." She pointed at her face. "My cheeks were bright red when I was born. Liza's an artist. She thinks that way."

"Hmmm." Ben gazed dreamingly toward the barn. "Yes, she would," he said before striding out the door into the back yard.

Rouge ran to the door and called after him. "Don't disturb her."

He was midway between the barn and the house, heading toward the car parked under a trio of big, scabby oak trees. His gait was clumsy.

"What?" He stopped.

"She's working." She pointed toward the back corner of the barn.

Ben shook his head and proceeded his journey toward the car, muffling himself appropriately. "The artist at work. Shhh!"

Rouge grinned. Was he parodying Liza's routine? She watched him reach the car and nearly fall in as he bent through the open window to rummage around the interior. She glanced at the back of the barn that Liza had converted to studio space a long time ago. There had been another man for that job executed when Rouge was what? About three. What was his name? She remembered only the curly red hair, a faint smell of wood clinging to his skin. Liza and he had worked together for what seemed a sliver of time in Rouge's recollection. It had to have been longer than that. Just the work alone. Building the walls that would define her studio within the large barn space, laying in the insulation doubly thick to protect against the cold Hudson Valley winters, nailing up walls, the ceiling, setting in the lights. This would all have taken two people a good deal of time. But in Rouge's mind, the space was created as if by magic with a wave of dabbled light dancing over scattered nails, spilled from the bag, sawdust like a cloud of mist that breathed structure into wood, tools singing in brisk cacophony, the busy mess of creation. In her memory, the studio emerged from the passage of one day. And then he was gone.

Ben finally backed out of the car and stood up, holding a worn brown canvas bag. The kettle let out a shrill whistle. Rouge ran to silence it and finish the coffee. By the time Ben stumbled in, letting the backdoor slam, a lit cigarette nearly falling off his lip, she had two steaming cups set out on the table.

"Hope you like it black. We're out of milk."

"Black's good." He took a careful swallow. "Great coffee. Where'd you learn to make coffee like this?"

Rouge's cheeks felt warm. She was sure she was blushing and giggled. "It was by accident, actually. I was trying to make coffee for Liza. I poured in way too much. She smelled it and said it would knock over a mule. But she took a sip and decided it was good."

"Nothing like a mistake to set you straight." Ben sucked on his cigarette, then blew out the smoke in a thick stream that twisted and curled in the space between them. Rouge eyed the smoke as it snaked itself thin.

"You run the show around here?" he asked.

She laughed hard this time, expelling countless possible responses. She could so easily be snide, angry, ironic if she did not check her words. Thank God sometimes they all came out a jumbled mess that people mistook for laughter. His eyes were green, she realized. Almost green. Hazel really. She wasn't sure what she should answer, so she shrugged and considered asking for a smoke. The fingertips on his right hand were stained deep brown, just like Liza's.

Normally she didn't like the men Liza brought home from the city, those she did bring back. Most barely noticed her, let alone had a conversation, ask *her* about her life. This guy was different. He reminded Rouge of Phil, Liza's sculptor friend who'd materialize from time to time to give a guest talk at the college. Or rummage around the country for discarded pieces of metal, forages Rouge loved to help with. She had to admit, she liked the attention.

"Yeah, I do. Sometimes. When she works, I do." Rouge paused, feeling her posture straighten. "You got another?"

"What, cigarette? Yeah, sure." He reached into his shirt pocket, pulled out a flattened pack. "You old enough to be smoking? How old are you?"

"Almost fifteen," she lied. Her birthday was nearly a year away.

Ben stared as if considering.

"I only smoke once in a while. It's okay. Liza lets me."

He held out the pack. "Long as I'm not the corrupting influence."

Rouge reached for the pack, took one out, held it tight in her lips and lit the match. She knew he was watching her. But she was smooth, she was sure of that. Liza had taught her many things. Some good, others maybe not. Maybe just useful. Like this now. How to strike a match and pull it fast to the end of a cigarette, catch the fire with her breath tugging from the other end to pull the flame through. He kept staring even as he leaned down to take something from his bag.

"Mind if I take your picture?"

"What?" She talked through the cigarette.

"Your photograph. Just sit like that."

He pulled a camera from his bag, leaned back in his chair and took several quick shots. Then he got up, stood behind her and took several more. She stayed cross-legged on the chair, exhaled some smoke, ran her fingers through her long hair, noticed the pale hair on her arms stand erect at the shutter of the camera. *Click. Click.*

"Do you think your mother will let me shoot her painting?"

"No." Her answer was emphatic.

"No. Are you sure?" He had moved to the back door and was concentrating on the glow of light from the barn's far window.

Rouge put out her cigarette, stood up to clear the table. "She doesn't like anyone around her when she works. No one. Not for any reason."

"What's it like?"

"What?"

"Her work. What does she paint?"

Doesn't he know? How could he not know? That's how Liza got their attention after all, sermonizing about her work and all her important artist friends.

"You don't know?"

"I have an idea, though I haven't seen anything yet. She was going to show me." He paused. "You tell me. How would you describe it?"

Well, she painted *things*. Big, gutsy things. About what Rouge had no idea. Painted and scraped and paced and painted for hours and hours. Not like the drawings of cats and snakes and wildflowers and naked, frolicking women that Liza could dash off so easily. Studies, she called them. "What's it of?" Rouge once dared to ask of a wet, glistening battle of reds, yellows and muddy browns. Liza did not answer right away. She studied the canvas, then picked up a scraper and smeared an unsettled glob of paint.

"It's not *of* anything," she finally answered. "It's about

something." With an impatient glance, Liza wiped her hands on her apron. "It's about what you feel it's about."

The truth was, Rouge felt confused, dizzy, nearly panicked, longing for her mother to pull something familiar out of the mess. A bloodied arm, a dead squirrel crushed flat by a car. Nothing so settling as a bundle of flowers, a bowl of grapes, even as that was what Rouge preferred to see. Wished, in fact, that Liza would paint.

Rouge wiped her hands on the dishtowel. "Sometimes it's the beginnings of figures. Like ghosts. Sometimes it's just color and shapes."

"Ah, an abstract expressionist." Ben was inspecting the sheer ivory curtains, running his hand up the backs, between the material and the light.

"Yeah, definitely abstract. That's it."

Click. Click. He looked from the window to the old stove. "Who's her favorite artist?"

"She likes Hank Bolton, de Kooning, too, and Arshile Gorky." Such odd names but Rouge knew they were important ones and was proud at how easily they slid off her tongue.

"Well." He was back scanning for photographs. "She's got good taste."

"Are you a painter too?" It was a question she had been meaning to ask. Of course he was a painter, some sort of artist. They usually were.

Ben laughed hard, almost despite himself. "No. No. I wanted to be, though. But I never learned to draw worth a damn. No, I just take pictures. Mostly of artists."

"Maybe you're better off."

"Maybe I am." Ben moved over to the table, put his

camera down, dug out the one remaining cigarette. "So, when is she done?"

"Who knows? It all depends."

"On how the work's going, of course. What else really matters if the work is going well, right?" He winked.

Pleasantly bewildered, she could not help grinning back. This guy was not like the others. Not at all. He gets it. Smart guy, this one. Unlike the others who would wait and wait while Liza painted, not realizing she had forgotten anyone was there. That often happened. She could get so lost in her work, abandoning the poor guy to Rouge and whomever of Liza's students happened to be babysitting at the time. Usually Emma. Not much would be said later, nothing like an apology when she finally reappeared. Liza would simply blame her work and its hypnotic power when she was fully engaged.

"That's okay, Liza," Rouge would respond.

But it wasn't okay. Rouge hated the awkwardness, feeling responsible for the poor guys and their broken hearts—those pathetic men who had been so easily swept away by Liza's beauty, her beguiling stories. Weren't they smarter than that? Even her students. How they bought her tales. Sometimes Rouge wanted to shake them to their senses. She's not that admirable, you know!

Ben leaned in and snuffed out his cigarette in the dregs of his coffee. "I should probably get back. I've got work to do. Is there a bus or something?"

"Yeah, there's one that leaves at two fifteen."

Ben looked at the clock over the kitchen sink that read quarter to twelve. A little time to kill.

"You ever take pictures?"

"What?"

He held his camera out to her. "Here, try it."

"I don't know how."

"It's easy," he said. "Look in here." He pointed to a tiny opening in the back. "When you see what you like, push this button here."

"Of what?" She held the camera up to her eye.

"Of whatever intrigues you from behind there."

Rouge slowly moved the camera across the room, viewing the kitchen in truncated compartments. The sink and stove. The big picture window. The refrigerator. The table. The light overhead. The open door of the pantry, shelves inside stocked with cans and jars of food. Isolated, what she saw revealed much more. An indelible weight and delineation. The harsh shadow of mullions like a heavy grate. The heaviness of light. Lines, clear and strong, etching graceful forms, aspects she had never noticed until now.

She moved the camera around, first at eye level, then down, running her vision along the floorboards, the edge of the braided rug under the kitchen table. Slowly. Thoughtfully. Finally, the view slid onto her feet, her toes long and thin, the nails trimmed straight across. Her feet on the rug, toes ready to spring, the curve of her arches, strong and determined. Bare, clean, appealing feet. *Click.*

She smiled, handed the camera back.

"No, go on. Finish the roll. I'll just go out and smell the flowers."

Maybe he did, Rouge didn't know. She lost herself looking through the camera, choosing to photograph the stairs, the bottom portion of a partially opened door, a chair, old shriveled lilies in a vase, a slice of her face in the mirror, a lock of hair hanging in front of her cheek. She shot until the film stopped advancing and was sorry to be done.

Just then she noticed the time. *1:20.*

"Damn, I have to get Ben to the bus," she said aloud. Cradling the camera in her arm, she ran downstairs into the kitchen. Not there. Out the front door. Nothing but the wide country vista. Around the house to the back. There he was, lying on the car hood. She grabbed his bag and camera.

"Quick," Rouge called out. "We've got to go. The bus leaves soon." She handed him his bag and camera. "Is this all?"

He rolled off the hood as though half asleep. Pale and wet from the hot sun, the skin of his torso was flabby, inching toward fat. He was a big man and he took his time wiping the sweat off his stomach with his shirt. "Did you get my toothbrush?"

"You brought a toothbrush?" He smiled his crooked grin.

"Very funny. Get in." Rouge climbed onto the driver's seat of the old station wagon, turned the ignition key several times before it took. It's the car, she wanted to say. So old. But he was staring off over the valley. The car jolted as she backed up. Too much gas. *Calm down.* Even Ben banged forward. Still he did not comment and she was glad of that.

"Lovely place," he said, looking over at her once they were on the way. Were her knuckles too white holding tight to the steering wheel? She opened and closed her fingers. "I see why your mother settled here."

"Yeah, she liked it because it was just far enough away from the college where she teaches. She didn't want to be too close to her job." Though students often came and went, many to babysit Rouge when Liza took off to New York, sometimes at a moment's notice, Liza had always insisted on some privacy and distance from her job, a quiet space to paint. She had discovered this old farmhouse forty-five minutes away from the college and not quite two hours outside of New York.

Tess, Rouge's godmother, thought the place 'divine'. She couldn't imagine a more serene retreat, she pronounced every summer when she came from Boston to trade her life as a doctor's wife and portrait painter for a month in the country to sketch and eat blueberries, wander through the fields in bare feet and, at night on the porch, listen to the conversations of the natural world. But mainly, she would say, it was to spend time with the two women she most loved.

"A little too quiet for me," Ben finally made his pronouncement. "You ever been to the city?"

"Yeah. A few times."

"You like it?" Ben was poking under the seat.

"Not really. It's noisy and dirty and crowded."

"It's that all right." He found a loose cigarette. That was what he was looking for. If he had only asked. Liza kept a pack stashed in the glove box. "But it's exciting too. Lots to do. Lots to see. You should give it another try sometime."

It was hot. Even with the windows down, sweat was sticking Rouge's dress to the back of the seat, clamming up the hair at her neck. But they were nearly at the edge of town, as far as she could go. Ben passed her the cigarette. She shook her head no.

"You're a ballsy little chick, aren't you, smoking and driving?"

Rouge felt herself blush.

"Just like your mother. She teach you to drive?"

"My neighbors, across the field. I've been helping them hay for the past few years. Since I can't throw the bales higher than the first row, they taught me to drive the truck."

"Liza know you're taking her car?"

"Yeah, she lets me drive around back roads once in a while."

"Ever been caught?"

"A few times. But not many people drive this road, and the sheriff says as long as I stay out of town and drive slow, he'll look the other way."

Rouge crossed the one-car bridge that connected the main rural road across the river to the settlement of stores and houses that were barely visible through the trees. She edged the car onto the side of the road. Town was a few hundred yards away. Even at the high point of day, it was relatively quiet.

"This is it. As far as I'm allowed to go. The bus station is on the other side of the green. See that clump of buildings there, that old red roof. Just head for that. That'll take you into the center of town. The station's behind Truitt's hardware."

Ben reached in the back for his bag. He opened the door. Before he swung himself out, he turned and grinned. "Thanks for the ride."

The car door slammed shut. He followed her directions, taking long strides along the side of the road. Quickly— how fast he moved—he was at the trees, nearly out of view. Just then he turned and waved back at her. Even from this distance, Rouge thought she could read kindness in his face.

She knew that if he could touch her, if he could reach out and push the hair from her eyes, she would cry. But he was so far down the road and she felt cold sitting here in the car under the bright summer sun.

*

It had been nearly two weeks since Ben had come and gone, and in his wake an oppressive heatwave had rolled in and settled over the valley. Life in the small town slowed to a standstill, people doing as little as possible. Though Rouge had other occasional babysitting jobs, she had a respite from the Donoghues as Mrs. Donoghue had taken the high-strung boys to her parents in Maine. Mary and Walter Simpson retired to shade-drawn rooms in their house just outside of town, leaving the store in the care of their son, Jerry. Hurley, the barber, closed his shop altogether, bent over and grumbling to no one in particular as he locked the door and hung the *Closed* sign; "Ain't no hair growin' in this weather." Even O'Neil's cows stayed close to the barn after milking, the journey out to pasture too far to go.

Liza slept during much of the day, her bedroom shaded by the big oak trees out back. By night, she would twist her hair up off her neck, tie her apron around her and head off to the studio to paint. But Rouge could tell she got little done. She knew just by looking at Liza's fingernails, how clean they stayed. The silence, well, that could be anything, but not the work, not when her hands were this clean. Rouge herself did only one thing each day. In truth, she did plenty of things but only this she would remember. Every day, first thing, she washed her sweat-drenched sheets and remade her bed.

At night, just before she slid into the crisp sheets, she'd fan her bed with the covers, because in this kind of heat, what she loved most was the zing of taut, fresh cotton against her skin, imagining snow and promising herself that this winter after the first blizzard she would fall naked on the ground and make angels with her bare skin.

If it weren't for the heat, Rouge might have considered her apathy as something worth noticing. She might have felt an unsettling emptiness, closed her eyes and observed how easily the image of O'Neil's barren winter fields floated into her mind—the dark, heavy dirt, raw and lifeless, no sign whatsoever of the impending mutiny lurking below the surface. Seeds that will grow and burst through come spring. If she weren't so flaming hot, she might have felt the stirring of that restlessness inside herself. But she didn't have enough energy to care.

But this last day of July, the summer's tenor finally changed. Tess was coming. In preparation, Liza was the first one up, had, in fact, not gone to bed, moving from the studio at dawn into her garden to fill baskets with vegetables and flowers.

"Get up, get up, Sleeping Beauty," she chirped through Rouge's half-closed door, swinging it open with her foot as she stepped in, a pot of yellow roses in one hand, a pile of folded towels in the other. "Tessie's here tomorrow. Get up. We have too much to do."

Rouge was sent to town to buy supplies early before the heat wore her down. On days like this, when Liza's energy became infectious, Rouge happily accepted her chores, spinning off on her bike to fetch the requested items as Liza preferred to clean the house herself and primp their surroundings—floral arrangements that filled tables in bursts of disarray, the curtains tied back just so, gardening gloves lying on the bench out back, the fingers hanging over the edge, stroking the lip of the watering can. At the center of the kitchen table, a glass bowl brimming with peaches and plums from the trees near the barn, tomatoes lining the windowsills, the large flat oval basket stuffed with zucchini, yellow squash and beans. The air inside was a soothing mix of rosemary and mint, hanging in decorative clumps that Liza had pinned to the walls.

As a child, these were the best days of Rouge's life, when the house came to life with colors and smells and her mother's creative touch. Later, as she began to babysit and see the plain, predictable environments others inhabited, she realized how magical Liza's touch could be. By evening, the smell of blueberry pie would take over as Liza and Rouge settled on the porch to sit and wait. Some years, they'd sing stupid songs and laugh; one year, Liza requested dreams. Not nightmares, just the good ones. Of late, Rouge took hold of these moments to gather what truths she could. This night, the notion of memories came to mind. They were leaning back against the wall, watching moths flap into the soft amber light.

"What is your first memory?" Rouge asked, breaking the silence.

Liza thought for some time before responding. She seemed lost in thought. When she finally responded, she spoke with that contemplative attention to detail that captivated Rouge.

"It's rather an odd one. I was alone with my father. He was going down to his greenhouse. It was foggy, almost like a dream. It must have been spring. And cold. Damp. I was bundled up and the wool scratched my skin. He held my hand as we walked. I remember being happy. That and the warmth of his hand. Fancy that."

The image held Rouge speechless. Liza paused to light another cigarette.

"We got to the door of the greenhouse. I could see plants through the thick windows. Papa took a while to find the keys. He let go of my hand to rattle his pockets. When he finally opened the door, it was dark inside. Not a speck of light. He told me to wait, then he went ahead and disappeared into the dark."

Goosebumps skittered across Rouge's arms. "Then what?"

"Then nothing. That's all I remember."

"How old were you?"

"I don't know. Little. Three or four."

"Were you scared?"

"Maybe. Probably. I don't know." Liza paused to knock a cigarette out of the half-empty pack that lay beside her. "And you. What is your first memory?"

Rouge hesitated, first running through the possibility of pressing more from Liza. But she knew Liza had given away all she would for the time being. She did not speak easily about her father, if at all. Her mother had died during childbirth so, of course, there were no memories there. Only the one photograph of her mother that she kept in the studio. If the woman's hair was longer and darker and the eyes were not so gentle, it could have been an image of Liza in her early twenties. She had a few photographs of her father, a pensive, thin man, and not many memories, at least that Liza would divulge. Rouge knew he was the town doctor in New Hampshire. He was quiet and methodical and seldom home. When he was, he preferred to settle into his chair in the front room and read. Liza, a wild child, would be kept away by Mrs. Carton, the housekeeper. Plump, stern Mrs. Carton. Liza spoke of her with a tone of disgust laced with gratitude. She had been her caretaker, after all, the one who kept her clean and fed, who minded her childhood by insisting that Liza keep herself busy—out of trouble really—by reading or drawing or playing with dolls. Keep yourself clean, child, quiet, and, under no circumstance disturb your father. He needs quiet. It was during such solitude in his reading chair in the front study that Liza's father died suddenly one day. A massive stroke, they said. Liza was twenty-two, teaching painting in town. And what happened to Mrs. Carton? Had she died too? Rouge had never asked. In any event, Liza had been left the house—which she sold—and an inheritance. Small, but enough, Liza would say, to buy her freedom.

Liza was staring at her now. Rouge could feel the ebb and flow of her warm, moist breath. "Don't think so hard. Just let it come to you."

"Oh, yeah." Rouge closed her eyes as if to follow Liza's instructions. But she knew her answer well before her mother asked, had stored it wrapped and cradled in her mind ever since the event took place.

"I remember butterflies. Lots of butterflies. I was swinging in a tree. You were underneath me painting the house, stopping every now and then to send butterflies up to play with me. You'd shoo them with your brush. Carefully, so you wouldn't get them wet."

Liza grinned. Her eyes sparkled. "You remember that?

You were still a baby. I tied you up in the tree, so you wouldn't wander away. What a memory you have."

Rouge smiled back, but as Liza looked at Rouge, her eyes began to change, growing narrow and cold even as they seemed to stay the same. Often, this was the harbinger of depression blowing in. Thankfully, Tess would land first and hold things at bay.

Rouge returned to the front porch the next morning to wait. She had a book with her, but she could not read. Instead, she stared at the words and waited, first for the purr of a car engine coming down the road, then the sleek, big car, the pink-scarved head, the owl-eyed sunglasses, a sleeveless arm rising up to wave, smiles and shrieks until Tess pulled to a stop in front of the house, everybody leaping up and out until they stopped in one long hug.

"Just look at you two," Tess said as she pushed back from the embrace, taking off her sunglasses for a better look. "Rouge, I swear you've grown three inches. I think everything I brought for you is going to be too small."

"That's all right," Liza answered. "We can get out the sewing machine and let things out if we need to."

"If Rouge even likes them. She's getting quite womanly." Tess winked at Rouge, slid her hand along the girl's hip. Embarrassed, Rouge drew her shoulders in, then noticed that Tess, a large woman to begin with, had gotten plumper since the previous summer.

"Rouge, honey, get Tess's bags. I'm sure she's dying of thirst. Tessie, I made some fresh lemonade. Let's go inside and sit in the shadow of something. There must be some coolness somewhere."

Rouge hung back. Normally, she would have taken Tess's hand and skipped in alongside her, eager to stay with the two of them as long as she could. This year, though, she found herself preferring to hang back as Liza and Tess walked arm in arm into the house, choosing instead to observe. Here was Tess dressed impeccably, as she always was, even in the country, in a fresh white shirt and lime green skirt. How startling she looked beside Liza, whose shirt was pulled out, her shorts tattered and faded, her apron splattered with paint. Strange, these two. How oddly joined, but not. Watching them, Rouge felt a scratch of sadness streak through her as though she were witnessing an accelerated walk through time. Two women, now mature, now old, now walking together, arm in arm, as though toward their deaths.

Rouge took a step backward then turned to collect Tess's bags. She could not help but think of the photo Liza still kept pinned to her studio wall, the small one with the crinkle-cut edges, the image now faded from age. In it, Liza and Tess are hugging in front of Liza's old station wagon. They are off to New York to art school, both of them so young—in their early twenties—so beautiful. Liza's long hair is tied off her face and her lips are split into a boisterous grin, as if at any moment she could leap out of the image. Tess seems quieter in her enthusiasm, more secure; her solid, curvy form anchoring Liza's wispy body. Looking at the photograph, Rouge felt light as a feather, sensing the thrill of life opening itself up to these women, young and fueled with only a hair of experience. The rest all possibility.

As Rouge lugged Tess's baggage up the stairs, chatter filled the kitchen, spilling throughout the house, gay, lighthearted banter punctuated by throaty laughter, floating through the air like a cool summer breeze. But the air was not cool and the suitcase was heavy, and by the time Rouge got to the top of the stairs and opened the guest room door, she was dripping wet. The shades were drawn to hold back the bulk of the midday heat. Would it be hotter to open the windows or leave them shut? She couldn't decide and sat instead on the wooden floor and leaned against the bed.

Maybe she closed her eyes for a moment. Maybe she actually fell asleep. The next thing she knew, Tess was beside her, gently shaking her shoulder.

"It's worse in Boston if that's any consolation."

"I don't suppose so." Rouge straightened her head, which had fallen crooked on top of her shoulder. Her neck ached. "What do you think is worse, melting or freezing to death?"

Tess shuddered at the thought. "I hope we don't have to find out. Ever." She let out a long breath. "We know it won't last forever. This godforsaken weather. Nothing ever does."

They sat for a few moments, almost shoulder to shoulder, the body heat between them pressing like a brick wall. Tess touched Rouge's face, turned her head to look at her as she spoke.

"Besides hot, how are you?"

"I'm okay, I guess."

"Try something more emphatic than a guess."

"I'm fine. Really."

Tess let Rouge's chin go. "Would you like to know how you look?"

Rouge shrugged, though she did long to hear.

72

"You look bored and restless, thinking that you'd like to get away. But where, for what? That is still a question. You look like you're growing up, my dear."

Rouge could have smiled. She could have cried, too, both at the same time, with the same intensity. Instead, her face stayed neutral and did not give away a thing.

"That's what I think, anyway. I may be completely off the mark. But, you know I'm here whenever you feel like talking."

"I know. I just don't have anything to say right now."

"Well, when you do. In the meantime, how is Liza?"

"She's about the same."

"Are her depressions any worse?"

Rouge considered them a moment. They were still complete, self-contained worlds in and of themselves that invited no outside visitors. They carried her away sometimes a week at a time, until one day, without warning, they spit her out and she landed as if from hibernation, refreshed and ready to wind up and go. Right then, thinking about what to tell Tess, Rouge imagined Liza standing in front of her father's greenhouse, watching her papa disappear into the dark. Leaving nothing but darkness in between.

"No, I don't think they're any worse."

"More frequent?"

"No, not that either."

"How is her work?"

Rouge shrugged. She never looked at it anymore. Liza had ceased asking her opinion. Her daughter's curt responses were answer enough to tell Liza that in this arena, Rouge was in the enemy camp. The big disapproval. For Liza's paintings made Rouge uncomfortable—sometimes the work *was* beautiful, sometimes it *was* enticing, but it always made her

73

dizzy. That was what drove those stupid compliments. *Nice.* Or, even worse, *Interesting.* What kind of answer is that? But Rouge could not help herself. She could not make her body and mind take a unified stance. She could admit this to Tess. Tess understood. Why, she would probably say she didn't get it too. But Tess always tried to make sense of what Liza showed her. That much was evident by the conversations the women would drop into for all hours of the night after Tess had seen Liza's latest work. For as long as Rouge was allowed to stay up, she'd hang on the nonsensical words. But now she had no desire to try.

"I'll be seeing for myself soon enough," Tess winked.

"Tess. Rouge. What are you two doing up there?" Liza called from the kitchen.

"We'll be down in a minute," Tess called back. Then to Rouge, almost in a whisper, "What about her drinking? And don't you dare say the same."

Rouge felt pressed. Tired. Sick of it, wanting to scream out, *I don't know. Stop it now,* she knew Tess's intentions were good. These were the concerns of her mother's best friend, maybe her best friend, too. Still, Rouge felt cornered and angry, and the look she shot back to Tess must have been tempered by desperation, because she did love this woman. Tempered, but enough to say, *Leave me alone.*

Tess stood up and smiled to indicate she would leave Rouge be.

"Later, can you take me to the river for a swim?" she asked, turning at the door.

"Sure."

"I'm calling this the summer of ennui," Tess announced over coffee, the three of them lounging on the front porch, Liza and Tess taking a break from a conversation that bored Rouge—the multi-faceted nature of love. They had been dissecting Tess's marriage, a happy one by most standards, Liza had been quick to admit, though Tess had more nuanced views. Rouge's attention had wandered off, pulled away by the sun warming her face as she lay on her back along the edge of the porch.

Hearing the words *summer of ennui* called her back, Tess's way of making the conversation about her. The summer of curiosity this past year, the summer of laughter before that, the summer of tantrums, the summer of sorrow—the year her pet cat Delilah had died—the summer of faded scarlet (at six, Rouge would wear nothing but her mother's pink cotton shirt).

"Ennui," Tess said again. "It's perfect for someone so clearly floating in that nebulous terrain called adolescence."

"What do you mean?" Rouge sat up.

Tess smiled. "Quiet, listless, introspective, sometimes hardly present." Tess looked first at Rouge. "Sound familiar?"

"That's it exactly," Liza chimed in.

Rouge felt herself flush. "Are you making fun of me?"

"Not at all," Tess said. "It's perfectly normal, darling. You're in that in-between place, limbo."

"Floating's a good word," Liza agreed.

Rouge looked first at Liza, then at Tess. Ordinarily, she loved being the center of attention, but now she felt exposed. In limbo, yes, though Tess had seen it first, and

Rouge was surprised at how the assessment hit her. The two of them started giggling and Rouge had a sudden impulse to lash out, yet caught herself. It was only teasing.

"It's not the easiest time," Liza said, quick to sense Rouge's discomfort.

"I disagree. It doesn't have to be difficult. Just because you were all over the place," Tess was talking to Liza, but she winked at Rouge, "doesn't mean Rouge has to be. She's more grounded than any teenager I know."

"I am?" Rouge thought of the other girls in her class, many having navigated the rocky terrain of freshman year with more confidence, knowing how to respond to the awkward attention of the boys, the slights to each other, while Rouge felt trapped, not wanting to even be a player in the game.

"Absolutely. You're on the next big adventure. You should be excited. Think of yourself as being wrapped in a cocoon, a remnant of what you were and as yet only a suggestion of what you will become."

"Brilliant," Liza said, nodding to Rouge. "That is you exactly, don't you think?"

Rouge felt strangely naked, pinned to a dissecting table with the two women gloating over her defenseless body. She wanted to cover herself.

"Maybe. I don't know."

Rouge made a move to leave, but Liza got up first. "We should get into town and do our shopping if we're going to have that picnic."

Tess stood slowly. "Sometimes I just hate having to move. You coming, Rouge?"

"No." The answer was quick and certain, just what Rouge needed. She was more grounded than she thought.

"Then would you start picking blueberries?" Liza asked.

"Please," Tess added. "Lots of them. I could do nothing this last week but eat blueberry pie."

Rouge waited until the sound of the car had disappeared before closing her book—*Bleak House*, so ponderous. Why had she ever picked it up? Because she loved *Oliver Twist*, that's why—and headed down to the kitchen. On the top shelf of the pantry, she found her mother's stack of baskets and chose the medium-sized one, stained a deep blue. Several jars of blueberry jam, clouded with dust, were neatly aligned on the top row. Some years Liza had dated. "Take the older ones first," she would instruct Rouge when sending her to fetch a jar for toast or pancakes. But Rouge had always believed the old ones lost their taste and pushed them to the back row instead. 1958, 1959, 1956. Who'd want to eat them now?

This had been a good year for the blueberries, and the bushes behind the barn were bursting with fruit that popped off the branches easily between Rouge's fingers. She could almost hold the basket underneath and tap off the berries. Sweet, juicy with the tart undertaste she loved, that zing of sour that startled the back of her jaw at first bite. She closed her eyes, felt the squirt of blueberry juice spread over her tongue. It was warm and sweet, the juice, her standing in the sun with no one else around. At that moment she felt happy.

The weather was pleasant now. A late summer rain had broken the humidity and the air was fresh with a tinge of chill—the imminence of fall—and golden light. She relished this time of year just before the heat dissolved into cold and the abundance of summer withered and dried. The cicadas were still noisy but their chatter had slowed. Across the road, O'Neil's land was bursting with hay so tall it used to bury her when she was small as she ran through the fields, feeling the long grass slither around her legs. In a few weeks, he'd have the tractors out to cut down the billowing blankets of hay, leaving the fields raw and crippled, the battered stalks of grass lifeless. Or so it seemed. Until spring, when green shoots burst through the dark soil and the cycle begins again.

It took her no time to fill the basket, which she emptied into the big tin tub Liza kept on the back porch. When she had finished harvesting—four baskets, enough fruit to fill the tub halfway—her fingers were stained deep violet, as were her lips and the front of her shirt. Damn! Liza's old shirt. Oh well, she shrugged, she could use it for painting.

Rouge was in her room drying off from a shower when Liza and Tess returned. The car rattled up the driveway, two doors opened and closed one right after another as insouciant women's voices careened into the silence of the place. Rouge slipped on a shirt and a pair of clean jeans. The screen door creaked open, slammed shut. Liza's voice rang out.

"Rouge, are you here? You have a package. From New York."

Rouge bounded down the stairs, zipping her jeans.

"Who do you know in New York?" Liza asked, holding out a large manila envelope addressed: *Miss Rouge Baker.* At the upper left-hand corner was scribbled, *126 Spring Street, New York.*

For a moment, Rouge had no idea. She was as perplexed as the two women hovering over her. Opening the stiff package carefully—it felt like a piece of cardboard was wedged in—she pulled out the contents; several large black and white photographs.

"What's this?" Liza tried to grab the pile from her. Instead, Rouge spread them out on the table as the images began to register. The crisp slant of an open door cushioned by its harsh shadow, a pair of feet slightly off-center, a close-up of a face cracked by thin strands of hair. These were the photographs she had taken; yet, blown up into large prints, they seemed formidable, bigger than her own vision of what she had shot, bigger even than her imagination.

Liza was edgy. "Rouge, what are these?"

"They're mine."

"What do you mean, they're yours?"

"I took them."

Liza laughed. "When did you take them? You don't have a camera."

Tess was studying each photograph. Rouge noticed a folded piece of paper that had fallen out of the envelope onto the table.

"These are wonderful, Rouge," Tess finally said. Then, to Liza, "Look at these. She is really good."

"Rouge?"

The exasperation in her mother's voice surprised her.

"Tell me." Liza was waiting.

"Okay, I'll tell you. Do you remember that last guy?"

Tess looked at Liza as Liza looked away and began to tap her foot. "Of course I remember him," she answered tersely.

"Then you'll remember what he is, won't you?" Liza continued tapping her foot, refusing to respond. So Rouge blurted out, "He's a photographer and he let me use his camera while you were busy painting, and these are the pictures I took."

"Well, they're very nice," Liza snapped back and left the room.

Neither Tess nor Rouge said anything at first. Rouge clutched the note in her fist as she gathered up the photographs. Tess held the envelope for her. As Rouge slid the photographs neatly in on top of the cardboard, Tess sighed. "That came out of nowhere, didn't it?"

Rouge simply smiled back as though it were nothing. Really. Then she hurried upstairs, closing her door snugly behind her. The note was short, the handwriting barely legible.

Rouge,

You've got a great eye. Hope you keep this up.
Ben.

Rouge found a piece of paper.

Dear Ben,

Thank you so much. I can't believe these are mine. They look so good. I'm really happy.

PS. Don't rot in New York.

Liza did not knock as she usually did, just burst in the room only moments after Rouge had folded up her note.

"What's going on?"

"Nothing. I just took some pictures. He sent them back."

"Jesus, Rouge, I slept with the guy."

"So, you must have liked him."

"Yeah, I liked him well enough."

"Don't worry then. He's a good guy."

"How do you know that?"

"You brought him home, didn't you? Would you have brought home a creep?"

Liza crossed her arms, stared at Rouge. What could she say to that? Rouge had her there. Liza started to answer but caught herself and left the room, calling behind as she shut the door, "Dinner's in half an hour."

Rouge woke early and rode her bike to town before Liza or Tess had gotten up. She bought coffee and a roll at the bakery, then sat outside the post office. She didn't have to wait long. The doors opened exactly at nine.

"Ah, Rouge, you're up bright and early." It was Mr. Nelson, the postal clerk, his uniform freshly ironed, his hair combed back and held in place by a dark blue visor. "Forgot the package, huh?"

"What package? I just wanted to mail a letter."

"Why, there was a package that came along with your envelope from New York. Your mother left here so quickly, I didn't have time to get it for her."

Mr. Nelson disappeared into the back and returned carrying a small box. "Here you go. It's for you."

The return address was the same, Spring Street. She could feel her face turn red as she hurried out the door. "Thanks."

Outside, she sat down on the bench and tore open the box. Out fell a large, heavy wad of newspaper that she unwrapped carefully.

"Oh my god," she almost shrieked. It was the camera. Ben's camera. Also a little booklet and another note:

Here are the instructions. You shouldn't have any problem. And send me your film.
   Ben.

81

THREE

Liza

(Summer 1951)

L iza was lying on her back when she opened her eyes. Waking slowly, she turned to find Hank sprawled beside her, tangled in the sheets, his head flat on the exposed mattress that their sex must have bared. How did she get here? Ah, the opening. Yes. The enormity of the night coming out of sleep seemed like a dream. And the Cedar Bar afterward? That felt like a dream slipping away— standing at the bar with de Kooning and Kline and others while Hank flirted with Elaine across the room. The eye contact back and forth. The gloating. The competition. Was she imagining it all?

His breathing was steady, soft, like a baby's she thought, as she ran her hand gently over his chest down to his penis, shriveled now like a fat, wrinkled worm. At her touch, he briefly smiled then rolled onto his side, not ready to be roused. She was sure he was having auspicious dreams.

Sweet, sensitive boy he seemed at that moment. Freed from his tough-guy exterior, here was such appeal. How alike they were. Liza longed to wrap her arms around him, tuck into his backside and drift into his dreams. How easy it would be to float into him. To lose herself in his familiar terrain. Too easy. The thought made her stiffen and roll away.

Pigeons cooed from the ledge outside the big open

window. Nestling back onto her pillow, she lay beside Hank and tried to recollect the previous night's antics. She smiled. Was this happiness freed of any constraints? She hated to name the sensation, could not bear to move lest she throw it off like a heavy blanket. Maybe she could paint this feeling. She'd like to try. Snuffing out her cigarette, she found some old crackers to give to the pigeons before she tiptoed away.

It was nearly dawn when she left the building, the sky beginning to lighten, the air fresh and cool. The sidewalks were empty, nobody anywhere, hardly even a noise, just the occasional squawk of a seagull cruising for garbage, a few delivery trucks banging over potholes on Fourth Avenue, well out of view. Liza inhaled the clarity of the city that existed in these early morning hours, no confusion of human forms or streaking traffic, the constant motion that distracted from the essence of the city. All those vertical lines of buildings, the rules of perspective that governed the layout of the streets. The fundamentals of drawing—line and form—the very bones of good painting upon which everything else would hang.

Liza hurried to the studio on 10th Street she had recently sublet from one of Hofmann's students, who was spending a year in Paris. The timing had been perfect, as Liza had begun painting bigger canvases—the more she moved into abstraction, the more she needed to put her entire body behind her brushstrokes to sweep on the paint—and she had outgrown the living room in the apartment she shared with Tess. Only a few blocks away, this studio was a coup for her both in its size and affordable rent. She was lucky to have found it.

Unlocking the industrial door took some effort, but once the lock clicked open and she shoved her way in using her shoulder, Liza entered the space filled with anticipation. A big sheet of canvas was tacked up on the wall, a painting she had begun just a few days before, some streaks of color, the beginnings of form. Her head overflowing with ideas, Liza stripped off her dress, slipped out of her shoes, and peeled off the fake lashes. Pulling on the overalls that hung on a nail by the refrigerator, which had stopped working long before Liza arrived, she lit the stove and started a kettle of water for coffee, then rummaged through a drawer to find some cigarettes. Unearthing a nearly full pack, she lit one and slid the rest into a hip pocket. Then she gathered up her hair, twisting it into a thick coil that she anchored with a pencil onto the back of her head.

Arms crossed, she stood in front of her canvas. Such a strange mix of brown and ochre, almost like vomit, she thought, hating the hue. It had started out as the Brooklyn Bridge, a civic wonder to which Hank had introduced her. The stately structure had taken her by surprise, moving her deeply. What was the essence of this magnificence? She knew the answer lay in the process that had not begun well. With one stroke of the scraper, she smeared most of the paint off, leaving a muddy film of brown. A touch of blue perhaps, the uplifting lap of water against stone.

She should have been exhausted after the delirium of the show. At least hungover. But she felt strangely rested and clear. Two huge windows in the studio were wide open and the city below was coming to life—horns honking, gates over front doors clanging open, the buzz of pedestrians early on a Saturday morning. Even on Saturdays, a palpable energy could be felt rising from the streets. Sometimes it was hard just to think. But not this morning. She felt hopeful, still inflated from the memory of the show. The bridge beckoned. Laying out globs of paint on her palette, mixing this one with that, she would let her instinct drive her. She loaded a fat brush with paint, approached the canvas like a willing partner and unleashed a long wave of color, then another.

She must have been at work for hours. The room was hot, the worn pine floor warm from the sun streaming through the windows, splattered paint glistening on the floor. But Liza had no feel for the hour, lost as she was in the confusion of form battling color, what to leave, what to scrape away. She barely noticed the noise from the street as its volume increased, or the repeated rapping on the door.

"Liza. Liza. Are you in there? Open up!" It was Tess banging, her voice growing louder, more recognizable, as if pulling Liza out of a dream.

"What happened to you last night?" she asked, waltzing in with two shopping bags when Liza heaved open the door.

"I was at the Cedar."

Tess eyed Liza, waiting for the rest. When Liza stayed silent, she said, "I trust you didn't sleep there."

Liza smiled a sheepish grin.

"Did you end up with Hank?" Liza nodded. "You two make quite the pair."

"Yeah," Liza admitted, putting down her brush. "Maybe we do."

Waving off Liza's cavalier attitude, Tess looked around for a place to set down her bags. She shook her head, sighed.

"It's filthy in here," she said, pushing a pile of newspapers away to find some room on the counter. "How in the world do you keep yourself straight?" Tess glanced at Liza. "I take that back. This is why you cannot keep yourself straight."

Liza shrugged. "It's why I have you."

"Well, thank goodness you do." Tess began fishing items out of one of the bags, laying down a loaf of French bread, some cheese and bags of fresh fruit. "Here, I brought you something to eat. I'm sure you haven't had breakfast yet. Or lunch. Though it's almost time for dinner."

Golden light filled the studio, clearly the light of early evening. Last night at this time, Liza and Tess were arriving at the opening. It seemed so far away, days since Liza had eaten a thing.

"I am starving, come to think of it." She sat at one of the kitchen chairs, cut off a hunk of bread and some cheese. Out of the second bag, Tess pulled a bottle of wine, a carton of cigarettes and some paper cups.

"You are the love of my life," Liza announced as she took a bite. "Marry me."

Tess chuckled. "Darling, you want a cleaning woman, not a wife. Now where is your corkscrew? Let's have a drink."

Rummaging through some drawers, Tess unearthed a corkscrew, opened the bottle and poured wine into the cups. Giving one to Liza, she took the other. As she leaned against the counter, she stared at the canvas on the wall, then walked over to look at it more closely.

"This is provocative," she said, her back to Liza.

Liza waved her away. "It's nothing yet."

"Not yet, maybe." Tess turned, came back and took a seat. "But it will be. I'm sure. Amazing. Full of life and passion. That's the thing."

Liza shook her head. "Are you ever not the optimist? Though I certainly appreciate it, a little doubt might do you good."

"It's hard not to be optimistic when one is as talented as you," Tess said. "Still, I can understand how this drives you crazy. How do you know when you're finished, where you're even going? I couldn't stand the uncertainty."

Liza knew Tess had always admired her audacity. She was a good artist, with the mettle to be bold. Even at the age of twelve when they first met, Liza could capture anything on paper—the glassy surface of the lake, sweeping floral bouquets that filled their house, even the cantankerous glint in their teacher's eye, the old high school art teacher, retired but still giving classes in the summer. Liza had dragged Tess along. When classes were over, they would take pads out into the fields. Picnics packed by Tess's mother, Liza's box of pastel pieces, Liza, her real teacher, instructing her how to draw.

Tess took a seat beside Liza. "Anyway, I'm amazed you're even working at all. After such an opening, I would still be walking on air. How you could even begin to concentrate is beyond me."

Liza deflected the enthusiasm with a perfunctory smile.

"Well, I, for one, admire your ambition. One day, I can say I roomed with the great Liza Baker."

"Right." Liza poured more wine into her cup. Tess raised hers.

"We should drink to that. To your success." She took a long swallow.

Yes, her success. Liza smiled at that thought, yet there was so much to do. Though welcome, Tess's enthusiasm was also unsettling. Liza looked at the painting, her rendition of the Brooklyn Bridge, a monumental structure that captivated her—the feelings of impenetrable solidity against the ever-changing flow of water. Such comfort, this anchoring that inspired hope. But elusive too. She thought of de Kooning's woman and how he could not get hold of her. She quickly swallowed the last of her wine.

"I should get back to work," she said, standing quickly.

"What you should do is get some sleep," Tess answered as she rose to pack her bags. "You look exhausted."

"I will," Liza promised. "Let me just work a few hours more. I'll be back soon."

Instead, Liza stayed with the bridge, painting as it grew dark and the noise of the city dimmed. Tackling questions the work elicited, she imagined herself standing on the bank, sketching with Hank as he entertained with stories of the bridge's inception. The first steel-wire suspension bridge that boasted a wine vault under one of the main supports. "That was one way they raised money to build the bridge," he instructed, "by renting out space in the vault."

How does he learn these things, she wondered, though at the time her attention had been captivated by the perfect balance between heavy granite and gossamer steel cables. Now, as she painted and scraped and painted some more, she swore she could feel his presence in the work, pushing her deeper, encouraging leaps of color and strokes. Finally, it was coming together. She stood back to be sure. Yes, it was good.

It was not as late as she thought when she finished, plenty of time for a drink at the Cedar, if people were there. Most of all, she wanted to find Hank and show him the painting. More than anyone else, he'd understand what she had wrestled through. He was not at the Cedar; she scanned the smoky room carefully, to be sure. After such a late night, he could very well be asleep. Should she wake him? If only to crawl into his bed and talk about the painting in the morning.

Liza hurried the few blocks to Hank's apartment and ran up the stairs. At first, she listened at the door, then began to knock, louder each time, until she heard a shuffling as he approached, awkwardness fumbling with the lock, then the opening, just a crack.

"Jesus, Liza," was his greeting.

"I woke you, I'm sorry. But you need to see the bridge."

"What bridge? Are you crazy?" He spoke in a whisper, stealthily glancing over his shoulder.

"The Brooklyn Bridge, our bridge. Let me in. We can sleep and I'll show you in the morning."

Hank put up a hand to hold her back. "This is not a good time."

Someone else was in his bed. Her stomach cemented. "I see," was all she could muster. He did not have to say anything more. Still he did, but his words were deafened by her humiliation as she hurried away.

*

Liza tried her damnedest to put Hank out of her mind. *Stupid girl,* she had chastised herself over and over as she fled from his apartment. *Stupid to even consider love, such thankless terrain.* The parallel with her father was painfully clear. She envisioned him late at night reading in his chair as she stood by the door, watching, waiting for him to notice her.

Why, Liza, she wanted to hear him say, *what are you doing up at this hour? Come,* he'd put down his book and eagerly pat his lap, *let me read you a story.* Welcoming her to him. Wanting her to approach.

But he did not notice, as long as she hung in the doorway. Or if he did, he'd take her by the hand and tuck her back into bed. The chore of it, his paternal duty. Nothing more than that.

Her guard had softened around Hank, all that they shared. She expected too much, she realized now. *Foolish girl.*

She could not bring herself to go to class the next week. Instead, she stayed in her studio and tried to paint her grief. *Here,* she thought, *manifest this and get it out of your system,* painting and painting in a fury, a thick wall of delirious color, not a crack for any emotion but self-pity to come through.

Hating this weakness, Liza walked the streets of New York, trying to lose herself in the energy of the city. She spent hours at the Met studying classic sculptures, marveling at the work of the modernists, reigniting her passion for paint. *Remember the success of the Ninth Street Show. The beginning,* she reminded herself. Now, there is so much work to do.

She'd return for the last week of class before Hofmann headed off to his summer school in Provincetown. Many of his students were following him there, Hank included. Earlier, he had tried to get Liza to come—the gang of them—but she decided to stay behind, everyone else making plans to escape the city. Tess was going off with her family to travel through northern Africa, a tour of Morocco and Egypt, then on to a rented villa in the south of France. Other artists were heading to the eastern tip of Long Island, a few home to the Midwest. It would be a quiet summer. Think of how much she'd get done.

Hank was in his usual spot in class when she arrived. A pretty young girl—Alice was her name—was set up beside him, the two of them in jovial spirits as they set up their easels. When he noticed Liza, he cut their conversation short and made his way around the other students getting ready for class.

"Where have you been?" he whispered to her. "I came to your studio several times. I was worried."

"You don't need to worry about me," she retorted, trying to hold her anger at bay.

"Meet me after class?" he implored.

"I'm busy after class."

He looked around. Only moments of free time to go. "Look, you and I…"

She put a hand on his shoulder as much to silence as to push him away.

"It's fine, Hank. You don't need to explain."

As May ended and June welcomed in the summer, the heat, held firm by concrete and metal, grew thick and pasty. Liza found it hard to paint, hard to do anything in such humidity. Liza tried to work through the night and sleep until late in the afternoons. But with the fan only circulating hot air, she was often drenched in sweat and did not sleep well at all. Tess was distracted, preparing for her summer trip. Liza's efforts were going poorly.

She lay in bed, thinking if she only stayed still, she might feel cooler. Another cold shower? A fresh idea?

The phone rang.

"Tess," she called out, hoping not to move.

No answer. Simply the ringing of the phone.

Liza looked at the clock. *2:55*. Time to get up. She rose quickly and reached the phone by the fourth ring.

"Hello."

A crisp British voice responded. A male. "I'm trying to reach Liza Baker."

"Yes, I'm Liza." She was suddenly awake.

"My name is Logan Mountstuart. I saw your painting at the Ninth Street Show. I thought it was terrific."

"Thank you," Liza answered graciously, hoping she sounded clear and alert.

"I hope you don't mind my calling. I got your number from Leo." He was speaking quickly, confidently. "I am the associate director of Leeping Fils Gallery. We're on Madison Avenue, an affiliate of Leeping Fils in Paris. I don't suppose you are familiar with us?"

"I've heard of the gallery, yes," Liza lied. Madison Avenue! Paris! Her pulse raced.

"I was wondering if I could visit your studio, look at some of your other work."

Liza's heartbeat accelerated. She tried to keep the excitement out of her voice. "Yes, of course."

"How about three tomorrow afternoon?"

"That would be fine." She gave him the address.

The next day, he arrived precisely at three. Liza had left the door open and heard his footsteps resounding up the two flights of stairs. She wished the building had an elevator. At least her studio looked good. She and Tess had spent the afternoon cleaning the place, putting things in order, setting out her best paintings, trying to make the studio look presentable for a professional eye.

Though Tess insisted she come back to the apartment and try to sleep, Liza had stayed awake most of the night. A little make-up would help, but not too much. Some mascara, enough to frame her large brown eyes. A dab of lipstick? She applied some, then immediately wiped it off, deciding the accent too formal. She should look more like an artist, she thought, choosing to wear Capri pants and a clean white shirt. Nothing fancy, but definitely fresh.

"Logan Mountstuart," he said, arriving a bit sweaty but not out of breath. He held out a hand. He had a round face, boyish, his appearance making him feel more accessible than did his voice over the phone. He was dressed casually and grinned when he saw her. Liza relaxed.

She offered him water or lemonade, which Tess had made fresh that morning and put into a thermos to keep cool. He accepted the latter, before taking a seat at the kitchen table.

He spoke about the gallery and its owner, Ben Leeping, an old friend from Oxford whose stepson Marius ran the space in New York. Because he was young, Ben had asked Logan to come on board, keep his eye on the boy, help him find emerging talent in New York to show along with the modernists from Europe. Liza tried to stay neutral and not give away her enthusiasm, but his interest was the jolt she needed.

He leaned back in his chair and finally asked her a few questions. Where she was from, with whom had she studied— "Ah, yes, Hofmann, of course!"—a few perfunctory things he rattled off almost in passing as he finished his drink. She gave succinct answers to his questions, eager to show him some work.

"So," he said, setting down his glass, "let's see what you have."

"I put out some recent work over here." Liza pointed to the far wall. "And over here." Out of the work she had done over the spring, there were only a few she was proud of: *Sunrise,* which was leaning against her painting wall just to the right of where she worked, as well as the small painting de Kooning liked. Tess had insisted on some others. Liza hadn't been so sure—many were good, damned good, but not great. Mountstuart walked around the room slowly, looking at everything without a word.

Finally, he glanced at her in approval. "I like the direction you're heading," he said, nodding toward the newest painting as well as the one from the show. She knew exactly what he meant, the simplicity of them both, not overworked like the other paintings seemed to her. "Suggestive," he noted. "Light but vibrant, I'd say. Do you have drawings?"

"Hundreds."

"Terrific. May I look at some?"

Liza pulled out a few sketchbooks from a pile of pads stashed beside a bookshelf and set them on the kitchen table. All contained a variety of images—street scenes, the bridge, a few faces, still lifes, even sketches of dogs. Many were realistic, though there were a few abstractions from class.

"These are good," he said as he continued to peruse the work. "Very good. I haven't seen many artists here who can draw. Only Todd Heuber and de Kooning. It's wonderful to see this skill in a painter." He closed the top of the last sketchbook.

"I would be very interested in seeing what you do over the next few months. If you keep developing as you have, we might consider a show."

Liza nearly fell over. My god, a show with a gallery affiliated with Paris! She was speechless. *Quick, say something. Don't stand there like a moron.*

He pulled a wallet out of his back pocket, drawing out a small card. "Here is my phone number and the address of the gallery. Why don't you ring me when you have some new work. We'll see where you've gone from here."

*

As Liza waited for everyone to leave for the summer—Tess to Europe, Hank to Cape Cod, Phil to work in a foundry in the Midwest, other students and artists to their various destinations away from the hot city—she convinced herself that the solitude would do her good. She could imagine forms emerging, color directing composition and movement, one painting after another. She only needed some time alone and space devoid of distraction, and inspiration would appear and direct her—those surprising movements of paint that seemed to come out of nowhere, tap her vision and say, *This is where you need to move, this stroke here, this color there.* Then she could seize it and make it her own and create something wonderful that she could stand back and adore. That's when she'd look up de Kooning again, inviting him this time to come to her studio, envisioning the place filled with paintings. New, big, exciting work, fit for a show.

She mentioned nothing about Mountstuart's visit to anyone, believing it would jinx her efforts. She couldn't keep the news from Tess, however. As she expected, Tess was thrilled, as much for the possibility of a show as the idea that Liza had a project with which to keep herself busy. Tess had been pressing her to get out of the city or to sign up for other classes at least, something to keep her on track and aware of time so that she would remember the mundane things she needed to keep going, such as food and sleep. Tess had been worried about that.

"I'll be fine," Liza promised.

"I'm sure you will."

Still, Tess left the cupboards filled with food and made Liza promise to take care of herself as she got in the taxi that would take her to the ocean liner where she would meet her mother and sail to Casablanca. Then she kissed her goodbye, holding onto the hat that matched her new turquoise summer suit as her lips touched Liza's cheek.

Liza stood on the sidewalk and watched until the cab pulled away, Tess's hat holding steady as the vehicle turned the corner sharply and disappeared from view. It was the end of June. She had almost two full months in which to work. Two months was a lot of time with nothing else to do. Much would get done, she reminded herself again, staring down the street, Tess's cab long gone.

"Okay," she muttered, "time to get to work."

Liza had prepared for this moment. She had stretchers and a roll of canvas and tubes of new paint. Though she didn't like the idea of hot, dirty air blowing around her studio, she had purchased two large fans in case the humidity became unbearable as many who lived here said it could be. It was pleasant today, though, clear and dry and not too warm. The city buzzed with activity as always, dependable background noise. She would start big, she had decided on her way to the studio, not small as she usually did, making sketches first, then transferring the movement onto bigger sheets of paper or canvas. The idea of a field of white over which to let her body, not her mind, direct with large physical movements appealed to her. This was what had created *Sunrise*. Her body letting go. Liza was glad to have the painting back in her studio to serve as a guide into new work. This would get her started.

Liza painted and painted. Several weeks had already flown by. She had five canvases going on at once, thinking that what would not fit on one would work somewhere else. In this way, she could keep a rhythm out of which something good would eventually emerge. But by the end of July she had nothing that satisfied her. Everything was overworked, exhausted and desperate. Horrible, all of it.

Standing in the center of the studio late one afternoon, she stared at the canvases, each an unbearable saturation of color and form. *Self-Portrait* is what she'd entitle each of them. If anyone asked, she'd cackle back, *Yes, this is a glimpse into me. A chaotic mess.* She should rip everything off the walls, take a few days off and begin again. Some rest would help. It was just fatigue, she couldn't stop herself, let alone muster clear-headed judgment about the painting process. When was the last time she had a good night's sleep? A day at the beach? She should go out to Long Island. Jones Beach was an easy day trip. There she could lie in the sun, float in saltwater and rejuvenate. If Tess were here, that's what they would do.

But Tess was in Aix-en-Provence now. After their tour

of northern Africa, her mother had rented a house where her father and brother would join them for a few weeks. Tess had told Liza she would seek out each of Van Gogh's haunts and sketch them all so that she could bring back a visual taste. Liza imagined her surrounded by sunflowers or lavender, rested, tanned, beautiful, at the very least content.

Several postcards lay on the kitchen table. Tess was a responsible correspondent, writing in tiny script to cram all her observations onto the small card. The medinas in Fez, Roman ruins near the border of Libya, the Nile and pyramids of Giza. More impressive than she could have ever imagined. But the poverty was overwhelming. All the beggar children and people lying in the streets, such a mix of life, the sublime and the decay. She'd have many stories to tell when she returned, and a journal filled with sketches.

There was nothing edible in the refrigerator, only a container of moldy cottage cheese and some overripe plums, their skins wrinkled and beginning to rot. Over the course of a month, Liza had finished off all the food Tess had bought. If she didn't have the energy to get herself to the beach for a day, at least she should go to the store and buy some food. But first a drink at the bar at the corner of Fifth and 11th Street. A shot of bourbon—it was nearly evening—then she'd find something to eat.

She intended to have only one drink, maybe two. There were a few people in the bar. It was a squalid place and she didn't care to notice much. Settling in at the end corner of the bar, she ordered a glass of Four Roses, drank it quickly, then asked for another.

He could have been there when she arrived, seated at one of the tables against the wall that was sheltered in shadow.

Or did he come in after her? She couldn't remember, hadn't spotted him at all until suddenly he pulled over a bar stool and slid in beside her. He was tall and lean and his hair was ash blond and thick. His pale blue eyes were sparkling and he had a dimple in his chin. These things she remembered about him as well as his deep, melodic voice.

But that was all she could be sure about. Nothing else really, not even his name. Though he presumably told her, nothing sounded familiar when she repeated a litany of possibilities later. He was just a good-looking guy in the bar.

He must have bought the drinks for she had only taken a few dollars when she left the studio. She remembered vaguely a discussion about the Impressionists and Cubists and some mention of Picasso. She didn't think that he was an artist, but he was informed enough to hold her attention or at least follow her in conversation and prod her to keep going, because it was very dark when they left and she stumbled going out the door and needed his arm around her to stand up straight and find her footing.

They probably fucked, but she had no recollection of that either, how he had felt inside her, if it was even any good. She would have been too drunk to come. Was he as well? No matter, whatever happened after they left the bar was all speculation. What she did remember was the sudden waking—it was early and the light coming in the window was still tinged with traces of dawn—as Liza opened her eyes in the strange bed, the man beside her asleep, breathing quietly. Both of them were naked. She recognized the blond hair and felt sick. Her head and stomach ached and her mouth was sticky. She thought she might throw up any moment, so she eased herself up and slipped on her clothes, strewn haphazardly around her side of the floor. Then she tiptoed out the room, down the hall, out the front door, and somehow found her way home, her vision off, her mind in a blur.

She returned to the studio later the next day, set out a fresh canvas and tried to work. But she felt listless and uncomfortably cut off from the world, which hummed outside her window and beyond—in Europe, on the Cape, in the Midwest, everywhere she was not. She was lonely now in a way she hadn't experienced before, the freshly gessoed canvas, which had usually been such an exciting adventure, now glared at her like the enemy, daring her to venture in. It is easier to obsess about the guy as she tried to ignore her thoughts and settle into work.

But his memory nagged incessantly. *Who was he?* Why did this bother her so? It was merely a fluke encounter, nothing, she told herself over and over. Forget about it. But she couldn't. Okay, she finally allowed after a few unproductive days, go back and find him. Then you'll know and can get on with it.

Liza retraced her steps to the building she had fled only a few mornings ago, a brownstone on 22nd Street. At least she had noticed the street number as she turned down Park Avenue to make her way home. Stopping in front of number 165, she considered the steep steps and the impenetrable front door. Was there a pot of geraniums outside the entrance? The building looked hazily familiar, but so did the one two doors down.

Climbing the steps with uncertainty, Liza looked at the outside buzzer, searching for a name she might recognize enough to jar her memory—none did—then rang the bell for the apartment on the top floor. She knew she had gone down at least three flights of stairs. And there were no stairs above her, nowhere to go, when she exited, but down. A woman finally responded to the second or third ring and claimed she knew nothing about a man living there. Liza must be mistaken.

There was no man living in the second building. Just another woman, this one perky and surprisingly polite.

"Well," she offered, "my nephew spent the weekend. But he's only thirteen. I don't think he's the man you're looking for. Sorry."

Liza looked up and down the street carefully. Nothing else seemed familiar. It was definitely not the large yellow house with peeling paint. She had come down dark steps—she was sure of that—and nothing else matched her recollection. She returned to the bar and asked the bartender if he knew of anyone fitting the man's description. But the bartender was no help, only giving her a smirk and muttering, "Good luck," as he dried shot glasses. She checked the place each night for a week, scanning the few patrons who sat at the bar or huddled around tables, a paltry lot, all of them. After several days, she gave up, though she eyed everyone she passed on the streets for some time just in case.

Forget about it. It's nearly the end of the summer, she reminded herself unhappily. Life was starting up again, people were returning in a few weeks, and Liza had nothing of any consequence accomplished.

"Think about what you'll say," she mumbled as she looked about the mess of her studio. "Forget the guy. It was nothing. Worry about the future."

But it was something. She could not shake her obsessing.

One week, two weeks, he haunted her, and it didn't surprise her that her period was late and she started to feel nauseous at the same time every morning, regardless of whether she had eaten or not.

When Tess finally returned, she was shocked at Liza's appearance.

"You look horrible." It was the first thing she said. No *Hello*. No *Glad to be home*, nor *I'm happy to see you*. No perfunctory pleasantries after all this time. She just launched into the truth.

"What have you been doing?" Tess spoke sharply as she set down her bags. "Or not doing, I should say. You look like you haven't slept or eaten in a month."

Liza was lying on the couch in the living room, exhausted, though she hadn't done a thing but sleep, it seemed, for over a week. She was thin and drug-tired and she looked like shit. She hadn't even bothered to change her T-shirt or brush her hair in days.

"Welcome back," she muttered.

Tess strode quickly across the living room and sat at the coffee table in front of the couch. She was everything Liza was not—tanned, well rested, thoroughly stimulated after a summer abroad, and, as usual, beautifully garbed in a yellow linen blouse and floral skirt, an old Moroccan beaded necklace around her throat, matching earrings and an arm ringed by silver bracelets.

"Are you sick? What is wrong with you?"

Liza waved her away. "Yes, that's it," she answered with great effort. "I haven't felt well for a few days." Tess stood. "I'll make you some tea. Would you like a poached egg? A piece of toast?"

Liza cringed. Eggs sounded disgusting. Thank God they didn't have any.

"Should you go see a doctor?"

"No, just some sleep and I'll be fine." Liza tried to sound reassuring, but that took all her effort.

"Let me at least help you to bed." Tess moved her legs off the couch, put a hand under her elbow to hoist Liza to a stand and led her down the hall into the bedroom.

"What a mess!" she exclaimed as she pushed open the door. Clothes were strewn everywhere, the bureau top a heap of books, scarves, overflowing ashtrays littered about the room. It was a knee-jerk response. Tess couldn't help herself. Then she remembered.

"I'm sorry to scold. I know you've been sick. Let me smooth out the bed and you get some rest."

It was good to have Tess home again.

*

A week after Tess's return, Liza felt no better. In fact, she was worse. She had thrown up the breakfast Tess had insisted on making her, four days in a row. By early afternoon, she felt better and could manage some food, but her energy remained flat. Tess insisted it was time to see a doctor. Tess would make an appointment with her family physician.

Liza was sitting on the toilet seat, holding her head after rinsing her face off with a washcloth, determined to get to her studio for an afternoon. Maybe some work would restore her strength, though she knew it was a futile plan.

"You needn't bother," she finally had to admit to Tess. "I'm pregnant."

Tess nearly dropped the brush she had been tugging through her long, wavy hair. "You're what?"

"You heard me."

"Are you sure?"

Liza could see Tess trying to get a grip on her reaction. She exhaled loudly and slowly. "Who's the father? Is it Hank?"

"God, no!" Liza rose quickly. That would be the last thing Hank would want. He had told her often that he hated children. The idea of them even, the crying and dirty diapers, the mess they'd make in the studio and everywhere else. At the time she had agreed. They had no place in a serious artist's world. Everyone knew that.

"How can you possibly paint when there is a baby crying?" Elaine de Kooning had commented one night at the Cedar Bar. Liza had found Hank seated beside Elaine at the bar last spring when she came to meet him for a drink. Elaine was surrounded, as she always was, by young men crowding in. Hank pulled Liza into the conversation. She immediately agreed with Elaine. As she did, she looked around and noticed Elaine's husband, Bill, with other painters at the far end of the bar.

"It's different for men," Elaine continued, turning back to her coterie of fans. "They know how to guard their personal space. How to devote themselves to their inner world. But," she added, blowing out a long stream of smoke as she spoke directly to Hank and a young male artist Liza did not know, "if a woman wants to be serious about her career, there simply isn't room for both."

Then she looked right at Liza. "Don't you agree?"

"Absolutely."

"Well then," Elaine chortled, "that's settled." She looked

up for a moment, noticed Bill and nodded his way. Then she smiled and turned to her crowd of boys. "Now, who's buying drinks?"

Liza gripped the edge of the sink as she stood a bit too suddenly. She was dizzy and tired and felt as though she was speaking through a sleeping-pill haze. How was she going to respond to this? She hadn't yet given that any thought.

"Then who?" Tess waited.

Liza couldn't yet answer.

"Liza?" Oh, she should just get it out and be done with it. She sighed and spit out, "I don't know."

"You're kidding." Tess rarely got angry but Liza could hear it in her voice. Disappointment as well. And disgust. Liza was quick to defend herself.

"Look, it was some guy I was drinking with in a bar. I fucked up, okay. I'm sorry. What can I say?" She left the bathroom. But Tess followed, speaking over her shoulder as she headed to the bedroom to get herself dressed.

"Don't apologize to me."

Liza turned. "Back off, Tess. I'll deal with it."

Suddenly Tess softened. Liza was well aware that Tess hated confrontation but more than that, she appreciated how anger was no help in finding solutions. It only inflamed alienation, and she needed to be on Liza's side in this. As she did over and over throughout their friendship, Tess stepped into Liza's space and offered to take charge.

"No, no, I'll help you. Look, we all make mistakes." She tried to chuckle, but it sounded more awkward than comforting. So, she put her arms around Liza instead. "I'll make some calls. We'll find a doctor to give you an abortion."

"Fine. Fine." Liza pulled herself free and lay down on her bed. "I'll think about it later. After I sleep."

Three days later, Hank called, just back from Hofmann's summer school, all exuberance, not a hint of the hurt that had scalded their last meeting.

"You should have come. The place was amazing, the light especially, dawn and dusk. I did eight new canvases and I think I have a dealer, John Myers of Tibor de Nagy. You must come over and see."

How easily his vitriol had died, now that he was on the verge of success. She wasn't surprised. Fuck you, she thought. But she couldn't help herself. She was curious to see what he had done. "I'll be over tomorrow afternoon," she told him.

Grateful his studio was a short walk from her apartment and located on the first floor, she had to knock loudly to be heard over the blaring of Duke Ellington on the stereo, a musician he had introduced her to last spring, now a favorite of his. They had disagreed about the inspiration of music while they work, Hank claiming that it galvanized his brush strokes, while Liza insisted on the music of her emotions as being the best muse. How they had argued!

And there he was in the doorway, tanned, taut, and full of life, nearly knocking the wind out of her. Such a handsome man, she thought as she caught her breath, wondering if she had made a mistake dismissing him so soon. Then her eyes traveled over his shoulder to the large canvases set up around the room. She tried not to look askance. This was going to get him a dealer? The paintings were more confident, yes, the colors stronger, but still felt unbalanced and unresolved. Then she saw the one at the end and stiffened. It was her painting, *Sunrise,* all the colors and movements but in the extreme, an imitation gone wild.

"So?" Hank asked after giving her a moment while he turned down the music.

What could she say? They had always been honest about each other's work. She was not about to fake enthusiasm now. Particularly now.

"It's good," she said. "Better, certainly. The summer obviously did you good. But much of it feels overdone. You've flattened out the tension. Especially in this," she pointed to the one at the end, "this one doesn't work at all."

Hank chuckled. "That's the one he liked the most."

"You're kidding." But he was not. He smirked.

"You're jealous, aren't you? Mad I might have a dealer."

Liza stiffened, tried to smile with enthusiasm, but she could feel envy distort her lips. This was revenge for her turning him down, she could tell.

"Of course not, Hank. I'm happy for you."

Did he believe her? His placid expression gave nothing away. Maybe he just didn't care. "How about a drink?" he finally offered.

"No," she said, "I have to meet Tess."

The sultry air lifted, finally, by mid-September, and in the lighter, cooler weather it was easier to breathe. Art classes had started again. Though Liza had enrolled, she hadn't yet attended a class. It all seemed too much to take on, lying about the summer and the lack of progress she had intended to make. Maybe next week she'd show up. She did not tell Tess she was avoiding class. Nor could she admit that she was avoiding pursuing an appointment for an abortion. She couldn't make decisions about anything, it seemed.

Mountstuart had called early in September. He had been away much of the summer and apologized for not staying in touch.

"It's fine," Liza responded, grateful for the continued interest, yet relieved he had clearly not been waiting for her work.

"And how was your summer?" he asked, the question sounding perfunctory, as though he were going down a list.

"Slow. I was a bit under the weather. Some virus or something. I'm only now just getting going again. I'll have something soon." She felt it was safe to put him off and buy herself a little more time.

"Just give me a call when you do."

She assured him she would. Now almost a month had gone by. Her energy had started to come back, at least during the afternoons and evenings. A painting in progress was waiting for her on the wall, a bit impatiently it felt to her; the outline of a figure that she had begun to sketch in a few days before out of a field of brilliant color, a tempestuous field, cut into chaos with vicious, choppy strokes. Out of this agitation, a figure was coming, of whom or what she could not yet discern.

But there it was, the tenuous thing, tapping its foot angrily—well, not its foot for there were no toes or ankle, only the hasty lines of a slight rectangle—demanding her to do something. Or to get it out of there.

Liza approached the work, touched the surface of wet paint. Out of where into what? she wondered as she pulled a brush out of turpentine and wiped it clean. This figure was taking her somewhere. It wouldn't let go. She tried to scrape it off and keep the picture abstract. Though it intrigued her as if it had a life of its own, she had to wipe it away. The figure was no longer the thing in painting. It was passé, too obvious. If she made figurative work, she'd be dismissed as second-rate and referential. She must stay with the abstract if she were to be taken seriously.

But the figure kept emerging out of any shapes or lines she drew. "God damn you," Liza yelled at the canvas and threw down her brush.

She pulled a bottle of bourbon out of the cabinet in the kitchen and took a swallow. Searching through her bag, she found a small piece of paper upon which Tess had written a name and number. Liza picked up the phone.

"Dr. Martin's office," a receptionist answered.

"Yes, I'd like to make an appointment."

He had an opening the next day. Liza explained her predicament, telling him only that she was a single woman and did not have the resources to raise a child. He was an older man, gentle and grandfatherly, and though she knew he performed abortions, she did not want to take the chance of any judgments, so she told him nothing else. Certainly, he would understand finances. And he did. He gave her no argument and scheduled her to come back in three days. Early in the morning before office visits started.

"Okay," Liza announced when she returned. "I've done it. I've made an appointment."

"When?" Tess asked. She was seated on the living room couch having a cocktail before dinner.

"Friday at seven."

"I'm coming with you."

"You don't have to. I can go alone."

"No, you can't go alone. Of course I'm coming with you."

Liza went to her studio the next day, determined to work and think of nothing else. No abortion, no invitation from Hank to come by his studio and see his new paintings, no meetings at the Club or the Cedar Bar, the latest gossip, Mountstuart waiting. She wanted to think only of the painting in progress and where it was going once the figure was gone.

But once she had scraped away suggestive lines—the remnant of a foot or a long bone that could be part of an arm—the mess of the turbulent color field made her feel lost. It had seemed so promising at first, the only inspiring work she had painted all summer, greens and oranges and creams colliding like tiny, crazy waves; a promise of something, she was sure. Now it seemed nothing, a hopeless storm of colors going nowhere. Liza pulled out the bourbon and sat down on the floor. As she drank from the bottle and smoked cigarette after cigarette, she stared at the few paintings that lined the walls of the studio. Trying to study them from the vantage point of being an outsider, she struggled to have some distance and find something hopeful in the work. Anything. A suggestion, an inference, some sign of promise.

There was nothing. She sighed. She had to be honest. Here she was in the thick of everything, doors open, people beckoning her to follow—de Kooning, Mountstuart, Hofmann, the New York art world—it was all here before her, yet she could not feel more hopelessly lost. She started to cry.

"You worthless piece of shit," she shouted into the large

empty studio. Then to her belly, she added, "You deserve a better mother than this."

She finished the bottle and must have fallen asleep in a heap on the floor. Unsettling dreams plagued her. She couldn't remember what, but when she woke, she felt warm tears streaking down her cheeks.

On the day of her appointment, Tess woke her early. "It's time," she said gently, shaking her shoulder. Liza rose thick from a sleep she had dreaded falling into and awoke feeling surprisingly clear-headed.

They arrived at the doctor's fifteen minutes early. The door was still locked. "I need to walk a little bit," Liza told Tess.

"I'll walk with you." She took her arm.

During the trip in the taxi and even standing at the locked office door, Liza had not felt a thing. Nothing. Just the logistics of the appointment and when they'd be done. But as she began to walk, telling herself that it would soon be over, she was flooded with feelings. No, these were not feelings, they were commands. No, not even that, nothing as cerebral as that. She was overpowered by an instinct; it must have been that. Unshakable, overwhelming, almost a cry of survival. She did not understand, had never felt anything of such force. All she knew was that she could not go through with it. There was no question at all. The decision was sudden and final. Stopping, she turned to Tess and announced, "I can't do this, Tess."

They were standing in the middle of the sidewalk. People were emerging from apartment buildings and brownstones and filling the streets. Liza and Tess stood, huddled together as people streamed by.

"How will you manage?" Tess finally asked.

Liza smiled. It did feel possible, suddenly truly possible then and there. She wanted to shout but could only answer in a whisper, "I'll get a job teaching somewhere in the country, where this kid can run barefoot and I can paint."

FOUR

Rouge

(1966-67)

As though it were an appendage, Rouge took Ben's camera with her everywhere, into town, to school, even the bakery where she worked on Saturdays and after school when extra help was needed. But now, with his camera and eye for reference—for all the film would be sent back to Ben—she felt paralyzed. Piqued by an image, say, Mrs. Paige hanging a garment in the window of her dress shop, her own clinging awkwardly to her large rear end, or maybe Hurley asleep in his barber's chair, his head fallen back, mouth wide open, his lips fluttering with gusts of snores, she would find herself losing interest as her eye neared the lens. As though an annoyed, clipped voice was the final judge. *Who'd want to look at that fat ass? Or an old man snoring?*

So she started with flowers. That seemed safe enough. Not the dead ones that had dried and were curling into crippled forms. There were still some chrysanthemums and cosmos in bloom. They would do. And a roll of film of O'Neil's barn near sunset when softer light soothed the cracked wood and peeling paint. She took pictures of fields dotted with large red dairy barns and clumps of cows, the grassy square that marked the center of town, its edges lined by a row of dogwood trees, the crisp, white steeple of the

Presbyterian church, the wheelbarrow in front of Simpson's store piled high with squashes and pumpkins. Rouge labored to pick out what was appealing, viewing her familiar surroundings through the lens as if she were a visitor. After a week, she mailed Ben four rolls of film, then rode her bike to her friend Shelly's for dinner.

Though she had been back for nearly a month, Shelly was still bronze from the summer spent on the coast of Maine at her grandmother's. With her tan, Shelly was dramatically beautiful. Large blue eyes, fleshy lips and cresting cheekbones. If it weren't for her wispy, brittle hair and ungainly nose—unfortunate genetic gifts from her unfortunately dowdy mother—Shelly would have been perfect, in Rouge's opinion. As it was, she seemed perfect enough for the mediocre boys at school.

Mrs. Monroe answered the door. A slight, stern woman, she made Rouge nervous, so different from her mother in just about every way. A teller at the bank before she met and married the branch head, Mr. Charles P. Monroe, eleven years her senior, she promptly got pregnant and retired from the bank to run the home and brood of three children. The Monroes lived in an imposing three-story Victorian three blocks from town, an intricately detailed house that sat perched upon a clipped lawn like overweight royalty. Everything about the place gleamed. Outside, its wood was painted white with dark green trim every five years without fail, before any cracks could be detected on the surface. Inside, the place shone like an old European hotel or what Rouge imagined an old European hotel must have looked like; chintzes and stripes and silk and sparkling wooden floors. Everything immaculate from the tall ceilings down to the mudroom out back. Mrs. Monroe's life was like that—immaculate—day after day, cleaning, directing Agnes, her cleaning woman, cleaning some more. Even the dinner table had good silver and candles.

"Ah, Rouge, Shelly is upstairs," Mrs. Monroe said, shutting the door. "Don't you two girls get involved in anything lengthy. Dinner will be ready soon."

Rouge nodded and hurried up the front stairs. Curled up against pillows on her bed, Shelly gave Rouge a devilish look as she came in the room.

"Quick, close the door tight." She beckoned Rouge closer. "Look what I've found," she announced, pulling something out of her pants pocket, a pink cloud of bubble gum quickly appearing out of her mouth. Rouge sat on the end of the bed and waited as Shelly extracted what looked like a pale brown-colored chunk of chewed gum. She grinned, grabbing the thing, and stretched it between her thumbs.

"Do you know what this is?" she asked, smacking her gum.

"A balloon?"

"Oh, you're so naïve. It's a rubber."

"You're kidding. Where did you get that?"

"I found it in the back of my dad's night table. It has to be centuries old. I can't believe they still do it." Shelly pulled it tighter, straining all the color out of the material. "Do you think they really get this long?"

"How should I know?"

"Hey, where's that camera of yours? Let's take some pictures so we have something to compare the real thing to. When the time comes, that is."

"God, Shelly, you're so weird."

Shelly leaned back on the bed. Rouge eyed her, thinking of a photo. Maybe of Shelly blowing bubbles with her gum. Would that be too stupid? Maybe an image of Shelly acting weird, which she liked to do, taking her cue from Liza, Rouge was convinced. How Shelly's mother disapproved of her; even though she was a college professor, she was still a strange bohemian woman—an *unmarried* bohemian woman—though Rouge was a nice enough girl. Mrs. Monroe did not relish Shelly spending a lot of time at Rouge's, but she would let her come out occasionally, the Bakers being preferable to the local boys who courted her daughter. Still, she knew Shelly dabbled in make-up when she went to visit Rouge. Why, that woman probably encourages them! And, was that cigarette smoke she smelled in her daughter's hair when she returned home? What do they do there? Wouldn't her mother just love to know?

"Girls!" Summoned by her mother's voice ringing up the stairs, Shelly slid the rubber back into her pocket and rose from the bed with theatrical effort, slunk downstairs and into the dining room and collapsed into her seat. The formally set table was unsettling. Rouge seldom felt comfortable, worrying that her hands weren't clean enough, if she was remembering to sit up straight. Did Mr. Monroe ever have anything to say? Would Mrs. Monroe stop shooting disapproving glances at the children, two boys younger than Shelly, sullen, all of them? Could anyone relax and enjoy a meal?

Rouge was often invited to stay for dinner. Every time, it was a similar scenario. Unless she was asked a question, Rouge consumed her meal quietly. Tonight, it was lamb stew and salad. A glass of red wine for Mr. and Mrs. Monroe, milk for all the children. Everyone ate so quickly that she had to focus on her chewing to keep up. Out of the corner of her eye, Rouge noticed Mrs. Monroe's stiff maternal lips, the pulled-back graying hair straining for freedom and a smattering of some interesting color, and longed to have her camera. But that would be rude.

"Tell me again, Rouge," Mrs. Monroe finally asked, "what your mother does on her trips to New York."

Rouge put down her fork before answering. "She goes to look at art, to visit artist friends. She is very close to Hank Bolton."

"Hank Bolton? I don't believe I know his work. But I'm not an art aficionado, at least of contemporary painters. Only the Hudson River artists. And Jackson Pollock, of course."

Rouge cleared her throat. Here's where she could impress, echoing what she heard discussed among Liza and her students, Liza and Tess, about the mysterious New York art world.

"Bolton is famous now. He was on the cover of *Life* magazine, just like Pollock. He's having a show at a museum in New York. He and Liza are good friends."

Why she chose to add this last bit of exaggeration, she hadn't a clue. It simply came out before she could catch herself. Rouge could not believe they were friends; all they seemed to do was fight, mostly over the phone late at night since he had moved to France. Though Liza tried to muffle her voice, Rouge could hear the anger, the slamming down of the receiver, soon afterward, her bedroom door. Some friend, Rouge always thought. He never came to help Liza. Not like her other artist friends. Said he hated the country.

She had only met him once that she could remember, a party in New York, the air heavy with smoke and loud voices, Rouge feeling so tired, nearly falling asleep on Liza's shoulders until she was finally put down onto a pile of coats. Kept awake by a game of darts, she went out to look for her mother only to be rescued by a warm, firm hand that led her through a jungle of legs. "This is no place for a child," the man announced as he turned the hand over into Liza's. Later, Rouge found out—another late-night conversation on the porch that wafted in through her open window— that Hank did not like children. But she already knew. She could feel it in the disapproving grip of his hand.

All of these thoughts flooded her mind in the wake of her lie.

"Hank Bolton," Reg, brother number two, muttered through a half-eaten chunk of lamb. "Sounds like a cowboy."

"Reggie, don't talk with your mouth full."

Mrs. Monroe laid her fork down on her plate parallel to her knife, signaling the end of her meal. "That's something. Isn't it, Charles? Isn't it something that Mrs. Baker is friends with such an important painter?"

"I wouldn't know such things about Mrs. Baker," he answered quietly. Then, turning to address Rouge, he continued, "But I do know that she is financially responsible. I'll say that about your mother. Often those kinds of people aren't."

"Mom, can we please be excused?" This was not a question coming from Shelly. It was a moan.

"Yes, you may. Don't forget your dishes."

"You have no idea how lucky you are," Shelly whispered to Rouge en route up the stairs to her bedroom.

Maybe, Rouge responded, but would never dare say so aloud to Shelly. Maybe, she thought, riding home later that evening, the stars unusually bright, the moon full enough to light the road like a dim candle, accentuating the trees and fences and buildings in the distance as if they were guardian angels in the night. Even in the chill of early fall, before the long season of snow made bike-riding impossible, clipped her freedom and left her dependent on rides from Liza or the bus, Rouge loved the route home, the bumpy dirt road that rattled up her spine, the invigorating air when she got up to speed, the peacefulness of a landscape whose every crooked tree limb, every broken fence and arch of rolling hill was so familiar.

As was the old farmhouse Liza had purchased a few months before Rouge's birth. Set back maybe a hundred feet from the road, it was a sweet place, peeking out from the grove of trees that loomed over it from behind, between the house and the barn. The opposite of Shelly's house. Anyone could drive by their home and barely notice it at all. But Rouge loved it, creaky as it could be, the original yellow paint now faded and peeling in so many spots. The big front windows that looked out onto the flowerbeds in the front, spilling over the fence in the height of summer. The warmth of the small rooms inside. Even the board on the ceiling of the front porch, popping its corner free from the frame overhead. That, too, made Rouge smile.

Her mood shattered the moment she walked through the back door. Liza stood cross-armed at the sink, two untouched plates of dinner on the kitchen table.

"Where the hell have you been?"

"I stayed at Shelly's."

"Thanks for letting me know! It's not as though I have nothing better to do than be your servant. As you prance around your day, you might take a minute to check in so I don't have to waste my fucking time!"

"Sorry. I forgot. I'll sit with you if you like."

"Too late for that. I put dinner away for tomorrow night. If you remember to come home."

"Jesus, Liza. What's your problem?"

The glare Liza shot back could have pierced Rouge's skin.

Rouge softened her tone. "What's up? Why are you so angry?"

She could have sworn the anger in Liza's eyes was dissolving into tears, but she looked away and pulled plastic wrap out of a drawer to seal up the food.

"It's nothing," Liza said, her voice suddenly deflated. It wasn't nothing at all. There would have been bad news, another rejection from a dealer, a missed event, most likely a difficult phone call with Hank. When were they not difficult? Liza often conciliatory at first, eager to solve the problem at hand, listening, considering, cajoling even to bring him around, his fragile moods despite his success. Always about him, Liza would later complain to Tess. Him, him, him, until she couldn't stand it and would snap.

Later that night, Rouge heard Liza in the front hall, whispering on the phone to Tess. Thank God for Tess, the one person who could iron out Liza's frustrations, help fend off her depressions. Most of the time.

A few days later, Rouge's batch of film finally returned. It had been nearly three weeks. Rouge could not wait to see what was there and rode home particularly fast. Liza was in the studio so Rouge ripped the envelope open at the kitchen table. But instead of finding large prints, she was perplexed to see all her pictures printed small, several crammed onto one page, in neat rows, laid out sequentially just as she had taken them. It took a moment to realize she was looking at each roll of film, one per page. The note that accompanied the work looked hastily written, Ben's handwriting bigger and sloppier than before.

> Rouge,
>
> If you're thinking of a career in the postcard business, then you're probably well on your way. But you seem to be too thoughtful and inquisitive for that. Before you shoot anything else, sit for a while and figure out what you're looking at. And why. Is it something you want to look at? Is there a story there? Or better yet, does what you're looking at ask you questions you can't answer? Don't send me any more film unless what you've got tells a story or leaves you hanging, longing for more. Think about that before you shoot.
>
> Maybe you want to start with people. Lots of stories there.
>
> Ben

Feeling tears well up in her eyes, Rouge set down the letter. She could barely breathe. She felt stupid and inconsequential. Postcard business? How embarrassing. She had only wanted to impress him with... what? Pretty pictures, wasn't it? An idealized life. He was right. They were postcard images.

But the other stuff, the things that she was interested in—butts and open mouths and dead flowers—would he like them more? They were stupid, too. She didn't know what to do. He had told her to tell stories, okay, here was the assignment, but what? She'd need to let it rest for now. There was geometry to review. She would worry about it later.

But all the while as she studied formulas and theorems, she thought of Ben, of his words. She reread the letter multiple times. It was late when she heard Liza slip up the stairs, come down the hallway, knock softly on her door.

"You still awake?" she asked as she stepped into the room.

"Yeah."

"I have to go to school early tomorrow. I have student critiques and I haven't even looked at the work." Liza paused in the doorway, staring at Rouge. "What's wrong?"

"Nothing." Rouge kept her eyes on her book.

"It doesn't look like nothing to me. Have you been crying?"

"No."

Liza stared, waiting for the truth. Leaning against the door jam, arms crossed, all the time in the world. Liza stood her ground and stared. Waiting.

Rouge was no match for this. This is where Liza always snagged her and yanked out the truth. That long, patient stare that cut through any pretense Rouge could muster. She hated herself for such easy transparency. Where did she give it away? A quivering lip, slumped posture, furtive gaze? She tried to set a defiant face, but it was nothing more than putty in front of Liza. Shelly pulled off lying to her mother so easily. Why couldn't Rouge?

Despite her effort, she caved. Rouge pulled out the envelope from under her pillows and threw it across the room toward Liza.

"These are from Ben?"

Rouge nodded.

"Jesus, Rouge, is something going on between you?"

Rouge leapt up to grab the envelope away. "Never mind. You wouldn't get it."

Liza cackled. "Don't be so sure. Let me have a look." She took the envelope and sat at Rouge's desk, studied the photos, holding them close and perusing them just like she would her students' work. Scanning the page took forever, freezing Rouge in animated suspension, but she said nothing. Afterward, she opened the letter. As she read, Rouge watched her tense and could feel questions brewing. Still she said nothing, just put the contents down and bit the inside of her cheek.

Rouge braced herself. For what? What was Liza thinking? She couldn't read her at all. Just when Rouge couldn't stand it any longer and was about to say something, anything, Liza made a move, pulling her cigarettes out of her pocket, lit one, then threw the pack to Rouge.

"He's right, you know."

"What?" she fumbled out. This she had not expected. What had she expected? Just about anything except Liza siding with Ben, moving into his camp against her.

"Meaning you can do a lot better." Rouge had heard this line before, something Liza often told students, especially younger ones. Those just beginning. *You can do better.* The kind of comment chosen to weed out the faint of heart, those without the talent to match the confidence. Art is hard work. Not for sissies. Not for those who back down easily when challenged.

Liza had said these very words to Emma when she was a freshman, bringing her to tears, she admitted to Rouge later on. "But it was the best thing anyone could say to me," she said in defense of Liza, the teacher, when Rouge was complaining about something. Liza, the mother. "It was an invitation to keep looking, questioning. To find new doors. It's her vote of confidence, her way of saying, *Yes, you can.* It's why we all love Liza, because she sees our potential and cultivates it."

"Tell me what you're thinking," Liza said. "You don't agree?"

"I... I... I..." Rouge looked around. Her dolls and stuffed animals, her bookshelf overflowing with books, the room crowding in on her. "Yes, you're right. He's right."

"And I bet those photos weren't half as fun to take as what you took when he was here." Liza smiled.

"No. They weren't."

"That's your best guide. If you pay attention, you know when you're pushing yourself and when you're being phony. Ben is absolutely right. These would look great as postcards in Simpson's store. Right there next to the maple sugar, stuff to feed the tourists. But where are you in the pictures? That's the question."

As unsettled as Liza was making Rouge feel, she was emboldened too. Seen, understood and encouraged.

"De Kooning once told me something that is essential for any artist, to find one's attitude and be able to put it into the work. Your mark, so to speak. That often what you convey is just a glimpse, the emotion of it. But clearly there."

Rouge had heard her tell this vignette countless times to her students, but until now it hadn't made sense. Yet, tonight, the words had meaning, enough at least to intrigue her and encourage her to try again.

Getting up, Liza kissed her on the forehead. "It's really important to keep going, even if you make hundreds of bad images. Sometimes it takes forever to find your mark. But, if you have any talent at all—and you apparently do—it will show itself eventually. If you work hard enough."

Before she left, Liza paused at the door, tossing back one more surprise punch.

"Ben gave you a challenge. I hope you'll rise to the occasion."

After the door closed, after Rouge replayed the conversation, after she got her bearings and picked up her camera to load it with a fresh roll of film, Rouge noticed the time. Nearly midnight. She should study for her math test. Forget the test. There was more important work to dream about.

*

Liza was late picking up Rouge from school. She was always late the afternoons when she taught her evening drawing class. Thursdays, this semester. Rouge knew she could have an hour or more to knock off much of her homework in the library, the only student there, working in silence until she heard Liza's footsteps rushing down the hall long before her voice called from the door. "C'mon, let's go." Miss Coleman, the school librarian, nodded at Liza with a grimace of relief. Now she could leave, too.

"Wait," Rouge called after stopping at her locker to throw in her ungainly history book. She hated being rushed.

"Let's go. I have to set up the still life."

Leaving the smell of cigarettes in her wake, Liza turned the corner of the main hall, passing Mr. Headley, the principal, sitting at his desk beyond his open door. "Good evening, Mrs. Baker," he said. Miss, she had corrected him on more than one occasion. There's no Mister.

The car was running when Rouge got in, warm from Liza's drive to school. It was dark outside, just past five; already a chill had claimed the evening air. Rouge swung around to look in the back and see what Liza had grabbed from the house this time, fodder for the new still life she set up every week. The reason she was always late, trying to find a cacophony of textures and shapes. Nothing easy or comfortable.

Cacophony. Rouge had loved that word when she was little, the way it rolled around the inside of her mouth. She thought it a synonym for clutter, as much of what Liza gathered was broken or useless—her old tricycle, a large cracked bowl, tools that were rusted from neglect, old wrapping paper from Christmas. Rouge had used this delicious word with aplomb wherever she could, until one of Liza's students corrected her.

"Cacophony refers to sound, not to garbage. Here, let me show you cacophony." He put John Cage on the record player in the studio. Hearing the noise, Rouge immediately threw her hands over her ears, refusing to utter another word.

"Oh, no, you don't." Rouge reached over the seat and grabbed a silk arm sticking out of the old milk crate. "You can't take Jezebel. I told you." Jezebel, a gift from Tess when Rouge was eight. Tess's favorite doll as a child, originally named Geneva, rechristened one night when Liza and Tess deemed her too spoiled by teenage affiliation to have such an innocent name. She absorbs all the energy around her, Liza had informed Rouge. She's special that way. But she's seen and heard too much to be a Geneva anymore.

"We should call her Jezebel," Liza had decided that night after dinner out on the porch. The two women laughed. Enchanted by the doll's delicate features and soft, silk skin, Rouge was ecstatic just holding her.

Liza was peering intently at the road. "You never play with her anymore."

"I don't care. She'll get filthy in the studio, covered with paint. Or forgotten." Rouge stared at her, fixed in her stance. "Have you found my elephant yet?"

Liza turned abruptly. "What? That was years ago." Then back to the road. "No, I have not found your elephant. I haven't been looking."

"Well, until you do, no Jezebel." Rouge stared out her window. She loved that doll. Still. She held Rouge's childhood, the secrets she had kept from her mother. From Tess even. The conversations with her father, wherever he was. Jezebel had approved of Rouge asking, sending her words out into the night air to be carried to wherever he happened to be. A whisper of her existence. No, it was Jezebel's suggestion, but Shhh! We won't tell Liza. She wouldn't understand.

Rouge crossed her arms, spoke to the window. "No Jezebel, period. She's special."

"All right, Miss Prissy. Have it your way."

Liza drove down to the back of the art studio, pulling up as close as she could to the loading dock. Though it was not a parking space, Liza always parked there, ignoring the occasional warnings from the campus police when they bothered to check the art building.

"Jonah," she yelled, heaving the milk crate up onto the landing, a cigarette dangling from her lips. How she could yell so loudly and not drop her cigarette was beyond Rouge. It was a joke Rouge had with Liza's students—one of the seven wonders of Liza.

"Jonah!" The building was brightly lit and Rouge could see students moving about the studio whose large windows faced the back. But no Jonah, Liza's teaching assistant for the past two years, someone Rouge was convinced Liza could not survive without. "Rouge, go see if Jonah's in the office." She picked up the milk crate herself, hoisted it onto her hip and disappeared into the studio.

Jonah was at his desk doing other work. He had recently grown his dark blond hair long enough to pull into a ponytail, and since he had seen the Beatles' movie *Help* he had taken to wearing a top hat and black cape. Nothing hugely out of the ordinary on campus where student fashion tended toward the New York beat influence—black skirts and tight pants, turtlenecks or striped shirts, the rare plaid jacket. Monochromatic with a splash of color. With his penchant for bright colors, in particular flaming red silk, Jonah was often the one to provide the splash.

"Plato," he mumbled as Rouge came in the door. "Thank God it's time for class. I presume Liza needs me."

Rouge gave her cocky, affirmative grin. Jonah rustled her hair. Though she was old enough now to stay home on her own, she continued to come to the evening class with Liza for precisely this—Jonah's hand on her hair, the attention from the other students who adored her mother. And by association, Rouge, too.

"Since you're not drawing tonight, would you mind working on my paper?" It was a private joke between them. Rouge never drew in class, never drew period, long immune to the appeals of Tess and Liza, the students, too. You're Liza's daughter. How can you not be a brilliant draftsman? Liza had long ago given up trying to interest her.

"Ha ha. Ha ha ha!"

The sound of his name careened down the hall.

"Off to the taskmaster." With a wink, he was gone.

Rouge followed him into the studio, looking to see if Emma had landed yet. Rouge had had many student babysitters over the years, but Emma was the one she had bonded to most. Thursdays, Emma had a late afternoon class and usually grabbed dinner on the run to get to the art building just before the evening drawing class began. It was only *6:45*; she'd probably not appear for another ten minutes or so.

Other students greeted her as they set up, having dubbed Rouge the studio mascot. Some brought candy, others strange foundling toys. Early in the semester, Sarah had turned over a dysfunctional wind-up monkey playing his symbols in a desultory fashion, if at all—their game of the moment, setting monkey Clyde atop her easel, winding him tight, then jostling him just enough to elicit one small clink.

Liza and Jonah were positioning the still life in the center of the room, Liza barking orders to the person closest to the lights. "Shut off the third switch, would you?" as she stepped back to eye the ensuing shadows that created what Liza deemed central to the composition. "More, try the next switch over. No, that's too much. Put it on again." She turned to scan the room, finding Rouge parked by Jonah's easel. "Be a doll and get my smokes from the car."

Emma was rushing in the back door as Rouge came to the exit, nearly running into her. Pausing to give her a hug with one arm, the other carrying a pile of books, Emma winced. "I'm in a rotten mood, be warned. I got a fucking C on a paper I slaved over. God, I sound like Liza. How are you?"

Rouge followed behind as Emma stashed her books in her locker, gathered her drawing materials, picked out an easel from the few remaining at the back of the studio and stood for a moment to find an advantageous spot. "Where shall we be?"

"Over by Jonah," Rouge answered without thought, her preference to be squeezed between her two favorite students.

Jonah always worked in the same spot, to the left of the center of the room near the exit to the offices, as he was often asked to come and go, fetch supplies or a book from Liza's office. Emma dropped her belongings beside him and set up her drawing pad.

As easels began to quiet from their scraping into place, Liza announced the night's challenge. "I want you to focus particularly on the shadows, the space in between. Think of it as the mysterious essence that gives form its defining shape."

Afterward, she walked to the record player at the back of the room and leafed through albums. Music was a constant fixture in class. Tonight, something dreamy, meditative.

"How's Debussy?" she asked, not waiting for a reply to put it on and fiddle with the sound until it was just loud enough to nudge thought but not interfere. Then she began her slow pacing around and between easels, correcting here, adding a line there, the students hanging on her every word.

Rouge was quickly bored. The attention had shifted to work and the desire to please their teacher. Leaving the building, she went out to the car to get her camera, stashed in her backpack. In the pocket was her last roll of film, two others done and waiting to be sent to Ben. She considered wandering around campus, but it was dark and windy and the lamps illuminating the walking paths were soft enough to make the place seem otherworldly, only a few bodies moving in and out of the shadows. It was too dark to take pictures. She'd just wander around.

Even in the dark and the cold, Rouge liked being here. The place emanated an acceptance she did not feel anywhere else, certainly not her high school, where social norms were harder to navigate. Here she was taken as a faculty child, someone inhabiting her own hallowed world, to be seen, coddled at times, allowed to do what she wanted simply because she was so in between.

But now it was cold. Checking her watch, she saw it was nearly nine. Class would be winding down soon. Only a few of the students were still at work at their easels when she sauntered back in. Most were gathered around Liza at the front of the room as she was doing her own rendition of the still life, rattling on about line and tension and other words Rouge had heard countless times. Rouge moved slowly behind Liza's easel so she could have a better view. Emma holding her chin in her hand, her eyes sparkling. *Click click.*

Jonah's top hat removed, strands of hair contorting in the air just above his scalp. *Click.* A young woman with long dark hair that covered half her face, only one eye visible, a strand of attention that Rouge framed to connect with the back of Liza's head. *Click click click.*

"Will you stop that?" Liza suddenly snapped. "That noise is distracting. Can't you find something else to do!" All eyes followed Liza's and landed immediately upon Rouge, who hastily put down her camera and backed away.

It wasn't long before Emma found her in the office, leafing through Jonah's Plato without trying to read a word.

"You're doing photography now? That's cool."

Rouge threw out a forced grin.

"Good to see you doing something creative, finally. Are you taking a class at school?"

"No, a friend of Liza's got me started."

"Someone from here?"

"No, from New York." Rouge hoped the edge in her voice that framed *friend* would not give the awkwardness away, prod Emma into asking more about said friend.

"She's a bit ratty now," Emma explained, nodding with her head toward the studio. "Andy asked about Bolton, his new direction. She gets so testy when anyone brings him up. Do you know why?"

"Yeah, she's jealous. He's famous and she isn't." Rouge's quick assessment startled her. She had never said or even thought that before. Not that clearly. Until this moment, it had only been a vague sense but nothing definitive enough to claim with words.

Emma sat back, pondering. "That explains a lot."

Liza's footsteps could be heard rushing down the hall,

carting the half-full crate with objects stuffed quickly in. "Let's go. It's late. I'm exhausted. Do you have all your stuff?"

Rouge nodded.

To Emma, "Make sure Jonah closes up, will you?"

In the wake of Liza slamming out the door, Emma grabbed Rouge's arm before she followed and whispered, "Let me see your photos next time."

The ride home seemed interminable, Liza glaring at the road, not saying a thing. Usually after class, she was chatty. Rouge sighed and played with the radio, but the reception was capricious this far away from any reasonable metropolis. She could not wait to get home and almost leapt from the car before Liza pulled it to a full stop.

"What's your hurry?"

"Homework," Rouge lied as she ran up the stairs.

She lay on her bed with her book open, scanning the pages while she waited to hear what Liza was doing. Coming to bed? Making a drink and lighting a fire? Rouge heard nothing, meaning Liza would probably be up for a while.

Dear Ben,

I'm sending you two rolls of film. The first one is of my neighbor, Dale. His dad owns the dairy farm across the road from our house. There are two sons, this one and the younger one, Tom. Tom is almost twenty-five. He'll inherit the farm one day. Dale is twenty-eight and spent three years in the navy. That's where he got all those tattoos on his arms. I think he's in love with Liza. No, not in love, but fascinated by her. But Liza thinks he's coarse and she's not interested, though she's nice enough when he brings over a few bottles of milk.

Anyway, he's pretty moody and sometimes he gets mean so you have to be careful around him. He's home now, working for his dad, but he won't be around for long. He's unhappy and searching and his eyes are looking for other possibilities. Just in case.

The second roll is of my friend Shelly. She's really pretty but I don't have to tell you that. You can see it for yourself. She's pretty popular in school and a lot of boys are in love with her. But she's kind of spoiled and can be a bitch and sometimes gets this hard look on her face. I like that look a lot. I like that she's so tough. But she isn't always. Like in these pictures. Her boyfriend just dumped her for some other girl. Shelly's never been dumped and the pain of it just smacks through her toughness. I know she's completely humiliated but she'll never let on. I doubt she'll even let herself cry. Not over this boy anyway. But right now her face is this mess of pride and hurt and anger and bitchiness and I love it.

I hope you like these better. I see what you mean. They were a lot more fun to take.

Rouge

*

As she did most afternoons after school, Rouge rode by the post office to pick up the mail. "Your mother was in earlier," Mr. Nelson said as Rouge walked in. "Quite a pile, too."

Damn, she thought, turning to leave then remembering her manners. "Thank you," she called out, in too much of a

140

hurry to hear a response. Just the sound of the heavy outer door slamming shut behind her.

"Damn!" she muttered to herself as she jumped onto her bike. Rouge was expecting photos any day. With her luck, they had come today, the one day she wasn't there to intercept the mail. She raced home.

Liza had a fire going and was curled up on the sofa, reading, or trying to. Rouge could tell she was slipping into one of her depressions, her lethargy beginning to weigh Rouge down. She had taken some students to New York the weekend before, trips that could exhilarate or discourage.

"There's mail for you," she mumbled as Rouge came bounding in the back door, cheeks flushed, her fingers chilled and numb.

The large envelope with its familiar handwriting lay atop a pile of art magazines and advertising debris. Rouge grabbed the envelope and hurried toward the stairs.

"Not so fast. Come in here." Liza's voice catching her just as her foot hit the stair. "Let's see what you've got."

"It's for me."

"It's your photos, I know. Let's have a look."

Rouge sighed and stepped back down to ground level, shuffling into the living room, flopping down in the ragged, sagging armchair next to the couch. "Well, let me at least look first."

Carefully, she slid a finger under the mail flap and broke it open, pulling out two sheets of what she learned were called contact sheets, several small images circled in red crayon. She breezed through the images, then, pleased at the initial view, handed them over.

Liza studied the images carefully as she would her

students' work, while Rouge fiddled with a loose thread dangling from the bright floral pillow Liza had sewn the summer before—a splash of color to hide the tired brown fabric of the armchair. Sat and waited. At last, Liza handed them back.

"Well?" Rouge demanded.

"Well, they're good. Very good." There was little enthusiasm to light her words. "What does he say?"

Rouge had purposely left the letter in the big envelope. "He likes the potential stories."

"Hmmm…?" Liza rose slowly to put another log on the fire, not in any mood, apparently, to talk. Rouge gathered up her things.

Just as she was leaving, Liza spoke up. "I'm glad you have a mentor. We all need one. But it's time for you to learn to develop your own film. I'll see if you can work with Jerry."

Jerry! The slimy old man who taught photography at the college. Dressed as he always was in a dirty apron, flannel shirt rolled up to the elbows, the bared arms below covered in rashes he claimed were from the darkroom chemicals. Long stringy hair pulled back in a ponytail. Did he ever smile? "No, thanks."

"Why not? He knows his stuff."

"He's creepy. And he smells."

"Maybe one of his students, then. There are plenty of kids who can teach you to print."

Liza was not even looking at her, just settling herself back onto the sofa. "I'm sure Ben's a busy guy. You should let him go about his own work."

She was right. Rouge's pride quickly evaporated. She hadn't even considered any other possibility than putting rolls in the mail. But for how long? She was embarrassed that she hadn't thought of that first, embarrassed at her dependence on Ben, embarrassed mostly that Liza considered this before she had. Ben's a busy guy. Of course! What was wrong with her? Rouge stood and gathered up her work.

"I'd better get to my homework. It's late," she grumbled, striding out of the room.

Rouge left school at lunch the next day to go to the post office and mail the letter she had written the night before. Only a letter this time. She had decided not to send the five rolls of film lined up on her bureau.

> *Dear Ben,*
> *Thanks a million for the prints and all your help. You're way too generous. I'm sure you're busy enough with your own work. It's probably time for me to learn how to do this myself. But you've been a great teacher and I really appreciate it.*
> *Thanks again,*
>
> *Rouge*

"Hey... hey!" Shelly had to call several times through the stream of students heading to class to get Rouge's attention. "Did you get the photos back yet?"

"Yeah."

"So, when are you going to show me? Let's go to your place after school. We can get Kevin to drive us." Kevin, her latest boyfriend.

"Probably not a good idea. Liza's not feeling well."

143

"Then let's swing by and pick them up. We'll go over to Billy's."

The bell rang. Students took their seats. "Maybe," Rouge whispered loudly across two other heads.

Shelly found Rouge again at her locker at the end of the day. "Let's go. Kevin's waiting in the car."

"Not today. It's my night to make dinner." This was a lie; Liza probably wouldn't be stirring even to eat, but Rouge was not in the mood to entertain anyone.

"When then?"

"I'll bring them tomorrow."

"Promise?"

It was too cold to ride bikes anymore, so Rouge took the school bus that waited in the front parking lot. Mostly it was filled with students from her class, those who hadn't befriended older students who could drive them home. There were only about twenty who lived on her side of town and Rouge found a seat next to Martha, always a seat available next to Martha, a painfully shy girl, not much to look at, not much to talk to, though she was the smartest student in her grade.

Martha barely glanced her way as she sat, her attention riveted on a book. How she could focus over the bumpy stop-and-go ride was a marvel.

"See ya," Rouge whispered, gathering her books as the bus pulled up to her driveway.

There was a light on in the living room but nowhere else. The studio was dark, no smoke from the chimney. If Liza's station wagon was not parked by the back door, it could have been one of her teaching days, forgetting, as she usually did, to light up the house before she left.

"Liza," Rouge called softly, closing the back door tightly to keep in the warm air. "Liza," she tried again. Nothing came back.

She wiggled out of her boots and threw them on the pile of shoes by the back door, slid on her heavy brown wool socks that she left on the shelf, then hopped up the stairs to turn on the small heater in her room. Liza's door was closed. She was probably sleeping or reading or whatever she did in her dark room where she disappeared into one of her holes. Rouge thought of knocking, sticking her head in the door to see if she wanted anything. But why bother? She wouldn't. She never did.

When Rouge was little, and Liza drifted into one of her moods, it frightened her, as though Liza had shed her skin and gone elsewhere, leaving only the shell of herself curled up in bed. Sometimes, she'd call a student to come babysit, claiming she was not feeling well, or would put Rouge in front of the television. There was seldom anything to watch and after Rouge tired of playing with toys or leafing through picture books, she would crawl into bed and lay beside her, Liza draping an arm over her small body and mumbling a sleepy "thank you," while Rouge stayed still against her in the dark, waiting for her mother to return, the warmth of the wool blanket knitting their two small bodies together, each hanging desperately onto the other for definition. For purpose.

Now, irritation met Liza's silence. No way Rouge wanted proximity to this. Liza could roust herself when she was ready, find her own something to eat.

It was a little after five. Realizing she was starving, Rouge went down to the kitchen to see what there was—leftover meatloaf that had gone dry, mashed potatoes in a bowl, some old vegetables, the usual stuff—eggs, milk, bread. Soup and tuna in the cupboard. Liza kept the place stocked in the winter. But nothing appealed.

Moving like a cat, though she knew silence was unnecessary, Rouge tiptoed to the hall and picked up the phone. "Shelly," she said when she answered, "can I come over for dinner? Maybe spend the night? I'll bring the photos."

"Mom," Shelly yelled over her shoulder, not bothering to put a hand over the receiver. "Can Rouge come for dinner…? I don't know. I think she's sick." Then to Rouge, "Do you need a ride?"

"I can ride my bike."

"Are you crazy? It's freezing. Mom says we can come get you."

They bounded up the stairs into Shelly's room. Rouge plopped down on the thick pink quilt covering Shelly's bed and pulled the envelope out of her bag. She separated out the page of Dale, whom Shelly could care less about, and handed over the sheet of Shelly faces.

Shelly held them up close, smiling at some, grimacing at others.

"Jeez, do I look like that?"

"Only when you're pissed."

"What a monster! I like this one." She held up the sheet, pointing. "Can you get a big one of this?"

"Yeah." Then Rouge remembered. "Maybe I can. I don't know."

146

It took just under a week for Ben's reply to come back. Rouge was only picking up the mail by habit now, the days she'd ride her bike, freezing or not, stopping at Simpson's for some peanut brittle first, and was taken aback when she noticed his scrawl on a small white envelope peeking out from between two art magazines. She zinged to life and did not wait until she got home to open the letter this time. Standing just outside the post office door, holding her breath to keep the icy vapors from clouding her view, she carefully slid open the flap and unfolded the letter.

Rouge,

I hope you don't stop sending me film. I enjoy watching you learn and it's no trouble to print your work along with mine. Besides, there is something you can do for me in return. I'd like to come back in the summer and take some photographs of you and your mother. There's some interesting portraits there. While I'm doing that, we could build you a darkroom. I'm sure there's a good space in your basement somewhere.

Ben

PS. Have you thought of photographing Liza?

We could build you a darkroom is all Rouge read the first go-round. The notion sent heat through her blood, firing her up for the cold ride home.

Liza was in the kitchen, making a pot of lentil soup. News of another group show at the college, featuring Liza's work, had pulled her out of her depression, flipping her into exuberance. The odor of wholewheat bread snaked out of the oven as Charlie Parker was horned in from the record player in the living room. The house was comfortably warm.

"Someone's quite pleased with herself," Liza commented as Rouge all but ripped off her winter coat and pulled off her hat, freeing her long hair into static war. She slicked it down with a sweep of her hand, not in the mood to dawdle over small talk, over anything at all.

Luckily, the phone started ringing. "I'll get it."

"Rouge, darling." It was Tess. "What's new?"

When did they last talk? A few days before, Liza having called to tell her about the show.

"Nothing." Rouge was surprisingly curt, for Tess at least, and softened her tone. "You know – school, work, friends. Nothing interesting. Liza, it's Tess." Normally, Rouge would hold the phone hostage, chattering away with Tess while Liza stood by, waiting, hand out for the receiver. Not this time. Not waiting even to hear a response, Rouge set down the phone and ran up the stairs.

Shutting her door against Liza's chatter, Rouge turned the knob until it clicked, then pulled the letter out from her pack and read it again. This time, it was not the *We can build you a darkroom* that leapt out. Instead, it was Liza. *Have you thought about photographing Liza?*

Coming from Ben, the idea of it stung Rouge. Damn, damn, damn, she thought, throwing the letter across her bed, watching it sail to the floor. Rouge was furious. "Why is everyone so fascinated with Liza?" she muttered to herself. She is all beauty and talk and beguiling exaggeration. God damn her!

She picked up the letter and stuffed it in her desk drawer,

then threw on a heavy sweater, pants and wool socks, so enraged that all she wanted was to get out in the snow. It was not her eye or talent, not her at all. "I would like to photograph you and your mother, ha!" She sneered, talking loudly to herself as she banged her dresser drawer shut. "It's all a lie. He's only interested in Liza."

"Who are you talking to in there?" Liza asked from outside the door.

Rouge quickly subdued her anger. "No one."

Liza opened the door. "Well, it sure sounded like someone from out here. Someone infuriating."

Rouge grabbed her gloves and the camera from the desk, avoiding her mother's eyes. "I just forgot something at school I needed."

"I'll drive you back." Liza was being strangely solicitous. It was not like her and, though Rouge would have welcomed the attention in the past, at the moment, it made her feel claustrophobic and even more agitated.

"No, it can wait. I'm going out for a walk."

"It's really cold," Liza offered as Rouge strode by her and out the door.

"I like it cold," she shot back, then disappeared down the stairs.

The air outside was dry and biting, and the snow crunched under her feet, the sound of it hard and crisp. A good, freezing temperature, the kind that pins everything still in time. Rouge walked briskly to the road and turned left, making her way down along the edge of the plowed surface, her pace keeping her warm, the cold and the motion mollifying her anger. Frigid air brought all awareness to her exposed face. Her cheeks burned; her nose tingled. The sky was overcast and the afternoon was growing dark, the only illumination coming from snow, clumped to every conceivable surface, the ground, the branches, the roofs and fences, every paltry blade of grass trying to find some air above the heavy white covering. Against such whiteness, anything exposed seemed bleak and colorless, a remnant of its original form.

She tried to photograph the trees but she could not stop thinking of Liza. Of Ben. Of the two of them together in one sentence. The two of them together at all.

"Forget it. Don't come for Liza. She doesn't care about you," she yelled down the white road as though her words could skim terrain, head south and reach Ben to correct his misguided mind. As if words from Rouge could warn men, any of them, away from Liza. If they could only hear her first and believe her, before their futile longing took hold.

But Ben was different, she reminded herself, moving along, pulling the collar of her coat up over her chin. How he acted in the kitchen, taking photographs, not minding Liza's absence. Not at all pining or sad, waiting for her to return. In fact, he seemed surprisingly nonchalant, as though maybe he had been done with her first. Rouge smiled, liking that idea. Wouldn't that have been something? And he was corresponding with her, not her mother. If he were still infatuated with Liza, he wouldn't be helping Rouge as much as he was. Rouge was sure Ben was different. He was smart and perceptive. She could tell by the way he studied her before he took her picture, remembering how he ran the curtains through his fingers, sliding them into the stream of sunlight. He was not foolish enough to come back for Liza. Not in that way. What had he said?

I would like to come back and take some photographs of you and your mother. There's some interesting portraits there.

She repeated his words again and again. You and your mother. No, she finally decided, Ben was sharp, enough to understand the complexities there.

The gray skies had nearly transformed into the dark of night by the time she returned. Coming up the driveway, Rouge could see Liza in the light of the kitchen making dinner. Smoke curled in parallel tracks from both the chimney in the house and the wood-burning stove in the barn, coiling up toward the trees. Rouge stopped by the car. She was not yet ready to make small talk with her mother, nor was she in any spirit to take on Ben's assignment. Even if Liza would let her. No, she'd warm up in the studio first, maybe take a few pictures of Liza's brushes and paints, her space without her.

The studio was warm, and Rouge set her camera down on a stool so that she could strip off her outer garments. Though Liza left her door unlocked, she seldom invited Rouge in and might be annoyed to find her snooping around. If she came out, Rouge would say she was looking for drawing paper to make a map for a school project. She moved through the big white room. Though the floor in front of Liza's workspace was splattered with paint, almost a thick, dried carpet from years of dribbled pigment, the studio was neater than usual. Several paintings were lined up methodically against the wall, and her painting table was clean, the brushes set up sequentially by size, the palette wiped clean. House cleaning, Liza would say, explaining to her students the importance of editing one's work. Often. Especially before a show.

Scanning the room, which was too neat—in fact, did not feel like Liza at all—Rouge was drawn instead to the photographs on the wall. The one she loved of Tess and Liza, and this other one that had captivated her as a girl. A portrait of a young woman yellowed enough to look more like a small painting, such serenity in her face as she gazed at the camera, her dark, large eyes soft and inviting, her skin aglow, her lips poised to break into a smile. It was the most exquisite face Rouge had ever seen. In its beauty certainly, but more than that, the tranquility and gentleness there.

This was a photograph of her grandmother, the one image that Liza's father had not destroyed after her death. Mrs. Carton had hidden it to keep for Liza. A girl should have something to remember her mother by, Mrs. Carton had told Liza when she gave her the photograph years later. Especially when they looked so much alike. The spitting image, Mrs. Carton had said.

And they were, almost identical. Which was why Liza believed her father always hated her, or so she said, not blatantly, she explained, for he was too much of a gentleman to express negative feelings, but deep inside he resented her profoundly for his wife's death. He had burned all the photographs. He could not bear to remember her, so, as Liza grew into the exact image of her mother, it made sense that he would push her away.

Funny, Rouge thought, moving closer to her grandmother's image as though it were a sweetness she longed to inhale. Yes, they resembled one another—the outline of the face, the cheekbones, the bright, wide eyes, but how could anyone possibly confuse them? They were so completely different. One so calm and peaceful, content in her skin, the other always on the edge of agitation, perched to escape. When Rouge was little, she'd pretend this was a photograph of Liza stripped clean of the chaos and uncertainty that tormented her. And of the sadness that stopped her nearly dead. It was the image of a strong, content woman Rouge was sure existed inside Liza, down there somewhere, just waiting until the way was clear of debris to float to the surface and be seen.

She considered taking a photograph of the photograph. That would confuse him, she thought. Then again, maybe not. How well could he possibly know Liza after only one night?

Just then, Rouge heard Liza calling her from the kitchen door. She hastily threw on her coat, scarf and hat, and slid into her boots, grabbed her camera and closed the studio door tight, leaving everything as she had found it.

*

Have you thought of photographing Liza?

For weeks, Rouge watched her mother. From under the curtain of half-closed eyes, a partially turned head, while she was supposedly reading or doing other things, she stared surreptitiously so Liza wouldn't question her. It was a meaty assignment Ben had given her and she felt as though she were his partner. She imagined the two of them looking through a lens at this woman, focusing carefully until he finally handed her the camera and invited her to take the first shot. Rouge watched her mother with this invitation in mind, with as much clarity as she could muster so that she would make him proud.

But it was hard. Studying Liza, she stumbled at times and ran several conversations through her head, possible letters to Ben. Yes, I've considered it and, No, I can't photograph her, because it's way too complicated. I don't know where to begin. I see one thing, and immediately it goes to something else. Then another, then another.

How about one part of her? Her feet or hands or her tiny ears? Something like that I could do, Rouge thought. I could do the mess of her studio, too. The things she leaves behind. But don't ask me to shoot her face, her eyes. That's precisely what I'm talking about. I get lost rummaging around in there.

Then Liza would be deep in thought or focused on drawing, oblivious to Rouge's presence, and Rouge was sure she could capture at least one worthy image of her. If only she could bend down and get the right angle.

Nursing a cup of tea, legs folded up to her chest, Rouge sat at the table across from Liza, waiting, watching, envisioning many possibilities.

Liza slammed her book shut. "What *are* you staring at?"

"I was thinking of taking some pictures," she answered, taking a sip of the now lukewarm tea.

Liza reached for another book. She had come home from the library with an armful that lay untouched for several days, neatly stacked one on top of the other on the kitchen table. "Not of me, I hope!"

"Yes, of you."

"No you don't. The last thing I need is for *you* to be watching me."

Rouge put down her cup, leaned forward. "C'mon, Liza. Let me just take a few pictures."

"No."

"While you're doing something else. You won't even know." Rouge paused to think of what, something that would engage her. Of course! "While you're painting. Really, I'll be quiet. You won't know that I'm there."

"Are you kidding? You'll make me a nervous wreck." Liza began reading, a sign, Rouge understood, that she was beginning to relinquish her resistance.

"No, I won't. I promise." Rouge waited. Liza was reading now and gave no reply. "If I do, kick me out."

"Maybe."

"Maybe you'll kick me out, or maybe you'll let me photograph?"

Liza began to hum. She said nothing more.

With the stove going in the studio, the large space heated in no time, its well-insulated walls an impenetrable barrier to the outside cold. It was late February with over two feet of snow on the ground. Very cold nights still, just a trace of warmth beginning to come through during the days. Liza had cleaned the space a month or so ago. She had ordered several new brushes and paints, and a large canvas had been started, its whiteness tinged by soft lines of charcoal and the first dabs of color. Another painting, only recently finished but still wet, was drying against the wall.

Liza usually stood while she worked. She would make a stroke or scrape off some paint, then step back to look and approach the canvas again. Rouge stood behind her, trying not to distract. From the stiffness in Liza's shoulders and the tautness of her arm muscles, Rouge could tell Liza was already engrossed in contemplation. Rouge stayed as quiet as she could, her camera poised and ready to shoot. Finally, Liza stepped up to the table and dabbed two brushes in paint, each a different color. Taking this as her cue, Rouge positioned herself behind her and took a few shots of Liza's arm sweeping paint across the canvas.

One or two shots, though there was nothing much there. Rouge put down the camera. Possibly from the other side, maybe Liza's face painting. Rouge tiptoed around the table and found a spot against the wall a foot or two from the canvas, holding stone still to see if she was noticed. Liza let loose a diagonal swath of amber. Apparently not.

Rouge stood for a while watching Liza's face betray struggles, the fierce gaze of her large, brown eyes mounting in intensity, then backing off from time to time—a temporary resolution possibly. Back and forth. It was a lot of energy to maintain. That fierce gaze, though, Rouge was drawn to the rigid concentration. But that wasn't it at all. Not the way Rouge was seeing it at that moment. It was every ounce of energy culled and waiting for the beginning of something. Or maybe the end?

Click, click, click. She inched closer. *Click.* How far could she approach before she was noticed and the moment gone? *Click, click.* Yes, she remembered now. She knew that look and where she had seen it before.

Dear Ben,

Here's a good story for you, but I swear it's true. I was maybe five. Liza got me up one night and took me to New York. My very first trip. I don't remember much of it, just all the noise and smells. It was dark when we got there. First, she took me to this big gallery, filled with tons of people. She talked to lots of them, holding me by the hand. I couldn't hear what she was saying, just mumblings of her voice. Most of the time I stared at knees and hemlines and some nice shoes as she pulled me around the room. Finally, we stopped in front of a wall with huge paintings, abstractions. Just like Liza's. At the time, I assumed they were hers.

I later found out it was a show of Hank Bolton's and those paintings made him famous. Liza didn't like them at all. I could feel it by the tightness of her hand holding mine. Her squeeze got hard and sweaty. I looked up at her then and she was staring at the paintings and had the strangest look in her eyes. Fear, anger, I don't know what. I think what I shot of her face here is about as close to that look as I've seen since.

We went to some parties afterward. I'm pretty sure I slept for most of it. When I woke up, I was on a pile of coats on someone's bed. It was really noisy, and the air was smoky and smelled bad, and at first I couldn't find Liza, though I knew she was around, and I wasn't scared. At one point, I stopped by this woman asleep on a couch. She had on a dress and it was pulled up high on her thigh, like she had to wiggle a lot to get comfortable. There was another room not too far away. The door was open. Inside, some guys were laughing and hitting something. It was darts shooting into a dartboard, though from where I was standing, I could just hear the noise. Just then, this dart came whizzing out the door, across the room and stuck right into this woman's thigh. I almost screamed, but I didn't. I think I was too shocked. The woman on the couch didn't even *wake up. I couldn't believe it. It was like a dream. So I walked up to her, really close, because I wasn't sure it was true, and I stood right next to her, staring at her thigh, at the plump trickle of blood that began running down her leg. I was absolutely hypnotized when all of a sudden this big, warm man's hand took mine and led me away. I followed him, though I'm looking over my shoulder at the woman who's still not awake, and he took me to Liza. He put my hand in hers and said to her, "This is no place for a child."*

Later, the next day, as we're driving home, I asked her who he was.

"That was Hank Bolton," she said, as though I should know.

But I didn't and asked, "Who's he?"

And all she said was, "He's a famous painter."

It would be nice to see you again. I hope you will come.

Rouge

FIVE

Liza

(Interludes, 1950s)

Since Liza had made the decision to keep her child, an enormous weight had lifted. She felt light, kindled, connected once again to her work, every ounce of herself flowing through it. The smell and lusciousness of the paint exhilarated her as she felt it fly across the canvas, then turn and ribbon itself out until there was nothing left on the brush. Such freedom of movement, as though she herself were sliding through cadmium red pudding, feeling herself let go and glide. Unrestrained, unhindered, complete release. She dabbed more red onto her brush, moved close to the canvas, applied another stroke here, a slight touch there. She stepped back to take a look and let the answer come to her.

There. It came there. Now some phthalo blue, a slither of it here.

She stood back to view the large painting from afar. Much of the canvas she had left untouched, the undercurrent of white giving the paint a field through which to move, as though it were dancing in delight. She would show Hofmann as soon as it was dry. Once she had a few more completed, she could call Mountstuart and invite him for another studio visit.

At first, Liza did not mention the pregnancy to anyone,

engrossed as she was in her painting. Too tired at night after a long day's work, she avoided the Cedar and the interminable talk that could easily captivate and exhaust her, especially now that work was going so well. She preferred a good night's sleep so she was fresh for the day.

A few days later, Phil knocked on her door.

"We never see you anymore. Hank says you're hiding. Everything okay?"

"Yeah, just busy working. Come in and see."

She was happy to see him. Though Phil had discovered sculpture—having been raised on a farm, he was more comfortable with tools and metal than brush and paint—he looked at a lot of work and had developed a discerning eye. That and his bear of a body and affable attitude made him a welcoming friend, easy, someone good to have around.

Seeing the work, Phil said nothing at first. He just stared, then whistled, then turned to her, grinning, "Jesus, Liza, some damn good stuff. Something's sure gotten into you."

"Yeah, I know." She could not help but beam.

Phil plunked himself down in one of the two old armchairs Liza had gotten off the street. "Let's have it. What happened?"

Distracted as she was by her enthusiasm over Phil's response, Liza answered before she had a chance to think. Am I ready to divulge this news? There will be criticisms, warnings. Am I ready for this?

"For starters, I'm pregnant," she blurted out.

Phil waved it off. "Talk to Elaine about dealing with that. She's had a few abortions—"

"I'm not going that route," Liza interrupted. Here it

comes, she thought, the judgment, the condescending advice. Better to start off with Phil, the least challenging of the bunch.

"Who's the father?" He furrowed his brow.

"No one you know. A guy I met this summer. Just passing through."

Phil said nothing for an uncomfortable moment. Feeling a sudden chill, Liza rubbed her arms.

"Does he know?" he finally said.

"He doesn't care." She was emphatic in her answer.

He paused, considering. "How are you going to manage? You know what they say."

"Yeah, I know." Liza needed water and got up to drink from the faucet, not even bothering with a glass. "I know it's crazy, Phil. I don't understand it. Not exactly. You know I don't want a relationship. Not with another artist." Not, she would admit only to herself, with another man. "I see what that's done for Elaine and Lee and the other women artists who spend more time promoting their husbands' work than doing their own. You know that, too."

"Yes. It's true."

"This feels different. It's something I need to do. I can't explain it more than that."

Throwing his arms over the back of the chair, Phil nodded. "Well, if anyone can do it, you can, Liza."

She filled a glass of water and brought it to Phil. "Thanks for the vote of confidence."

Phil finished his water in a few quick swallows. "So, what are your plans?"

Oh yes, plans. Liza sighed. Painting had been so distracting. Thank you, Phil. It was time to start thinking about plans. Though it was nice imagining that she could make a living off her work, few artists sold much of anything, other than Pollock. Even a master like de Kooning struggled. His show of black and white abstractions at Charlie Egan's two years ago, hailed by the critics, had only one sale. To Egan's mother-in-law for $750. Egan was one of Elaine's lovers, convenient for Bill, though Egan never paid him a cent. Liza would need to find more dependable sources of income.

"I have a little money from my father put away. That will pay the bills for a few years. I'll probably get a job teaching."

"Have you talked to Hofmann? He'd have connections to that sort of thing."

"No. I haven't. But, that's a great idea. I'll ask Hofmann."

But there was the new work. Though her expanding stomach was about to give her away, Liza had a few more weeks where she could hide herself with big shirts and fall coats. She had made Phil promise not to say anything. Not yet. Five new paintings had been completed by the middle of November that wanted attention first. She called Mountstuart, who agreed to a studio visit.

"Marvelous," he pronounced. "I am very pleased. Let me take these to the gallery and see how we do. If I can sell any, we'll have a show."

First, she'd tell Tess. Always Tess first, though she was seeing less of her these days, as Tess had announced her engagement and would be moving to Boston after her wedding. Tess was thrilled about the new work, of course, but also pragmatic, eager to talk about her future, where she'd live once Tess had gone.

"Not now," Liza said. "Let me talk to Hofmann first and see if he can set me up with a teaching job. I'm going to the Cedar tonight. I haven't been in a while. Care to join me?"

Tess waved her away. "You know I hate the noise of that place, that unbearable smoky air. Not terribly healthy for you either at this point, I would imagine."

"Probably not. I won't stay too long."

As she hoped, she found Hank at the Cedar, seated at a table with Phil and a few familiar artists, his arm around a young woman she did not recognize. Liza pulled up a chair from a nearby table.

"Boys," she said, ignoring the girl.

"Ah, Liza, come join us." Phil slid his chair over to make room.

She had not seen Hank since he had returned from the summer, though she heard he had a new girlfriend. How quickly they seemed to come and go. Liza slid in beside Phil, and without acknowledging Hank, she reached her hand across the table to the woman. "Liza Baker," she said.

"Ellen McNaffy," came the response.

"We met this summer at Hofmann's," Hank interjected. "She's a terrific painter and also works as an assistant to Myers at Tibor." He turned to her, smiling. "I have her to thank for the introduction."

Undaunted, Liza acknowledged the connection with a nod, then asked, "You must be familiar with Logan Mountstuart then. From Leeping Fils."

"Yes," Ellen said. "We've done business with the main gallery in Paris."

"Well," she said, looking purposefully at Hank, "looks like he's going to be my dealer."

Phil clapped his hands. "Well done, my beauty!"

Hank tried hard to hold his composure. "You've done some new work, obviously. I'd love to come see."

"Any time," she answered. "You're both welcome."

Hank appeared the next afternoon, without Ellen. At first, he said nothing, just stared at the paintings. Liza curled up in an armchair, waiting, a strong inkling of the conflicting thoughts going through his mind.

"It's good," he finally announced. "Lively in your loose brushstrokes. All the white gives it air. But, they don't feel quite done. Still unresolved."

Liza stiffened. You shit, she thought, those are my words about your work. She knew right away that he was beguiled by her paintings' spirited vitality. It was what he was after in his work, always just coming up a bit short. So close, but he just couldn't let go. She smiled.

"Very much done," she said instead. She might as well give him everything she had. "I've found some meaning, you see."

"What meaning?"

"I'm pregnant and I'm going to have the child."

Hank's response was exactly what she anticipated. "It's not mine, is it?"

Liza let out an angry laugh. "Absolutely not."

"That's good. You know how I feel about children. They'd only tie you down, especially now when things are just beginning." He paused, enough to give her a genuine look of concern. "It will be worse for you. How are you going to paint when you're a mother? Where will you find the time?"

"I'll figure it out."

"Yes, I have no doubt you will." He held out a hand, an offering of a nominal goodbye, though Liza understood that it was just a stance—an I'm-not-with-you-in-this—not a farewell. But definitely a parting in the journey.

*

Despite his enthusiasm, Mountstuart could not sell Liza's work. Nor could two other dealers who subsequently took her on. Though she would never admit it to anyone—not even Tess—she understood why. With a baby, she did not have time to play the scene, to make the connections, get herself known.

With a glowing recommendation from Hofmann, Liza secured a teaching job at a college an hour and a half outside the city. They were expanding their art department, wanting to develop a more modern approach. What better candidate than one of Hofmann's star students. Liza was offered as many classes as she could handle.

Before Rouge could toddle, Liza brought her to class, propped her up on blankets surrounded by a field of toys, and let her be the focus of attention as the students set up to work, someone always available to keep an eye out and entertain. But soon, she had to rely on the babysitting service provided by the college. Rouge hated the chaos of other toddlers and clung to Liza in tears.

"You'll be fine." Liza knelt down to wipe her face, kiss her head, free herself from desperate arms. "Rouge, c'mon, I have to go." Handing over the red-faced child to one of the students helping out, she rushed away, the ordeal often making her late for class.

Once her guilt had dissipated—she had to get to work— once she had dumped her things and finagled with the still life she had started to put together at the end of the last class, once she had given her day's instruction and got the students to work, she could wander around and engage with each individually, giving corrections, solutions, new directions, hope. The mentoring of so much potential gave her great satisfaction. She understood why Hofmann loved to teach. When she found herself complaining about not having time to do her own work, she tried to remember this. If not in her own studio, at least in class she could be a star.

There were still the weekends, time between the chores of life. It was easy to find a student to come and stay over and scoop Rouge away, until they wore out all the distractions and came knocking on the studio door.

They always did, eventually. Why should this evening be the exception?

"We've done everything you suggested," the exasperated student said, clearly exhausted herself and ready to leave. "I can't keep her away any longer."

Liza sighed. She had just about reached the point where she could lose herself in her work, forget everything but the essence she was about to capture. So elusive, this glimpse. So fucking elusive.

"It's okay," she said. "Let her play in the corner and draw."

But she was done for the day, the glimpse having vanished even from memory.

Time to clean brushes, pay the student, pick up her child, and make some dinner, mustering what energy remained to play with dolls, read books, and get Rouge to bed; so tired that she often fell asleep beside her.

It was not that late when the phone rang and rang and rang. "What is it?" Liza woke hard, stumbled out of bed and into her own room to answer, if for no other reason than to stop the annoying noise.

"I was just about to hang up." It was Hank. "Where were you? In the studio?"

She didn't dare admit her fatigue, not when she knew he painted well into the night. Every night.

"Yes. Thanks for the interruption," she said. He had been drinking; she could hear it in his voice.

"I'm in the Whitney Biennial. You have to come down and see."

Most people would note this announcement as pure bravado. *A few solo shows at my gallery and now this.* Liza alone seemed to be able to pick out the tinge of insecurity, the 'you have to come and see' as a plea for her approval. This odd little dance in the midst of their bigger lives; how far apart they were drifting, yet he still longed for her eye.

"Hank, it's Tuesday. I have to teach tomorrow. I can't get away. You know that." She was clearly exasperated. "Why don't you come up here?"

"I don't have the time. I have to make a decision by tomorrow." He never had the time of course, hated the country, hated her life away from the city, the child, the endless distractions. Besides, there was nothing else to do. At least in New York there was a world of art.

"Then get Ellen to help you."

Hank grunted. "We broke up a few months ago."

"Ah," she said, no surprise really. All that drinking and sleeping around even among those who were married. It was a wonder anyone stayed together.

"Come down when you can. I want to show you the new work."

"Maybe this weekend, if I can find a babysitter."

"Oh yes," he retorted. "That."

Liza was wide awake now. Even though she had to get up early, she would not be able to fall asleep. Checking to make sure her voice had not woken Rouge, she went instead to her studio.

A large canvas had been nailed to the wall. Still wet from the day's work, the painting glistened, the movement of big brushwork beckoned, *Come back, come back.*

Liza stood and stared and tried to draw the energy out of herself to follow, to catch hold and get back into the chase. But she couldn't do it. She was absolutely drained.

Instead, she grabbed a brush soaking in turpentine, aimed and threw it hard as she could at the heart of the canvas.

"Goddamn you. I'm too fucking tired to do this."

*

"You're coming, of course?" It was Phil on the phone.

Liza sighed. She was so tempted. "I haven't decided."

"What? How can you miss Hank's big show?" Phil said. "He invited you, of course?"

170

"Yes."

"When was the last time you saw him?"

A long time, has it been two years already? His success at the Whitney nearly four years earlier had catapulted his career to countless solo shows and big dollar sales.

"Just before he moved to Paris." Girlfriend number what? Six, seven? She had lost count, though this one, Isabella Rouault, well connected in Paris, would help shape his international career.

It had been snowing the night he told her, bundled up against the cold, hurrying from one gallery to the next. Just happened to mention it.

"What?" Liza stopped dead in her tracks.

"What do you mean, what?"

"Jesus, Hank, do you have no shame?"

"What the hell are you talking about, Liza? I can't have my relationships, just because you won't?" He was standing square in front of her, arms crossed tightly. "You know damn well that if you weren't saddled with that kid, you'd be down here sleeping your way to connections."

"Fuck you, Hank."

His move had been over a year ago, though he had sporadically kept in touch, as if nothing had really changed, just as he always had, phone calls late at night. Talking about his new work, long discussions about that, only at the end asking about hers. Now, speaking to Phil, Liza twirled the phone cord tightly around her finger. How she wanted to see his new paintings. The man himself, she wasn't so sure.

"You can be my date," Phil said.

"All right. If I can get a babysitter at this short notice."

Liza called and called. Those students who were competent enough to care for a six-year-old were all busy on a Friday night. There was Mrs. Wilson, recently widowed and most likely happy to have something to do. If only Rouge did not balk at her presence, insisting her gnarled arthritic hands were claws meant to pin her to the ground the second Liza left.

"She's not that bad. Just a lonely old woman."

"Yes, she is. A monster. Don't leave me with her." Rouge was apoplectic, standing at the door. Liza pulled her outside.

"Now you stop this. She's a perfectly nice woman. You need to behave. I need you to behave." She gripped her hard. "Promise?"

Rouge glared back but managed a nod.

God damn it, Liza all but shouted as she got in the car, determined not to think about it anymore. She'll be all right for one evening. Mrs. Wilson is perfectly nice.

Though the opening was packed, she found Phil easily, his thick unruly hair and recently grown beard sticking out amid the more dapper crowd. She recognized many of those who had carved out successful careers, yet she clung to Phil's arm, focusing her attention on Hank, surrounded by admirers and deep in animated conversation. Lovely, polished Isabella was by his side, relishing the spotlight.

"Let the current art star bask in his glory," Phil said, sensing Liza's distress. "Come, let's have a look at the work."

Big, dramatic blocks of color adorned the walls. Over the years, Hank had begun moving away from gestural abstraction to simple form. The contrast of hues was almost meditative. Striking. Deceptively calm, the chunks of thick color hiding an agitation she knew haunted him, though he would never admit it. Liza was moved by the work, yet she felt strangely halted in her tracks, teased by the mystery of what lay below the surface.

"How about a drink?" Liza said to Phil. "We can connect with him later."

"When was the last time you were at the Cedar?" he asked when they hit the street.

"It's been a while."

"To the Cedar then," Phil grinned. "For old times' sake."

Even at this early hour—it couldn't have been much past nine—the Cedar was crowded; everyone talking, laughing, drinking, the place suffused with smoke. Liza noticed the old clock on the bar wall, reading *3:25*. The time meant nothing; the clock often ran backwards if it worked at all. Liza squinted to look into the room and find familiar faces among so many who were new.

"Hey, there's Randy," Phil shouted over the din. "You remember Randy." He grabbed her arm and led her over to the booth.

Ah yes, Liza thought, the kid from Hofmann's class, the cute guy from the Midwest.

"You remember Liza?" Phil said. Randy's eyes sparkled in recognition as he patted the spot next to him.

"Liza Baker," he all but crooned. "How could anyone forget you?"

"Randy just closed a big show at Charlie Egan's. Big black and white paintings. Damn good stuff."

"Good for you," Liza smiled.

"You were quite the painter yourself. I remember your work. Where did you go?" He had to shout to be heard as she leaned in close.

"Upstate to teach."

"I hope you're still painting."

"Definitely. Much as I can."

Phil went to the bar to get the two of them drinks, hurrying back to get Liza's attention. "Hey, look who's here. Your old friend Bill de Kooning, over at the bar."

One of their group, a young woman, somebody's fuck no doubt, perked up, stood to see. "Where?" she asked.

"There," Phil repeated, taking her head in his hands to point her face toward the man in the knit cap crowded in at the bar. "Liza knows de Kooning. Hey, Liza, go say hi. Bring him over for a drink."

"Yes," everyone clapped and whistled. "Bring him over."

What could Liza say? She felt put on the spot. She hadn't actually seen Bill in years. The last time had been, what, two years after Rouge had been born, at an opening where de Kooning had cornered her, asked how she was doing. He never saw her around town anymore. "But," he had said, embarrassing her then, "I always remember a pretty face."

If she had been more sober, maybe she would have laughed it off. Phil helped her up. "C'mon, Liza, show your stuff." Sure, why not? Impress them all, she could do that, she thought, as she eased herself up and out into the crowded room.

Bill was visibly agitated as she approached, leaning over the bar baiting a guy a few feet away, snarling as he yelled, "Yah, subconscious, hell! Sure, I paint women," he shouted, banging his hand on the bar. "Why not paint them? They are everywhere. Look," he raised himself a bit, struggling to stand, and lifted his arms as though he were gathering in a flock. "Look, girlies everywhere."

And there were, many, beautiful young women around him. Liza had heard that he and Elaine had split and Bill had had a daughter with another woman. Maybe she was there among them. Liza stopped and turned, thinking this was not the time.

Suddenly one of Phil's friends was behind her, breathing on her shoulder, giving her a push toward the bar. "You don't really know him, do you?" Liza turned. He was jeering at her.

"Of course I do." She whirled around and approached Bill, pushing through the young women. "He's an old friend," she muttered to one.

"Hey, Bill, remember me?" The words came out so fast. *Remember me!* She bit her lip, though she couldn't help smiling at him. But then he turned her way and it shocked her to see how pitiful he looked, his eyes red and weary, his face unshaved. He looked at her, perplexed.

"I... I was in the Ninth Street Show with you." She sputtered her words. Maybe she should turn around and leave. But he was reaching out for her, grabbing her by the arm and pulling her to the front of him, right in front, staring at her face, searching for recognition, so drunk, his eyes seemed to shake. There it was; he did know her for suddenly he beamed. Ah yes!

"Yes," he shouted as he spun her around to face the baiter. "And here's one now. Look, can't you see, the big eyes, that wide grin." He leaned down to her, speaking in her ear, though loud enough for those around to hear. "Smile for the man, show him your teeth." But Liza was frozen. The light overhead was like a column of heat, illuminating her horror as everyone gathered around. "The hair. Well," he paused to look over her shoulders and down her front. "Not much there in the tits, is there? Well, you take them from somewhere else. Some other girlie will have tits."

The bar erupted. Bill as well, letting her go as he knocked over his glass. "Sam," he all but yelled at the bartender, "give me another." Laughter filled the room and sliced through the smoke. Nothing but laughter; the place was saturated. Liza backed away toward her table. God, they were laughing at her, too, her crowd. Voices rang in her head also, shouting, Get out of here. Get out. Grab your coat, get out. But there, the clock. What does it say? *2:50.*

That clock! That clock was all she could think about as she fled the scene. Time was a joke at the Cedar. Under her breath, Liza wished time really could move backward. If only things could be erased.

*

Though Hank had relocated to Paris, he kept his studio in New York and visited often to work a deal or, as he admitted to Phil, to have a break from Isabella's perpetual demands. "Hank and his women," Phil had winked to Liza, the two of them laughing over his capricious involvements, how quickly he'd go from one to another.

She had long gotten used to his sporadic calls, inviting her down to the city when he was done with his work, the courting of buyers, of various dealers. Weary of his young little art tarts. When the glow of success had burned itself out, and he felt desperately alone. That's when he'd call.

And she'd agree; she could not help herself. Always she would make the time, even if it took several days to put together the necessary childcare. She could give countless reasons why she shouldn't go, *please don't*—he was so self-absorbed, his success was unbearable, the way he used people to enhance his career, he was so good at that, with his infectious charm. But she could not say no. Okay, okay, if she were honest, his success did have its allure. Her hope that his influence would sway a dealer to take her on. It had opened many doors, she'd give him that, but as quickly as they opened, they shut. As one dealer pointedly told her, abstract expressionism had run its course, for the most part. That *for the most part* implying unless you're someone, which clearly she was not.

So, what was the pull? Such push/pull between them. Hypnotic, it felt. She always had to go.

It had been nearly a year since she last saw him, and his new paintings had taken a brooding turn, the colors, once bright and hopeful, had darkened considerably. Whereas his earlier works had felt nearly devoid of feeling, these radiated a quiet despair. Yet, they were surprisingly beautiful. Liza felt a chill run through her.

"You want a drink?" he offered.

He had turned into quite the drunk, she had heard. Not mean-spirited like de Kooning and Pollock. It was that kernel of sadness she knew he hid that, freed from distractions, would flare up and push him to drink. More and more it seemed, for he was drinking to destructive excess. Drinking and isolating. But then coming out of it to create such work.

She knew his journey. She could easily follow it, too.

"It's early yet. Maybe later."

"Suit yourself." He shrugged and poured himself a shot of Scotch, swallowed it quickly. "Let's see your slides."

He always did ask to see her new work. There was a genuine curiosity, at least for the work. Mostly compliments—their styles were so different now—how much he admired her energy, her talent with color.

"I'm happy when I paint."

"Yes, it shows." He poured himself another drink. She decided to join him. Maybe just one. They did not talk much about the art world, of which he had grown weary, nor of France, though he loved the countryside and his studio there. Erik Sati played on the stereo as they made small talk and they continued to drink.

At one point he put down his glass, reached over to stroke the hair off her shoulder, touch her face. Like the old days, how natural it would be to spill from this into bed. Though he had gained some weight, Hank was still something to look at, those beguiling dark eyes that could pierce through any hesitation. Easy, too easy to succumb now. For a moment she felt herself giving way, but then something held her back. Surprising herself, she stiffened at his touch. Things were different now, she realized as she pulled away. There was no going back.

"It's late," she said, rising quickly. "Time for me to get home."

It was well past midnight when she returned. Rouge had been asleep for a while, she was sure. Liza should go to bed, too, but she was not yet ready to sleep. Instead, she went to the studio and pulled out a drawing pad stored between the wall and her bed. Propping herself up with pillows, she opened the pad to leaf through the work.

Images of Rouge, all of them. Portrait-like sketches, as

true as photographs. Tess would love them, but these were for Liza only. She had not shown them to anyone, even to Tess. This pad was recent work, done in the past month. In the stalls, behind the rolled-up paintings, were many more sketch books, charting and preserving Rouge's childhood. Other people had photographs. Liza had drawings. Work that occupied her when nothing else would. Kept her busy, kept her drawing skills honed, the only realistic work that interested her. The only image she locked away in her brain, indelibly, so that she could summon it whenever she needed, draw her daughter perfectly just from memory.

Rouge restless in the late winter, reading out of boredom, discontent written in shadows across her face as she forced herself to look down at the book.

Rouge asleep—so many of those—angelic in her peacefulness. Liza had painstakingly worked to catch the subtle hue in her long blonde hair, lighter at the ends. Her hair was getting darker as she got older. Dirty blonde some called it, though it never looked dirty.

Rouge gripping the apple-faced dolls Liza had made her, drying out the surplus fruit until it caved into a wizen face that they'd decorate with make-up and outfits sewn from old scarves and Rouge's outgrown clothes. Rouge running through a field of wildflowers, tucked up on the sofa, leafing through books.

The last one was unfinished and she worked for a while on Rouge's hands holding a book. She had everything right but her pinky—it was too big, then too small. As Liza put down the charcoal, she noticed the early morning light through the window. She would work on it later, after a few hours' sleep.

The house was cool. Liza tiptoeing gingerly up the stairs and down the hall toward her room. But first she looked in on Rouge. She had not pulled her shades before going to sleep, and pale light spilled in through her windows, illuminating the interior. Asleep, she looked so young, her head cocked across her pillow, wisps of long hair floating around her as though she were underwater. Innocent, a little doll in this subdued morning light. She was such an easy child, eager and responsive, and Liza had surprised herself in discovering how much she, as a mother, had to give. Where had that come from? She had no clue. Not from Mrs. Carton certainly. That rough, crude thing. After all this time, Liza could still see her chapped cheeks, stiff black shoes and crackly gray hair. Not maternal in the least. A disciplinarian was more like it, though at times she could be kind.

Maybe it was a gift from her mother, though not through experience. There had been none, only the ghost of her presence. Other people's memories. Maybe all the maternal energy was like an old bag packed to the brim and left at the door between life and death, set there by her mother as she departed, leaving it for her daughter to open when she was ready, to find all that love, generosity, patience and strength come spilling out. When she had a child of her own and needed these things. But not until then.

Who knows? Liza thought. It was not anything she would have expected. But her effortless connection to Rouge had come, as if by magic. As if out of nowhere. As had her painting *Sunrise,* and so many others.

SIX

Summer

(1967)

It was the end of June. Shelly had left two weeks earlier to spend the summer with her grandmother on the coast of Maine. Lucky girl, Rouge thought, wishing one year she would be invited too. But not this one; an insufferable summer it was shaping up to be. An unusual amount of rain had fallen. Normally, this was the month where spring's timidity blossomed into dazzling summer light and warmth, but this June was nothing but a dark, dank letdown. After the long Hudson Valley winters, everyone craved the heat of summer. Rouge was not alone, though she felt unusually bitchy about the weather. Liza made light of it, for the profusion of rain seemed to suit her this season, driving her happily into the studio.

"It's a good time to get to your summer reading," she said, responding to one of Rouge's irritable remarks, filling her thermos with freshly brewed coffee, en route to paint. But Rouge was not in the mood to settle into bed and plod through dense texts, page after page of type that she could barely decipher as the rain tapped monotonous rhythms on the roof. She wanted the skies to clear. She wanted the wait to be done.

It was not early summer anymore. Where was he? Ben had said he was coming. Why wasn't he here?

The photographs of Liza popped into her mind. She had not looked at them since they had arrived. That was in April. They had spooked her, spilling out the envelope onto her bed as though it were a madwoman landing there. This woman with animated eyes so black, the whites around the pupils so white, at first Rouge did not recognize her. Of course it was Liza with her long hair curling behind her, her shoulders stiff, a fierce concentration rippling over her face. But the eyes? They looked disturbed and treacherous, as though at any moment they would leap off the page. It was a trick, surely. Ben must have done something to them. But what? Whatever it was, she didn't like it, so Rouge had packed up the pictures, retaped the envelope and hid them under a stack of sweaters. They were safe there. Liza never went into her closet anymore.

As she closed the closet door, she noticed Ben's note that had fallen on the floor. In it he made no mention of the enclosed work. Not a word this time. Only that he would arrive in early summer to help her make a darkroom and teach her how to develop and print. If that was all right with Liza. In the meantime, she should keep shooting. And hold onto the film. They would develop it together.

Rouge had written him back instantly—of course it was all right. She got out of school in mid-June. That would be a perfect time to come. They would love to see him again, though she was speaking her own mind for Liza's. If Rouge had asked, Liza would have answered no. She had brought him home with her once, but was done with him. And even if he was coming to work with Rouge, Liza wouldn't like someone hanging around watching. That was, unless she could control the situation, keep the conversation where she wanted it aimed, show what she wanted seen. Only Tess ever had access to more.

And no way would Liza tolerate him taking pictures. That would absolutely infuriate her. But that was what he wanted, Rouge knew, to photograph the two of them. With Liza, that was going to be tough to promise. Yet, Rouge wondered, if Ben could shoot them nonchalantly, from afar, Liza might not notice. Working in the garden, in the kitchen preparing dinner, driving the old car to town, lying around on the front porch having an evening smoke. There were many opportunities to casually photograph. Liza hardly had to know at all.

It had to be the photographs, Rouge decided. They must have spooked him, too, and he had decided not to come. Rouge got up and dug into her closet to pull the prints out of hiding. Laying them out sequentially across her bed, she studied each for some time. This was the last of Rouge's life that Ben would have seen, her mother engaged in her work—for there were several shots on the roll of Liza painting—the devotion, the passion, how she would put her whole body into the movement of the brush. And that look. If you didn't know she was studying a painting, that look could really floor you if you stared long enough. Rouge scrutinized the last image she had taken of Liza. Even if it was a painting, or anything provocative for that matter, the look was eerie. So intense, it made Rouge feel as if Liza was staring at death driving toward her fast as a train, terrified and welcoming of it all at once.

Rouge closed her eyes. The rain rat-a-tat-tatted against her window. The air was damp and cold to the bone. She felt the dampness chill her skin as she had a freezing thought.

What if Ben had kept copies and, in the time in between, he had looked again at the photos? What if what he saw was not terror nor intrigue nor passion even? What if all he saw was a woman helpless before the void? Here was this woman painter who has come to the country to do her work. She worked and worked but what came of it? Nothing, a few small sales, a handful of what Liza claimed were in reality only inconsequential dealers. If she was so good, why didn't her paintings grace the covers of the art magazines she collected, like Hank Bolton's and all the others? If she was so good—and Tess had always sworn that she was—why did the work end up rolled and stacked in the empty horse stalls? Maybe Ben had looked again and all he had seen was failure or worse, the illusion of hope. Maybe he was not coming after all and this was why. What was here for him? Rouge had wrapped herself in her blanket and had gotten up to stare out the window. There was nothing in the sky but gray. Not even a sliver of light.

Later that night, Rouge heard Liza rummaging around the kitchen, making herself a late dinner. Realizing she was thirsty, Rouge went down to get something cool to drink, finding Liza seated at the kitchen table, eating a sandwich with one hand, drawing something on a piece of paper with the other, her fingers dirty with charcoal. Once again, she was cultivating a dealer in New York, a connection made through Hank. *I knew he'd be good for something,* she had almost sung to Tess over the phone. Since the spring, she had been working hard; drawing, painting, buying new canvas and grumbling about having to teach and review endless student work. Thankful now that it was summer and she could be in the studio with three months' of uninterrupted time.

"Why don't you do something with Shelly?" she said, not looking up from her work. Instead, she rubbed her nose, leaving a smudge of gray.

"Shelly's gone, Liza, remember?"

Liza looked up, reorienting herself. "Yeah, that's right. Too bad."

She drew for another minute, held the pad up into the light. "What about the Donoghues? No babysitting this summer?"

"They moved! Tell me you don't remember that?" This had been a big discussion only a few months ago. How could she forget?

"Ah… yes, I do." Clearly she didn't. "Sorry. Simpson's? Weren't you going to get a job there?"

If Liza weren't so distracted, Rouge might have told her then about Ben. She should say something, but at the moment, she had given up hope that he would ever appear.

"I'll go see them tomorrow," Rouge answered lethargically. She could have been enthusiastic, pissed, resentful. She could have been anything; it didn't matter. For Liza was someplace else, distracted in charcoal.

The rain stopped early the next morning. The clouds miraculously abandoned the sky, leaving a clear field of blue, and the sun felt so hot and cleansing that, instead of going to Simpson's, Rouge chose to spend the day clearing weeds from the garden.

Two nights later, she was awakened by the bang of a truck engine's backfire followed by a squeak of wheels bumping over the uneven surface of the road. It came from a distance, but in the quiet of early morning, the noise was loud, and as Rouge sat up in bed, startled by the abrasive sounds, she could track the vehicle coming closer and closer. At first, she thought it was Dale O'Neil sneaking home in the old farm truck from his girlfriend's place, south of town. It has to be Dale, she decided. No way would he sneak anywhere making that racket. She looked at her clock. Not quite five. But as she slid back under the covers, the noise moved past the entrance to the O'Neils' and continued its slow journey up the road, in front of their fence now, pulling to a stop as the engine sputtered and purred, then started up again as whatever it was turned into their driveway and bounced its way in.

"Oh my God," Rouge shouted, leaping out of bed and flying down the stairs. "He's here, he's here!" As she passed Liza's room, she heard her mother stir, snorting a confused, "What the hell is that?" as she, too, got up. Rouge paused in the kitchen to collect herself and walked slowly to the back door. It was Ben. She could make him out in the driver's seat, barely, in the paling darkness. After turning off the ignition, he leaned his head back on the seat as if to go to sleep.

Suddenly she felt Liza behind her, apoplectic at the intrusion. "What is going on?"

She moved to go outside and scare off the intruder, but Rouge caught her by the arm. "It's Ben," she said, trying to sound firm but hindered by guilt. Why hadn't she cleared this with Liza earlier?

Liza turned, stunned. "What?"

"Ben. You know, the photographs." Rouge's voice was shaky. She took a breath to shore it up. "He's come to help me make a darkroom and teach me to print."

Liza glared at her. "Why didn't you tell me?"

"I meant to."

"Fuck!" Liza marched to the sink and put her head down in her hands. The silence was frightening. Rouge should have said something earlier. She hoped Ben wasn't hearing this. She moved closer to her mother to speak more quietly.

"I'm sorry."

"I can't believe you didn't say anything."

Suddenly Rouge felt she would break down. She felt unbearably irresponsible. And weak. Her trepidation would ruin it all. How she longed to have substance, to feel the weight of inner strength. If only there was something to her. If only she were more than just Liza's daughter.

Just then, Rouge heard words coming out of her, the faintest whisper, as though a little child were talking in the shadows.

"Please, Mama, I really want to do this."

Liza swung around. Rouge had not called her that since she was seven and had gotten it into her head that she was all grown up and could call her mother Liza like everyone else. Liza seemed surprised, but the words did soften her. Rouge could see it. She was no longer angry, but she was contemplative, working the logistics of his presence around in her mind.

Finally, after what seemed an interminable period of quiet, Liza nodded her head. "All right," she said impatiently, but not enough now to be a threat. "But once the darkroom is done, he has to leave."

"All right." Rouge did not dare mention the photographs he hoped to take. It was enough that Liza agreed to this.

"And where will he stay?"

"I was thinking of the room off the kitchen," Rouge said, nodding toward the closed door beside the pantry, the room that had once been known as the sewing room when Rouge was little and Liza made clothes for her dolls. Of late, debris had taken over. Neither of them was sewing much anyway, and empty boxes and piles of books and old magazines now filled the small space. "I could put that old cot in there and move the junk down into the basement."

Moving softly across the floor, Liza stood at the back door gazing out to the spot where the truck had stopped. She stared for a moment into the darkness that was lightening into dawn. Then she sighed.

"It seems he's fallen asleep in the truck. Looks like you have a little time. C'mon, I'll help you fix up the room."

*

After the room off the kitchen had been emptied of clutter, the space swept clean, the small sewing bureau cleared for whatever stuff Ben might have, a thin red blanket retrieved from the attic to cover the cot, the two of them working silently, in accord about men's simple taste, quickly lest he wake up from his crooked-neck sleep in the front seat, after Rouge had given her mother a long hug, after all of this that took them into the middle of morning, Ben had yet to wake.

"Shall I get him up?" Rouge asked as they stood together by the back door, staring at the truck.

"No, he's obviously tired. He'll wake when he's ready."

It had been good working with Liza, an easy connection she had not felt in a while. How quickly they agreed and moved together almost as one. If only she could freeze this brief time, but no. Sooner or later, she'd have to blow the tension open, because it was right there, brewing.

"You really okay with this?" Rouge had to ask. They were standing at the back door looking out at the truck, and the air had changed palpably. Where moments ago it had been Liza and Rouge seamlessly connected, she could feel the energy of Ben move between them and could not look her mother in the eye.

"I don't know. I should have had some warning." Now the truth. Liza was angry. Summer was her prime painting time. No way she'd want Ben, or anyone really—except Tess—hanging around.

"I know."

"As long as he's just here to help you, I'm okay with it." Rouge felt a huge wave of relief run through her.

"You've had students help you build things around here." Liza would relate to that. How easily she would talk her students into helping with building projects at home. Sure, she paid them, but that's not why they'd oblige, and Liza was well aware of the power she had.

"Yeah, but that's different."

Liza didn't sleep with her students, far as Rouge knew. It shouldn't be different. "Is it?"

Rouge instantly regretted the tone of her words. Liza was letting her have this; don't snap at her. Don't stir things up.

"Yes, Miss Wise Guy, I would say it's different. It's awkward as hell."

Rouge thought of apologizing, but Liza was quicker. "I was going to go shopping later, but since you have a guest, you can go into town and buy some food. Go on. I want to have a talk with him once he's up. Then I have work to do."

That Liza would disappear into her studio and leave

them be was exactly what Rouge had hoped for. "What should I get?" she answered with a sigh of relief.

"I'll leave that to you."

Happy to disengage, Rouge bounded onto her bike and pedaled fast into town.

Mrs. Simpson was out in front of the store when Rouge rode up, arranging lettuce and spinach in big baskets tucked under the shade of the awning. Smiling at the girl, she pushed on her back to straighten herself up. She was old but supple enough for the hard daily work. Her apron was bleached white. The store had just opened its doors.

"Why, Rouge, you're up bright and early," Mr. Simpson said, greeting her as she came inside. She was the first one there. "Are you keeping yourself busy this summer?"

"Yes, sir."

"And how's your mother?" Why did everyone always ask her that? She knew that Liza made them feel ill at ease. Rouge could see it in their eyes, the way they stopped and stared when Liza was coming down the street. Well, she was strange, compared to the others at least. Her life, her attitude, her comments, even the way she dressed. Not like anyone else here, that was for sure.

"She's fine, thank you." Basket in hand and distracted by Mr. Simpson's perfunctory questions, Rouge stood silent. The issue of what to make for dinner had plagued her all the way into town. She thought that it would come to her once she got to the store. But she was at a loss. It was easy with Tess. She liked everything. This time of year, it was lots of salads, bread and cheese. But Ben? Probably not salads, most likely something more. Rouge considered chicken, pork, hamburgers, spaghetti. What?

"Can I help you with something?" Mr. Simpson finally asked.

Rouge looked at Mr Simpson. His hair was graying, and his thin, compact body was beginning to sag. Yet, he was always busy, always kind, giving children slices of bologna or a small piece of maple sugar.

"What do you like to eat for dinner?" she blurted out. As soon as she did, Rouge felt stunned. What a stupid thing to say. But he smiled and took it in stride.

"Well, the pork's good today. And I always love a good piece of chicken. Mrs. Simpson cooks it up with a sprig of rosemary and some garlic. Real simple."

"That sounds good." It did. It sounded perfect. "We'll try that."

She followed him as he shuffled to the meat counter. "Which one you want, the chicken or the pork?"

"Both. And maybe some bacon, too."

Ben was up when Rouge returned, sitting on the front porch drinking coffee, and he waved as she rode her bike up. Unshaven and still in his rumpled clothes, he looked like he had just rolled out of sleep.

"I see Liza made you some coffee," Rouge said, jumping off her bike.

"Yeah. We had a nice little chat."

Rouge stiffened. "What did she say?"

His pensive look shifted to a smile. "Just to mind my Ps and Qs, so to speak. She was perfectly civil. Nothing I wouldn't expect." He got up. "Here, let me help you with those bags. Then I should probably take a shower."

Showered and changed into fresh clothes, Ben looked

so much better, ready for work. He found Rouge waiting impatiently in the kitchen.

"So," he said, "let's see about the space for the darkroom. You have a basement?"

"Yes."

"Let's take a look."

Leading the way, she took him downstairs. The main room was littered with boxes and debris from the past, old toys and clothes of Rouge's mostly, many books, a few broken windows, old tires, spare doors. Beneath the kitchen, there was a smaller room, once used as a root cellar, a musty space now poorly lit by a bare light bulb overhead.

"This will be perfect," Ben said. "I can access the plumbing from the kitchen. It won't be too much work. A few walls, a sink, a little cleaning, and we're set."

Rouge shivered in the space, but it was not from the cold. "A lot of cleaning, I would imagine."

They got to work that afternoon unloading the chemicals and boxes from the truck into the storage end of the barn. He had even brought an old sink, salvaged from a friend's place in the city. Afterwards, they drove to Truitt's to buy some lumber. There'd be other trips, he informed her as they drove home, but this was enough to get them started.

Liza made her appearance around dinnertime. The kitchen was warm and smelled of rosemary and garlic. Ben had laid out a large piece of paper across the kitchen table and was drawing plans for the small room while Rouge cleaned up the last of the day's debris. From below, she could hear Liza's entrance—the squeaky kitchen door swing open, bang close, her light, quick footsteps breezing across the floor, a savory greeting to Ben, her voice amiable. Rouge was relieved.

She could sense her mother's position from the tapping of her feet overhead. She would be standing over Ben's shoulder, looking at his sketches.

"So, this is it?" Her words drifted through the floor like dust particles falling. "And where is it going?"

"Right underneath us."

"Ah, that makes sense. The dark room." Liza chuckled. She was moving around the kitchen now, remarking on the good smells, her appetite. Ordinarily, she would be offering Ben a drink—isn't that what one does when there are guests? That's what she did when Tess was there. They would be having cocktails by now. But she had been painting intently, morning to late night, and Liza did not drink when she was working. Rouge smiled. Things were beginning well. She swept the last corner of dirt into a neat pile, took off her apron and shook it out, then bounded up the stairs.

They ate at the kitchen table. Earlier, Rouge had made a bouquet of phlox and asters with a small branch from the apple tree stuck in for a backbone of shape—a trick taught to her by Tess. Liza found a candle to place in the center between them and, for the duration of dinner, animated light danced across her face. She was dressed in a button-down shirt, unbuttoned just at the neck, the sleeves rolled as high as she could. The shirt was covered in splatters of paint, but in the candlelight the stains became an intriguing design. Thin strands of Liza's hair hung down along her face—she had pinned the bulk of it up—sweeping under her chin, moving delicately with the rhythm of her head as she ate and talked. She was so pretty in this light, like a spirit. And how easily Liza could converse when she wanted to.

"I understood the impact of black and white when I first

saw *Guernica*," she told him, moving bits of food around on her plate, more inclined to talk than eat.

Rouge noticed that Ben had cleaned his plate.

"The impact of such tragedy stripped of color—"

"Would you like some more?" Rouge butted in.

Liza glared at her askance. But Ben smiled and held up his plate.

"You cook this?"

Rouge nodded.

"What a wonder girl. Yes, I would."

As she refilled his plate with chicken, a neat mound of rice and crisp green beans, Rouge heard Liza return to the glories of black and white. There was vanilla ice cream and peaches for dessert. Should she ask now or later?

Now. "Save room for ice cream."

"Rouge, stop interrupting. Dessert can wait." Liza smiled at Ben and picked up the conversation. Rouge plopped down at the table and wiggled her leg as she watched the candle dance light over the flowers, waiting, interminably. Waiting.

Finally, he finished, pushed back his plate and found his cigarettes, offering one to Liza. "So, why did you leave New York? Why here?"

Liza leaned back in her chair and smoked dreamily. Rouge rolled her eyes. Here we go again—Liza's romantic answer as to why a single woman with a child would move to the middle of nowhere, knowing no one.

"Because of the light," she finally answered. "Because of the quiet and the smells and the colors. Because I need solitude to feel what I am trying to paint."

Rouge looked at Ben. He was staring at Liza. Was he captivated? Jesus, did he buy the pretty picture? They always did, stopping there at the imagined magic of it all, forgetting to ask about the dirt underneath. Rouge stared at him and added silently, the words echoing inside like shouts in an empty theater, *And because she can't stand being around most people. Because she's weird.*

Maybe Ben heard her. Maybe he didn't buy her crap and that look was disbelief. Whatever he was thinking, he managed to ask the one thing that would bring Liza down to size. "So, where do you show your work?"

Liza sat up, looking down at her empty plate. "I'm in between dealers at the moment, working on a new one." She got to her feet, took her dishes away.

He called after her. "Which one? I might recognize the name. You'd be surprised. I know a lot of them."

"I'm not ready to say. I don't want to jinx it. Why don't you two clean up. I have more work to do." She left quickly.

Ben said nothing for a moment while Rouge cleared the table. He was obviously uncomfortable and Rouge felt sorry for him. Liza could change so fast. If you didn't expect it, it could be unnerving.

"Don't worry," Rouge finally offered.

"I didn't mean to annoy her. Did I?"

"No. She just gets weird about her work." Clattering the plates into a precarious pile, she turned back to Ben. "It's just that she doesn't have a dealer. Hasn't for a while. She's been in shows but her work doesn't sell much. It's always a battle."

"I see," Ben mused, leaning back in his chair. "Maybe I could help. I could make an introduction." He looked up. "I photograph work for many of the galleries. If she wanted, I could set her up with some dealers."

Rouge shrugged. "Maybe this one will work out."

"Maybe." Ben got up and walked toward the door. "I'm pretty tired. Mind if I hit the sack early? We have a long day ahead of us."

"Not at all. I'm tired too," she lied.

Closing the door to her bedroom, she stood for a while leaning into it, harder than she realized, until she felt the strain of her body and noticed her toes had turned white, as though she were barricading herself in. She breathed deeply several times until the flow of air regulated itself into slow, cleansing currents. The agitation dissolved, her toes relaxed. The windows had been left open and the temperature in the room had cooled. She closed each window, drew the curtains shut in an effort to block everything out—the night air, the insects' repetitive lullaby, Liza's incessant grip on every part of her. But not here. Not in *her* room, her enclosed space. Here she felt protected, secure enough to strip off the exterior coat of herself, like a cicada skin. So defensive, this shell that held her tight. Rouge could feel the weight of it slip off as she eased into the softness of herself, the pleasure of solitude. How light and enervated she could be, exposed in this space, a beating pulp of a thing, ready to take flight and soar. She could feel the wind beneath her, holding her aloft, a dip of intention here, a turn there, free to travel the streams of air. To go anywhere. Everywhere. It was all possible, this side of these walls.

*

They began work the next morning. Ben had been up earlier to move the wood from the truck to the basement and was measuring the space, when she tumbled down the stairs. A big carpenter's bag hung around his hips, dragging with the weight of hammers, nails and several other tools. He looked professional.

Rouge jumped right in. She wanted to learn everything and help him do it all. "What can I do?" she blurted out, forgetting any perfunctory morning greetings that should have come first.

He had positioned one piece of wood on the floor and was kneeling over it, measuring and marking it with chalk. Hearing her offer, he laughed.

"You want to learn how to frame?" She shook her head avidly. "Well, why not," he answered, getting to his feet. "It's a handy thing for a girl to know, how to build a room."

He stepped over the nearby pile of wood and looked around. "How are you with tools?" he asked, stepping toward a dark corner.

"I'm pretty good with a hammer and a saw, if that's what you mean." She peered after him.

Out of the mess in the corner, Ben pulled out something metal with a cord attached. "Here you go. You can cut these pieces up." He handed her the tool. It was an electric saw, heavier than it appeared, and she had to brace herself not to buckle under its weight. Reaching down to find the tail of the cord, he plugged it into an extension cord he had run from the functional part of the basement.

"Think you can handle this?"

There was a note of sarcasm in the question. Was he testing her? The heavy tool intimidated her, no question, but she stood her ground. Yes, she could handle it. She would. "What happened to the regular straight thing?" she responded with a smile that said instead, *I'm with you.*

Ben was laying a piece of marked wood on top of two sawhorses. "Way too slow. This is a skill saw. You ever run a skill saw?"

"I've never even seen one." She was holding it fast, gripping it tight with both her hands.

"Here, let me show you." He came up beside her to support her hands from behind and direct her as the motor flicked on, and the saw buzzed. It would have jumped away from her, but Ben kept her hands steady, his grip gentle but tight as he guided her through the first cut. Zip! The end piece fell to the ground.

He let go. "Now you try."

She positioned the blade at the edge of the next mark, keeping the wood steady with her knee, and concentrated hard to maintain the line. Zip! She stood, smiling, yelling over the whir of the saw. "This is fun."

"Yup." Wiping his cheek with the back of his hand, he left a streak of tan dust. "Electricity's a good thing."

Ben let her saw everything he marked. Then he showed her how to fit and nail the pieces together to form the skeleton of a wall. Rouge loved the work. More, she loved being near him. In the cool of the basement, helping Ben, working alongside him doing just as he asked, she hoped she had impressed him with her dexterity. When they stopped several hours later to eat, he stood to inspect the frame of the wall lying on the ground, ready to be hoisted into position. She could sense he was pleased, for he took off his tool belt, nodded his head, then reached over to grab her hair and shake it gently, setting free a cloud of sawdust that was snagged in her locks.

It was hot in the kitchen. While Rouge opened the

refrigerator to rummage for lunch, Ben waited by the back door, staring off at the barn. What was he thinking? Was he...? No, she did not want to imagine. They have too much work to do. There isn't time enough to share with Liza. Besides, Liza was busy. For once, Rouge welcomed her mother's obsession with her work.

She put together tuna sandwiches and lemonade and called him to the table. They ate their food and drank most of the pitcher of lemonade, then decided to take a swim before returning to the basement. A water break would be a nice jolt, he said. It would clear the sawdust out of their heads.

Rouge had three different bathing suits; two were leotards, one was a bikini that she wore sunning in the back yard with Shelly. Yellow with pink flowers, its petite cups just enough material to cradle her small breasts and lift them into a hint of cleavage. Studying herself in front of the mirror for what seemed like hours, she couldn't decide. She was thin, but the slight bulge in her breasts thrilled her. And made her feel shy. What should she do? His footsteps were shuffling around the kitchen; the back door opened and closed. Come on, come on. Make a decision.

"What are you doing up there?" Ben called from outside her window.

"I'm coming," she yelled back. This is what she'd do. Wear the bikini, but cover herself with a T-shirt.

He was in the shade under the maple tree, dressed in cut-off jeans. "I thought you had fallen asleep," he remarked as she bounded out the door.

"Sorry, I couldn't find my suit." She blushed and hurried ahead of him.

They wandered down through O'Neil's field to the swimming hole in the river. With the excessive spring rain, the pool at the bend in the river was deep enough to hold currents of water that stayed cold below the surface. They could use the rope swing that Mr. O'Neil had tied on the big limb of an oak tree years ago for the boys, and, drawing up into a ball, drop in without hitting bottom. At least someone as light as Rouge could; maybe not Ben.

Instead, he waded in at first, then paddled out to the deepest part of the pool, protected from the currents by a wall of boulders. There the water stayed cold at the bottom. "Bet this is a great place to fish," he called after her, flipping over to float on his back. "You ever fish?"

"Nope," she called after him. Rouge peeled off her shirt and leapt through the water until it was up to her waist. All the while, he continued to float, eyes closed, smiling at the sun.

Just as she reached the pool, he plunged his head back into the water as if to wash off his hair, then pushed himself to a dripping stand, the water reaching his shoulders. From where she stood, Rouge could barely touch bottom.

"Maybe I'll take you sometime." He fell back into the pool and let his body float. He seemed content here. Rouge was pleased. The water that sparkled in the sunlight could blind her at the right angle, but underwater, just below the surface, it was dark and busy with tiny, whirling specks of river life—dirt and bugs and fish crap and weeds. And fish, if she could keep her eyes open long enough to see them darting in and out of visibility. But Rouge didn't. She preferred to submerge her head and shut her eyes to concentrate on the varying water temperatures at different parts of her body. Just where does the cold turn to warm? There, at her knee. Now, there on the thigh if she moved just so. And if she floated, the surface became one warm layer of water. A bath.

They swam for some time, then lay on the bank in the sun. How effortless it was to be near him, easy to be in her skin. She was glad she had worn the bikini. Ben had stretched out on his back, his arms crossed to shield his eyes, and she wiggled closer. His belly looked pudgier this year and collapsed into itself like a soft pillow, and Rouge stared at his torso, wishing she had brought her camera. Next time she would, she told herself as she watched him doze. Many questions were waiting at the back of her throat. Everything about him intrigued her at this moment. Keeping her questions at bay was exhausting, so she focused on the gentle, rhythmic movement of his chest hair as he breathed in and out. Quietly, she chewed on pieces of grass.

Suddenly he let out a deep, loud guttural snort, and they both jumped.

"Jesus, did I just snore?" he asked, propping himself up on his elbows.

"You sure did." Rouge was grinning at his embarrassment.

"I hate that." He winked. "It scares the hell outta me when I do that."

He sat up, scratched his head and stared at the river. Without looking at her, he asked, "Say, I've been wondering about your father. He isn't Hank Bolton, is he?"

Now he turned toward her, and she gazed away and responded with the lie that had become her token answer. The truth, or what Liza had always told her, was embarrassing. That her mother was drunk and could not remember who he was. The implication that Rouge was a mistake, though Liza *never* admitted so. Quite the contrary. What her mother insisted was that the two of them were fated to come together, and the momentary partnering was Rouge's way in. It was all ridiculous and absolutely humiliating.

"He died before I was born," Rouge answered perfunctorily, the lie she was more comfortable telling. "He was killed in a car accident."

"How tragic. I'm sorry." He scratched his head again, clumping his thick hair.

Rouge shrugged. "It's okay. We've managed." Funny, she wondered, that he mentioned Hank Bolton. She had considered that herself, the way Liza got all prickly when she brought him up in conversation, quick to displace the subject. Yet, whenever Rouge asked her mother about the identity of her father, Liza stared her straight in the eye and said, "I don't know." Such an assured response, it couldn't possibly be a lie. But still?

"Why did you say Hank Bolton? Do you think I look like him or something?"

Ben studied her for a moment. "No actually. Not at all. You look like Liza, except for your blonde hair and blue eyes. I've never seen anyone with such light blue eyes. And you're much taller."

Trying not to let herself beam at his observations, she remembered her bikini and considered putting on her T-shirt. Would that be too obvious? Silly?

"It's just the way Liza talks about him," he continued. "And, they all slept around in that community." He blushed a bit. "Well, you're too young for that. We probably should be getting back anyway. What do you think?"

"Fine with me."

They walked more briskly back to the house, Rouge hopping in and out of the tall grass that threatened to smother the narrow path. As they approached the road, Ben put his hand on her shoulder, as if he were a parent reaching for a child to hold her back from traffic. It felt like an instinctual move, yet the steady, warm grip of it sent a shiver deep into Rouge's belly and she wanted to move away. No, not away. She wanted to stand tall and lean in closer, to feel even more of the warmth of him. Her body was tensing at his touch.

But then he dropped his hand to cross the road, and they kept a slight distance walking back to the house, agreeing to meet in the darkroom after they had changed. She raced up the stairs.

Even with the windows left wide open, her room was hot and clammy. She peeled off the bikini and sat abruptly on the bed. She envisioned Ben touching her shoulder, moving his hand down her body and over her breasts. Feeling suddenly hot, then cold, she shuddered. She didn't dare imagine further. What did she know? Rouge had kissed a boy once, at the end of a school dance. Only a peck on the lips. An inconsequential boy. But Ben was different. He could melt her on the spot.

Though she eyed her clothes from the morning lying in a heap, she felt clean from the swim and decided to change. As she moved across the room, she caught a reflection of herself in the long mirror on the closet door; a tall, thin streak of flesh. She turned back and faced the mirror square on and, for a moment, was startled by what she saw. As though it were a stranger; a slim, supple body she did not know. The eyes looked bigger than she remembered her own; transparent gems of blue staring back. With barely any effort, she could tug up the corners of her lips and dip dimples into her cheeks. Not her mother's dimples, these wide chasms of flesh, nor the blue eyes, nor the height, for she was now, at fifteen, a good five inches taller than Liza. Maybe these features came from her father. Whoever he was.

But what of this person in the mirror? Rouge was attracted and put off at the same moment, and she wanted nothing more than to touch the form, watch her own hands draw slowly over the belly of this vision, touch the heat of its skin, the firmness of the breasts, gently push back the hair. For no other reason than curiosity.

*

They spent a little over a week finishing the darkroom, working throughout the mornings and for much of the afternoons. The framing went smoothly, as did the walls and the placement of the long, shallow sink. Rouge tried her hand at much of the labor, and he seemed pleased to let her do whatever she could. She was a natural with tools, he told her. A girl of many gifts. That compliment delighted her, but she tried not to let it show. And though he often hovered over her while she worked, close enough that she feared she could hit him with the hammer with an overzealous swing, she relished his proximity, even though her heart beat faster, her hands turned sweaty. She was sure her swing of the hammer would go all to hell.

Could he read her? He gave her no clue. His eyes, green and opaque, gave nothing away—no flirtatious glow, no confusion, nor awkward attraction. No, the way he looked at her had not changed one bit. It was still warm and kind, the gaze of a friend. Please, oh, please, look at me a little differently, she found herself craving. Still, she was young, and he nearly twice her age; what could she possibly expect? He had been Liza's lover once, though she knew it was only a drunken fling, almost a dream, nothing, at least for Liza. Or him. Or was it? This was all ridiculous, some dream-like fantasy, she reminded herself. Where was reality in all of this!

Besides, he was agitated about the plumbing. Everything had gone so well, until now. His large body wedged in under the sink, the space below brightly lit by a clip-on bulb, he was getting tense and angry. The fittings were not right.

"Shit," he grumbled, cocking his head and shoulders to pull himself clear. Rouge had been sitting on the floor watching him through the lens of her camera, waiting for the emergence of the frustrated face, the brow furrowed, his thin lips clenched tight, the eyes that remained flat through the fury. All exaggerated by the overhead bulb that illuminated the small room. *Click!*

He looked up at the noise, and instantly everything changed as a smile wiped away the hardness of his face. "Very funny."

"It is. You look funny, especially in this light."

"Yeah, well, maybe you'd like to try your more delicate hand at making this fit." He held out the small pipe joint pinched between two large fingers.

Rouge reached for the piece. "Where does it go?"

"Right there," he answered, dipping his arm under the sink and pointing into the lighted area. Rouge ducked in and attempted to screw in the joint. Once, twice, three times twisting and twisting as the joint spiraled around and went nowhere. She would have kept trying, sure that what was wrong was not getting the screw lined up straight, when Ben called out.

"You pissed yet?"

"Almost," she replied, about to try again. She would get the thing to screw into place.

"You just keep on working then while I go into town and get the piece that's the right size."

What? It took only a flash for her to realize his joke on her. She pulled herself out, angry at her stupidity, not yet ready to laugh. *Click*.

He put down the camera. "There. We're even. Let's go take a drive and get the right piece." He held out a hand to help her up and she reached eagerly for it, relaxing her hand into his, relaxing her body as well to let him hoist her to a stand. He lifted her effortlessly.

Two days later, the darkroom was ready. The enlarger was installed, the trays for the chemicals set neatly in a row on the shelf above the sink, everything from Ben's truck unloaded and installed. They finished late in the afternoon, and Rouge could not wait for her mother's break from work. She hurried to the studio, knocked on the door and called Liza's name, her wiggling legs charged with excitement, uncomplicated and hopeful, as though she were six.

Liza opened the door. She was her typical painterly mess. Rouge grabbed her hand, not even considering that she would have to warn Liza not to touch anything in the pristine workspace.

"Come, I want to show you," she said, pulling Liza along into the kitchen, down the precarious old stairs through the mess of the basement into the clean, new room. Ben was putting the last of the boxes of papers away and continued his work while Rouge explained the set-up hurriedly—the trays set out for chemicals, Ben's old enlarger that he was giving to her, the drying rack, the timers and thermometers, the film canisters, even the red safe light.

"Look at this gorgeous ruby color," Rouge said, the words tumbling out of her mouth as she turned off the overhead light and started flicking the red on and off. This was the safe light they would use for making prints, she explained, repeating what Ben had told her, safe because photographic paper was not sensitive to red light and would not be exposed in its deep illumination. Not so with film, though. Film was sensitive to all light. That they would have to develop in complete darkness.

"Isn't that amazing?" Rouge asked, more to slow herself down than to solicit any validation.

She held Liza's hand under the light, her long, thin fingers wrapped around her mother's, the two delicate appendages distinguished from one another only by Liza's multi-colored blotches. In the mystical ruby light, the interlacing of fingers, one hand resting willing in the other, was an exquisite sight, and Rouge paused to study it. Beautiful, those hands together. She did not have the time to conjure any words, only the sensation of tranquility that flowed through her. Likenesses and differences, tenderness, connection and separation. Possibly love. All the things the moment held, harmonious, if only for an instant.

From over her shoulder she heard a long, drawn-out sound of a camera shutter release—was Ben seeing it too?— then, following the progression of the sound wave, Liza's hand stiffened and pulled away. As she did, Rouge turned. Ben was still looking through the viewfinder, pointing at the space where their hands had been. She hoped he had captured them, before Liza's movement fogged the image.

*

The next morning, Rouge made a pot of coffee but did not dare drink any as her nerves were already up and running. Six am. Should she knock on his door? The light in Liza's studio was still on. She had not come to bed yet. Nothing new. Either she was engaged in work or she was avoiding Ben. It didn't matter, though her absence made things easier.

Rouge decided to go down to the darkroom and leaf through the books Ben had brought, struggling to understand the technical language. It would make sense when she actually did some work, he had assured her. She hoped so. The reading alone was confusing her—reducing the contrast, increasing the contrast, playing with the highlights, overexposing, under-developing, negative density. It sounded incomprehensible.

Footsteps overhead broke her consternation. They were heavy ones, definitely Ben's. She hurried upstairs. He had poured himself some coffee and was sitting at the table, realigning the seven rolls of exposed film she had left there.

"Good," he said as she appeared in the doorway. "We have a lot to work with here." He looked over at her. "I see you're up and ready to go."

"Are you kidding? I can't wait."

"Then let's get started."

Scooping up her film in one hand, he took his coffee in

the other and, once downstairs, placed all carefully in the dry area of the darkroom.

"The first thing we have to do is get our chemicals up to temperature." He began running hot water from the faucet. She stayed silent and let him speak, restraining her questions to watch and listen as he explained about development times. Ben moved with an expert's ease, testing the water temperature with the thermometer, setting up the water bath for the chemicals, diluting the developer, preparing the trays. Watching him, she was thrilled, believing, yes, she could do this.

Finally, he rubbed his hands together and reached for one of the tanks. "Now this is the hardest part," he told her, unscrewing the top of the small metal tank and dropping out the reel it held inside.

"Getting the film onto the reel," he continued. "I'll show you later. You'll need to practice with a dead roll to get it down." He had taken one of her rolls of film and laid it beside the dissected tank, along with scissors and a can opener, before reaching overhead to turn out the light. "I'll load it for now so we can move along."

In the instant zoom of darkness, she felt lost for a second, not sure of where she was in space, though she knew she was right next to Ben. She put her hand out to hold the table and steady herself. Her vision was absolutely black, not even a crack of light, yet it was titillating believing that such difficult things could be done in the dark. Hearing him grope with the can opener, the film, picking up the scissors, snip, snip—all this he could do without sight—Rouge was captivated, prickling with curiosity.

Ben flicked on the light. The tank was sealed, the empty

shell of the roll of film lying on its side. He swept the mess into the wastepaper basket, then stepped sideways toward the water bath that held the chemicals in glass beakers.

She watched him work, sequentially treating the film with each of the chemicals. Finally, he rinsed the tank in water, opened the lid and took out the reel. Holding it carefully, he unwound the film, hanging it by one end on the clothesline he had strung between walls, anchoring the bottom with another clothespin. It was the roll of film she had taken of the old tractor in a field. The image looked odd, completely backward, the sky dark, the tractor light. She had known what to expect but had not yet seen it, though Ben could read the film with ease.

"It's a bit thin," he mumbled as though to himself. Then, looking at her, he added, "Underexposed. But not by much. We can correct for it when we make the print."

Over the course of the morning, Ben developed all her rolls, loading the tanks himself, but letting her take it from there as he coached her through the process. He was a good teacher, holding her hand firmly to show her the motion of agitation, complimenting the well-developed rolls of film. Just being there, working in the small room together, Rouge had never felt happier. Nor more confident, even though there was so much to learn. Here in the darkroom or standing behind a camera, there was none of the awkwardness that had confused her before. This is what Liza means, Rouge thought, when she says she gets lost in her work. This must be exactly how she feels. Rouge wished she could have frozen this moment with the development of the film, the two of them here. There was no sense of time, for without any natural light, it was hard to guess the hour, only the hand of the timer to mark the passage of minutes, moving forward, then pushed back to zero with each new roll of film. She could have been there for days.

But Ben was hungry. It had to be near noon, he informed her, time to get something to eat. Over lunch, they could talk about the work, pick the negatives they wanted to print. Get some fresh air and clear the chemicals from their heads. He cut the negatives into sections and slipped them into wax paper sleeves, then carried them up to the kitchen and laid them out across the table. Rouge made sandwiches as Ben stood at the window, eyeing each roll of film through the midday light, making small marks with a red wax crayon next to a couple of frames.

He ate quickly—he really was hungry—pushed back his plate and lit a cigarette.

"There's a few here we can work with, to learn the process at least, but…" he paused to inhale a breath of smoke "…I have to say, the images are a bit flat." He held the smoke in as he talked, the restraint of air sucking tone out of his voice, making it sound light, tentative.

"You mean underexposed?" Rouge had found it difficult to eat and had spent more time pushing food around her plate.

"No, I'm talking about the context." She was perplexed. "It's a bit boring," he said, leaning forward to snuff out his butt on the plate. "Safe. I only say this because you're capable of more."

Rouge did not speak. She had nothing to answer, though she longed to make an excuse. What could she say? That the images of her mother had frightened her away from images of people. The stuff he had said was good. God, that sounded stupid.

Ben gathered the plates, took them to the sink. "What happened to your portraits? They were quite fine."

"I don't know. I ran out of ideas." The stiffness of her answer sounded, to her, like a lie.

He chuckled. He knew. She felt him looking through her and, in response, she hunched her shoulders in tight. He had been so proud of her up until now. She could not stand the disappointment. But maybe she was wrong, for suddenly he was behind her, holding her shoulders and giving them a shake.

"I say we get our cameras and take some fresh stuff. You model for me. I'll model for you." Then he chortled, "Some model, me, huh?"

"Well," she said, "at least you'll be hard to miss."

Ben did not pose her much that afternoon. Instead, he instructed her to dig weeds in the garden and he knelt down close to shoot. With his camera trained on her, she was painfully aware of herself, of every move she made. Was it stupid? Awkward? Bending down over tomato plants, she was sure she looked ugly. When would it be her turn behind the lens? Time inched by. She hated the attention. And loved it too. That's what made it difficult, the ambivalence that was barely appeased by concentration as she pinched small, stubborn grass shoots between her fingers and tugged out the roots, freeing the space for the delicate new growth of beans, carrot and beet tops they had recently planted. *Click, click.* Think of the warm, damp soil. The pungent, sweaty heat. Think about that.

It seemed forever. She was hot under the sun, and beads of moisture were tickling her face. Finally, he finished the roll and handed her the camera.

"Tell me what to do," he said, as she rewound his film.

She thought immediately of asking him to take off his shirt—that inviting, soft belly— but caught herself. Take off your shirt! How forward, something Liza would say. She dropped her eyes and looked around for a location. Scenery floated by as she turned her head—the cluster of oaks with its intricate, mottled shade, a slice of light in the open barn doorway, the shadows under the porch ceiling.

"There," she pointed toward the barn. "In the doorway. Maybe you could stand there and have a smoke." He followed her eye, saw the clean, strong beam of light, and nodded.

"Good choice."

But tricky. In those shadows, the background would be a strong black and he instructed her how to capture it right. "Focus right on my face. Don't take an average reading for light, the contrast is too strong." Then he leaned back against the wood, lit a cigarette as she shot.

They developed the film right away. Afterward, Ben methodically inspected the images, standing out on the porch. Hovering close beside him, Rouge had trouble reading the tiny details, had no idea if there was anything good.

He had almost finished scanning each roll, frame by frame, first the roll he had taken of her, marking one or two. Then Rouge's. He stared intently at the first two.

"There's some good stuff here," he pronounced. "We'll use these two rolls. After dinner, we'll make some prints."

If dinner would ever be over, she thought, as she tried to rush him through the meal. Liza had whipped up pasta and tomatoes and a salad, but Rouge did not have the stomach to get any of it down. Ben had drawn Liza into a heated discussion about contemporary painting. Liza hated the work—too controlled and preconceived. Ben took the opposing view, the two of them accelerating one another further into a battle of opinions going nowhere.

Clearing the table quickly, Rouge took Ben's arm in the middle of the conversation. "Time to go," she told him. "We are going to print." She looked up at Liza, imploring her, no, demanding. Stop this nonsensical talk. Liza would get Rouge's glare announcing the conversation was over.

"Ready?" She tugged at his arm. Liza took that cue to cut short the argument and stood up to clear the table. Rouge didn't care, this time, if Liza were angry at being cut off. But surprisingly, she wasn't. Instead, she took Rouge's side. Lifting her plate, she threw back her head, tossing her curling brown mane behind her shoulders. "Better not keep an inspired artist waiting."

He shook his head and stood as well. "I know. I know." Then to Rouge, with a sigh of resignation, he motioned, "Okay, let's go."

As he followed Rouge down the stairs, she noted that his enthusiasm had waned. Clomping slowly down the steep stairs, he shuffled his feet as though the weight of his body tilting just a hair forward was enough to carry him down. Rouge had taken the steps in long leaps and was standing at the bottom. Maybe she should have waited. Liza would have ended the argument on her own soon enough. Disappointed thoughts collided with Rouge's excitement, quiet reprimands that dampened her mood. She and Ben had been having fun earlier. But look how animated he had been at dinner, his eyes sparkling in the candlelight as he engaged with Liza. And hers on him. Every time they talked about art. Now Ben was reluctant to work. He would rather have stayed with Liza. Was that it?

But the notion of making her first print overrode her worries. As soon as she was in the darkroom breathing the smell of chemicals, all else washed away. It did not matter if he wanted to be elsewhere. He was coming through the door, closing it tight, working beside her, warming up chemicals, setting out the trays. She had him now.

She listened with every ounce of concentration as he explained the enlarger and showed her how it worked. They had picked an image of him blowing out smoke, and once in the enlarger, his face reverted to its positive self. Ben opened the lens, projecting the image four times its size onto a strip of paper on the easel below. He cleaned up the focus, balanced the whites of the edges, then turned off the overhead light and flicked on the safe light.

He showed her how to make a test strip to determine the time of exposure, a narrow swab of his face, developed into varying degrees of darkness. Ben was so skillful, Rouge dutifully awed. Could she manage as easily as he? All in the red glow of light.

He removed a full sheet of paper from its protective box, slid it into the enlarger frame, turned to her. "Ready?"

"Ready," she responded through nearly paralyzed breath.

He flicked on the enlarger and set the timer. The seconds beat loudly, his face frozen on the paper in the harsh enlarger light. The room was cool and chills fired through Rouge's body. Tick, tick, tick, tick. Ding.

As soon as the bell went off, Ben lifted the paper by its edge, his big, chunky fingers moving like a lithe dancer, and slid it into the developer tray. He tipped the tray gently back and forth, once, twice, then gave it to her. "Here, like this. You do it."

Taking hold of the edge of the tray, she continued the steady motion, the clear liquid running back and forth over the surface of the paper. Instantly, tones began to appear as though swirled on by the moving developer, darkness here and there rippling out of the white, lines miraculously emerging and giving form to the shadowy mysterious markings. Suddenly converging into a face—it happened so fast—Ben appeared as if out of nothing, crystallized now in the liquid. There he was, large and strong. Rouge could not help herself. She gasped.

Ben reached across her and grabbed an edge. "We have to work quickly now." She took a step back to let him rescue the print, hold it above the developer and drip off the excess, then plunge it into the stop bath.

When they were done, Ben turned on the light and examined the wet print. It was a miracle to her, but he only let out a grunt. "It's good enough for now. Let's do a few more, so you can get the process down."

They printed several other images, some from each roll, working well into the night. By then, Rouge had begun to feel comfortable with the procedures and with handling the wet, slippery images. She marveled every time an image materialized out of the white paper, thinking that with all the precision and the timing and the measuring, there is still this. This moment of magic. This instant when, even if she thought she knew what was coming, it took her by surprise. Every time.

*

Some nights around midnight, Liza would go outside as the summer air cooled to wander in the darkness and feel the moist grass slither between her toes. She'd inhale the night air. It was serene, the darkness comforting, only a few bright stars overhead. She did love this place, she reminded herself; even as she needed to visit New York from time to time, she was grateful that this was her home. This simple old house. This space. She could not imagine trying to work in the city. It was noisy and busy. Too much distraction. No wonder Hank had settled in the countryside in France; over the years, the two of them had lost touch—his impressive career sidelined by alcohol and depression. She had little to respond to his occasional letters that grew darker and darker until they stopped coming at all. So very sad considering how well he had done.

Three good canvases glistened in her studio. Another big one ready to begin. The work was coming strong and fast. She stepped outside for a break, just to finish this smoke. She paused at the side of the barn, leaned against the rough planks of wood and closed her eyes. A few more minutes and she'd go back to work.

But Ben was here. Unsettling, his presence, yet so important to Rouge. Still.

The morning he arrived, Liza had woken him as soon as Rouge had pedaled off.

"What the hell are you doing?" Her voice was sharp, enough to snap him awake.

Ben shook his head, confused. "I came to help Rouge build a darkroom. Didn't she tell you?"

"No, she did not."

"Jesus, I'm sorry. I thought she had cleared it with you."

He paused. "I didn't intend it to be a problem. I only wanted to help."

Liza eyed him. "You have nothing better to do than to help a kid you barely know?"

"She's a great kid. And she's talented." Ben was miffed. "Besides, it's blistering hot in the city. I'm happy to get out for a while."

Their night together nearly a year ago flashed through her mind. Meeting at the Met where she had gone for inspiration, thoughtful conversation in front of modernist work. Yes, she knew de Kooning, Kline, Bolton too. She knew most of them. He was intrigued. And intelligent, too. Smitten enough to invite her for a drink, to listen to her relish the memories, embellish others. He had hung on her every word. She had not realized how badly she had craved such attention and had drunk too much, not thinking sensibly at all, obviously, because he had ended up home in her bed. Was the sex even any good? How she had cringed when she woke a few hours later. God, what had she been thinking?

Here he was again. What was going on? Liza had poured them both coffee, the last of the pot. "Just so long as we're clear. I'm not looking for a relationship."

Ben laughed awkwardly. "That's not what I'm after."

"And Rouge is fifteen, highly impressionable. This better just be about photography."

"Are you kidding!" Ben slammed down his coffee cup. "What kind of monster do you think I am? I have a little sister, for Christ's sake." He rose suddenly. "I'll leave."

"No, no, stay," Liza said. "It means the world to her. Just don't fuck things up."

He would be leaving soon, and she would not be sad, though what a mentor he had been for Rouge. She'd give him that. Her musing was interrupted by Rouge's muffled voice, laughter coming through the open kitchen windows. In the soft glow of the overhead light, their forms were muted, Rouge leaning back against the sink, Ben making himself something to drink. Earlier, they had disappeared into the darkroom right after dinner. It had been a little over a week, but time had lingered, and his presence felt longer. At first, Liza had thought nothing of it. If anything, she was relieved that Rouge had found something engrossing to do.

But everything looked different from this angle of darkness. Liza felt like she was watching a play. Here were the characters, a tall, blonde-haired girl—not a girl anymore—a young woman with a hulky older man. Liza snuffed out her cigarette and squatted, sliding down the side of the barn. What an appealing creature. Liza's attention went to Rouge first, observing her grace as she glided through her motions, turning in and out of the light, flicking back her long hair, reaching over to get an empty glass. She crossed her arms in front of her chest, craned her neck to one side and listened carefully, smiling from time to time, her shoulders thrown back. Liza could read no hesitation in her gestures. An actress fully prepared for her part.

And he? This ungainly man? Older and sure of himself in his experienced way, delivering his lines in a gentle tone. Through the open windows, Liza could hear the purr of his voice and began to stare harder as he reached out to touch Rouge's shoulder or stepped in and out of the center of the room. Liza stiffened every time he brought his body near Rouge, who did not flinch at his touch. Was his hand familiar? Was she intimate with him? Or simply unaware?

Why had he come back exactly? Liza had wondered since their conversation. She hadn't bought everything he had told her, though at the time it made sense. Making Rouge a protégée. That was too simple. Surely he had more interesting work of his own in the city. Still, it felt as though there was something else he wasn't revealing. Something was missing. But what?

She said this to herself, to the darkness, as she watched them. The dialogue had grown serious. No more laughter. He reached across Rouge, stood to smile. Was he satisfied at the work? Or was he in love? That thought chilled Liza. This unattractive man with his chunk of a fat nose, Mongolian eyes, too-big ears; nothing fit, none of him looked inviting. Could it be that the only woman he could attract was a sweet, young thing lured not by him, but by what he had to offer, using shared interests to casually slide in? Was that it?

Liza had to know. Opening the screen door just a quarter of the way, the quiet part before it squeaked, Liza slipped into the kitchen. Their backs were to her at the kitchen table, and their conversation masked the sounds of her movement.

Liza took a heavier step, speaking as she did. "Can I see?"

Rouge and Ben startled like dance partners nearly stepping on a snake. Liza would have laughed, but she was busy scanning eyes. Surprise in them both, but not embarrassment, not caught in any inappropriate moment at all.

"God, Liza. You scared me. Don't do that." Rouge let

out a sigh of relief. Ben grinned tentatively at first, but more warmly, Liza noticed, once the surprise waned.

"I ran out of cigarettes and thought Ben might have a few," she said with a shrug. "You two seemed so engrossed, I didn't want to disturb you. May I see?" Liza took the print off the top, held it up to the light. It was one of Rouge in the garden, a shaded profile of her face. "Nice," she judged, reaching for the next.

The work was good, especially Rouge's photographs of Ben under the eaves of the barn. She handed the photos back, trying to smile, knowing she should be grateful for all he had taught her. Rouge was turning into an exceptional talent. But laced with Liza's pride, shoving it over, was a burst of jealousy. Liza was mortified. How could she be? She should be thrilled—Rouge's future so promising and wide open. Anything was possible. She remembered just how terrific that had once felt.

Liza stumbled to restore composure and noticed Ben's nearly full pack of cigarettes on the table. "Can I have one?"

"Sure, take the pack."

She was certain her hand was shaking, though maybe they didn't notice. *There's plenty of potential still here, things can still happen,* she reminded herself as she grabbed the pack and hurried back to her studio.

*

Rouge rose early every morning, well before Ben who, by his own admission, was not respectable at all until ten am at the earliest. Rouge might have argued otherwise. After all, he had seemed quite functional with a hammer and nails first thing in the morning. Maybe, he explained, for something vocational he could function, but not for critical stuff like photography. Like art and such. You know, those things where you need your eye sharp, your head clear, he had added, mussing her hair with the palm of his hand. Early mornings? Not my style. No way, baby.

She lay in bed, wide awake, replaying conversations with Ben in her head, mimicking his words, the gruff and tumble of his voice when she was teasing him. Or he, her. She would try to ape him out loud, but her voice did not have the breadth to reach his edge, and her imitations sounded feeble. But she could hear his voice in her mind, and the echoes of it coated her arms in goosebumps. She could not wait to see him each morning. There were only a few days left before he had to leave, just a week until Tess arrived. What would she do after that, she wondered, a thought that brought her back down to earth, back to the wafts of manure from O'Neil's fields creeping in from her open window, the drudgery of school not far off, and Shelly's boyfriends. God, those endlessly boring conversations about pimply-faced boys!

Couldn't he stay at least somewhere in town? Liza and Tess could paint, and they could continue their photography.

No, of course not. That was the condition Liza had set that first day—Ben could stay until the end of July when Tess would be arriving. Grateful that Liza allowed his presence at all, Rouge had promised there would be no argument. Crossed her heart and hoped to die.

Besides, she recollected this morning as she watched the clock skip to another minute, he also said he had to leave at the end of the month. He had an assignment to get to.

Rouge let out a long, pained sigh. The notion of following him back to New York, asking for work, offering to cook and clean, anything to stay with him, crept through her thoughts. Instantly, she laughed it away.

"Hah! Liza would like that."

As there was plenty of time, Rouge got up and showered, then stood in front of the mirror. Hers was no longer the body of a stranger. It was familiar and much in need of improvement—her legs too skinny, her breasts too small, her hip bones sharp and crooked, her shoulders off. Couldn't she stand more level? At least her arms were strong and tanned and her hair she could still call blonde. Guys liked that. That's what Shelly always said. "You've got the hair, Rouge, but the boobs need some work."

Rouge practiced her facial expressions, trying out different reactions to surprise, delight, elicit consternation. Surprise? Open your mouth just so. No, too much. That looks stupid. Less, there, not too bad. Now, turn your head just a little to the left. Much better. Okay, now he says something sarcastic—oh, he's good at that. Do suspicion. Hum. Relax the eyelids just a little, let them begin to slip down, and then purse your lips, like this. Yes, but more. Nice. That's good. She thought to herself, pretty, she could actually approach pretty with a look like this. Rouge practiced the expression again in the mirror, then one more time to get the feel of it down. Now the smile. Oh God, there's that slinky left side. The corner of her mouth pulled up all wrong. It's a cute little grin with the dimples, but she had outgrown cute. She was ready for something more substantive, more mature.

Remembering that Shelly had left some of her make-up

in the back of the bathroom cabinet—Shel's mother hated her wearing the stuff and was constantly throwing it out—Rouge thought it might be worth a try. She had looked so silly when Shelly, too heavy-handed, had made her up for school dances and those stupid, awkward boys, transforming her into a caricature of a teenage girl, without the curvy, sexy body. The fact that no one asked her to dance should have been proof enough. *See, Shel, I told you the eyeshadow makes me look like I have black eyes.* That, of course, and unlike a lot of the other girls in her class, including and mostly Shelly, Rouge would not let anyone touch her. None of those swampy, drooly mouths near hers, breath that smelled of stale smoke and peach schnapps. And flailing hands, desperate to claim the tempting flesh of a girl's breast. No, thank you.

She had found some eyeliner and mascara, and Liza had lipstick. A bit dark, but Rouge applied it lightly and smeared it into her lips. She stood close to the mirror and held down one eyelid as she tried painting on a thin line of black. Her hand shook a little and stumbled. Damn! The line wasn't even close to her lashes. She rubbed it off and began again, slower, going for just a trace. There, nice and thin. Now the other. She opened her eyes, took a step away. They did look larger, older, yes. She bit her bottom lip. Now a little mascara. This could add a year or two onto her age.

She tried the lipstick but it was too red. Even rubbed out a little, it was excessive. It was not her style to bring awareness to herself in that way. But the eyes were all right. Subtle enough that Ben might not even notice exactly… what? That something was a little different. A little more appealing?

There was nothing to wear but old work clothes. The chemicals might destroy anything nice. So, she put on what she always did—some cut-off blue jeans and an old painting shirt of Liza's—and wandered downstairs.

A pile of recent prints had been left the night before on the kitchen table, images from both their rolls of film. Rouge had been learning to dodge and burn, to highlight and enhance the print's tonal quality. To heighten the mood, Ben had explained. Or, at times, to clean up the mistakes. That was it, Rouge realized then, seeing the effects of burning in a section of one of her prints. That was how he had made Liza's eyes so dramatic. That and a little bleach to bring out the whites. Just a little tampering with the image was all that was needed to make it pop out into something fantastic.

Like the photograph of their hands together. Softened in the dark light, the image strengthened by darkening the shadows and brightening the whites at the tip of the nails. Or this section of background behind Rouge bent over and working in the garden. She could make the gentle summer clouds denser, more foreboding if she burned in the sky, the leaves of weeds in the foreground etched in with more light.

"See the difference," Ben was instructing, laying out each of the prints—the befores and afters. "A little more drama to hold the viewer's eye."

There must have been nearly thirty photos left on the table the night before, the compilation of three days' work. A neat pile that suddenly looked smaller than Rouge had remembered. Leafing quickly through the images, she realized all the photographs of Ben were missing. About twelve of them, including her favorite—just a slice of his nose sticking out from dark shadows against the barn's rough grain of wood.

Her heart leapt toward the back of her throat. Ben had said they were only work prints, though, he added, a few of them were close to as good as they would get. Still, they looked perfect to Rouge. Where did they go? She ran down to the darkroom. Maybe Ben had taken them down during the night. But the space was clear and only three rolls of newly developed film hung in the corner. It didn't seem possible that Ben would discard the work. He had even joked that her pictures did him more than justice. "God," he had laughed, "in some I even look good."

It had to be Liza. Rouge couldn't think of anything else. Leaping up the basement stairs, she ran out to the studio. The door was open ajar. Rouge stuck her head in.

"Liza," she called, softly at first. She looked about the room, at the mattress in the corner. Liza wasn't there. Funny, Rouge thought, she never leaves the door open. She stepped in. The space was cool and eerie in its stillness. There was one big painting nailed up to the wall, two others on stretchers around it. They were more sedate than other work Rouge had seen, the colors somewhat muted, the brushwork less severe. Rouge looked around quickly for the missing prints. Nothing there.

She hurried back to the house, through the kitchen and into the hall. As she was about to bound up the stairs to Liza's room, she caught a glimpse of her mother, sitting up against a wall of the living room.

Liza had heard from the dealer the afternoon before. Another *No*. She had told Rouge but made her promise to say nothing to Ben, then put on an impressive show of normalcy at dinner, before retiring early for bed.

"Liza?" she asked, her voice whittled down to a whisper by surprise and fear.

Rouge stepped into the room. Liza was seated on the floor, against a wall, sandwiched between a reading chair and a bookcase, leaning back. Transfixed, she stared straight ahead at all of Rouge's prints tacked up on the wall that Liza had cleared by pulling away the sofa. Ben, Ben, Ben; images everywhere with only a nod toward order. Ben's photographs were tacked up crooked, a shoddy large rectangular collage that made him look fractured, confused, a nose this way, a profile there, his full-on face scattered about the mess as though to mark the sense of it all.

"What are you doing?" Rouge asked. Liza stirred, letting her head twist and turn sideways toward the intruding voice. She looked incoherently dreamy. What had she done? Was she drunk? Depressed? Was she even present at all?

Rouge spoke more emphatically to wake Liza from whatever state she was in. "What *are* you doing?"

Liza pulled her straight leg in underneath her into a cross-legged sit. She leaned forward to push the hair off her shoulders. She came to quiet life. "It's quite remarkable," she mused, pointing a finger at one of the prints. "Maybe better if you move that one over there."

"What?" Rouge was well into the room now, relieved that Liza wasn't drunk or depressed, but what? She was acting odder than normal. She stared at her mother, then at the wall of prints. All of the images together were confusing. What was wrong with looking at each, one at a time?

As though suddenly revitalized, Liza stood. "Here, let

me show you." She strode across the room, removed one print, then another and re-tacked the two. Stepping back to view the difference, she nodded. "What do you think?"

"I think it's weird," Rouge answered right away. "How long have you been here?" There was no plate of cigarette butts. It couldn't have been long.

But Liza only shrugged. "Well, you're still young. The images alone are quite good." Suddenly Liza stared at Rouge, scrunched up her eyes to better focus in. "Are you wearing make-up?"

Rouge could feel her face flush.

"You are," Liza said again, this time more loudly. Rouge looked down at the floor. Liza stepped closer, cupped Rouge's chin in her hand, pulled her face toward her. "Let me see."

Click.

Liza and Rouge turned instantly toward the noise. *Click.* Liza still held Rouge's chin. *Click, click.*

Ben was in the doorway, taking a step into the room, the camera shielding his face. "Don't stop," he begged.

But Liza already had. She had separated herself from her daughter and taken a few steps back like a mouse trapped by a cat in a corner, stunned by the intrusion, turning her face away. In a flash, she regained control.

"Are you out of your fucking mind? You can give people heart attacks like that."

Ben lowered the camera. Now it was he who was caught off guard. "I… I… I'm sorry," he stammered. "It was just an incredible shot."

Liza stormed past him. "You peeping freaks will drive me crazy." Her angry voice forged a hot escape down the hall. As she rounded the corner into the kitchen, Ben quickly raised his camera and took another shot.

Rouge started to laugh. He looked over his shoulder at her. "What's so funny?"

She laughed some more, spilling out relief, guilt, defiance; she wasn't sure. Ben's face turned red. "Stop it. You're making me a nervous wreck."

Gripping her sides, she tried to suck in air. Did she sound hysterical? She began to calm down. Tears were forming in her eyes. Ben raised his camera again, but she held up her hand.

"No. Don't." Her voice was sputtering, she was quietening down. "I'm sorry. I haven't a clue what was so funny. But it was." She dropped her hand. "I think."

"Well, one thing's for sure. My welcome is probably shot to hell."

"Possibly, but you never can tell." Rouge moved toward the photographs, aiming to take them down and put the room back to order. As she did, Ben held out his arm to stop her.

"Did you do that?"

Rouge chuckled. "Are you kidding? Of course not. That was Liza's idea."

He continued to hold her as he studied the wall. She leaned into his arm just a bit, longing for his warm skin to melt into hers.

"I like what she's done," he said. Then he let Rouge go.

*

Liza went right to the studio—where else would she go?—and locked the door behind her. How he had unsettled

231

her. She felt she was coming undone. What was going on? Pain beat in her head, behind her temples, under her eyes. She loved this space. She hated it now. Hated how even something silent, like pain, could be heard echoing through the room. Such a big, empty room. Except for the canvases, and the vacuous forms therein. Her audience, her creations. If they were so good, why couldn't she interest anyone in her work? Maybe she had been deceiving herself all these years.

"What?" she asked, standing in the center of the room, rapidly scanning each canvas, round and round and round, trying hard to keep her eyes moving, darting as if one step ahead of the pain.

"What?" she asked louder now. "I can't hear you. Who the hell do you think you are?"

As Liza stared at each, desperate for some confirmation, something, nothing, came back. Dummies without voices, work without life.

Liza slumped down to the floor. She was too exhausted any more to stand. It always came to this, didn't it? Always. One minute, pure elation—yes, she has finally done something good. Yes, it was all for this, this one moment when she could shout to the world, "I am a great painter!"

Then it would be gone, not even the memory of elation to linger. Nothing but doubt, derision, despair. Only the register of accomplishment in her brain. Just a moment ago, you were happy.

"Whatever the fuck that means," she spoke again to her audience, the paintings. She waited a second, as if for a response, while a distorted, pained smile drew across her face. "Oh, I forgot." Fumbling to get up, she staggered toward the table, to her brushes and paints, taking up one brush and smearing the end of it in cadmium red. "I forgot to give you tongues. How inconsiderate of me."

But she did not advance. The pain in her head held her back. Instead, she wandered over to the mattress and lay on her back. She had made her choice years ago and had missed her time. What had moved her in painting was no longer important, except for those who had become famous. Their work still sold.

"It's too much. I can't do this. I can. Then I can't. Even Rouge has some clarity of vision. It seems so easy for her. Simple. Why can't it just be simple?"

More than anything, Liza wished she could cry to release the sludge inside her and let it spill out. Allow herself some relief. But she couldn't conjure tears. She had begun to shut down; she had no desire to move. Soon she would be gripped by despair, held under the surface of life, of sensation, even sorrow. She would not feel sad. She could not even feel. Soon, like the forms in her paintings—her own creations—she would be completely empty and dull. To everything. Even the voice of her own daughter.

"No." She forced herself up. "No. Not again. I am finished with this."

She would get up, drive into town, to the liquor store, and find something to drink. Anything would do. Something biting that would permeate her body, jolt her with warmth and an inkling of hope. With a drink, she could dream again. She could fancy herself alive, glowing, prospects within reach. At least for a while she could rekindle a vision of that.

No one was outside. She slid into the car, turned on the motor and backed out quickly, before anyone could stop her. Rouge or Ben. What do they know? She tried to drive quickly to the store, yet her senses were dull, and she had to push herself to get up to speed. Walk at an exaggerated pace, speak faster in the store. Ignore people's comments, if at all possible. Get in, get out.

The day was hot, the sunlight diffuse in the humid air, though still bright. Liza had to squint. She should have remembered sunglasses.

"And aspirin," she said out loud, tapping her fingers on top of the steering wheel, speaking up against the air blowing in the window, as though she were dictating a shopping list to someone sitting in the seat beside her. Anyone at all. "Don't forget the aspirin."

*

Ben had gone right to the darkroom, developing the first of what he hoped would be his series of the two women, he told Rouge, who had followed him to watch. For as long as she could, Rouge stayed with him, framing his every move through the lens of her camera—his straight, engaged shoulders from the back as he made his way down into the dimly lit basement, his face in profile, stern in concentration, full-faced as he turned to reach over her for chemicals as a hint of excitement glowed in his eyes. *Click, click, click.* Even in the dark as he loaded the film, she kept her lens pointed toward the noise of him at work, popping, clipping, snapping, the round and round drone of film winding up, the shallow in and out of his breathing. Waiting for the end, for him to reach up and turn on the overhead light, for that instant where his face materialized out of the darkness. *Click, click.*

Her arms began to ache from holding the camera, but she had no desire to put it down. Instead, she pulled her feet up to the edge of the chair and propped her elbows on her knees, letting the rhythmic sound of fluid sloshing back and forth in the film canister hold her in place, help give direction to the turbulence that also sloshed inside her. Back and forth, round and round, pushing hard against her skin, making her hot. If she could hold it all, maybe she could give a name to what clashed and collided in there, but that was too much work, way more satisfying to funnel it all toward her eye, into the camera, out the other side, watching, watching. *Click, click, click.*

He held the newly developed film up to the light. Rouge bent down in front of him to catch the edges of his chin, black lines against the light.

"You're sure busy there," he said.

"Uh-huh." She hopped backwards to get out of the way.

Looking at his film, Ben said nothing, but now he was setting up to print. Rouge couldn't imagine what—the two of them startled, one upset. What could be there?

"I can't believe you got anything worth printing," she said.

"Oh, yeah," he answered as he poured developer into its tray. "Yeah," again riding out with his breath. "Yeah," now turning toward her, giving her a wink. "There's some stuff here all right."

Later, once they were dry, Ben tacked up six out of seven of his photographs on the living room wall. First in their sequence, tracking Liza through inquisition, surprise, defense, and flight, the changes rich and definitive in her face, in the tension and swirl of her body. Until the last when her form was only a blur in the distance. Throughout Liza's rapid movements, Rouge stayed steady. Standing, looking full-on toward the camera, almost in relief as her mother contorted around her. One, the hand on Rouge's chin, pulling their faces close together as Rouge tried to look away. Two, both of them directed forward by the sudden noise, evident in the flash of surprise in their faces. Three, the hand drops, Liza pulls back, separates. Four, eyes big, growing defiant, pushing away, the shape of her beginning to blur, all but the eyes. Five, Liza's face in profile, an out-of-focus flight, turning around, turning away. Six, only Rouge left, looking right into the camera, unwavering, the movement of a smile beginning to curl the edges of her lips. Behind her, the white blur of an exhausted storm ripples in the air.

As he stood at the wall, Rouge photographed him, his lips pursed tight to hold onto tacks, thick, dark eyebrows pushing down hard on his face. One, two, three, four, his mouth now empty, his lips released. *Click.* Another handful of tacks, two more prints to go. He took several steps back and viewed the wall. *Click.*

"See here," he finally proclaimed as though a revelation to himself. "Look how the focus is on you the entire time." He was smiling. "It makes her look like she's in a dance, doesn't it? Moving fast until there's almost nothing left." *Click.* He paused, took a thoughtful breath. *Click.* Then nodded in satisfaction. No, delight. *Click, click.* "Except her ghost."

Ben stepped up to the wall and removed all the prints except the last. Moving back to the center of the room, he stared at it for a while as Rouge shot several more images. Only a few more remaining in this roll of film.

"You know," he said softly, "that might be the best photograph I've ever taken."

Rouge lowered her camera. "Really? Are you serious?"

With a second thought, his response was more assured. "Absolutely. From what I've seen so far, this is *the* portrait of the two of you."

Rouge glanced at the image, then studied it carefully. She looked so… herself, but not exactly. She was unquestionably strong and the clarity dominated the image. Rouge would not say she was beautiful, though she was pretty enough. Nor was she exotic or mysterious. Far from it. But even though Rouge was seeing an image of herself, a figure that might ordinarily bore her in its familiarity, she was drawn to the assured stance and the firm edges of that mouth, those elements that held steady amid whatever mystery was whirling behind her.

"Huh," she muttered.

Ben sat on the sofa to have a smoke. Rouge moved closer to the print to inspect how he had exaggerated the whirl of Liza's form, how he had blurred her out, when the sound of footsteps scampered overhead. A door closed; water began to run.

"Liza must be taking a bath."

Ben approached the wall. "Maybe I should put this work away."

"Good idea."

They took down the prints together, and Rouge carried them downstairs as Ben replaced the sofa against the wall. They were in the kitchen thinking about dinner when Liza finally appeared. All traces of anger appeared to have dissipated. If anything, she looked surprisingly relaxed.

"I seem to be out of cigarettes again," Liza said to Ben, her voice softer than usual. "May I have one of yours?"

As Ben fumbled with his pockets, Rouge took a few steps around the room. She could muster no words, though that was not what she was after. Instead, she found herself moving toward her camera on the sideboard. As though by instinct. There, on that side of the room, she was facing Ben. Liza stood off to the right, leaning toward him for a light.

Click.

Liza turned over her shoulder and, with her lit cigarette held firmly in her lips, threw Rouge a strained smile. *Click, click.*

She stepped back, shook her hair with her free hand, then started for the back door. But halfway out, she stopped and turned to Ben.

"Maybe it's time you see what I do," Liza said.

Rouge nearly dropped her camera and gripped it hard in response. Ben leapt up. "I would love to," he answered, beaming from ear to ear.

Click. Click.

Rouge followed them through her lens, stepping after them to the door, one final shot of their backs ambling together across the driveway into the barn. A tall, lunky man; a trim, determined woman.

The film stopped. The roll was done. Rouge put down the camera and watched them disappear into the barn. Through the camera, she could look at everything in relation to light, depth of field, composition. She could separate all she saw into concrete components. But not now. With just her eyes, everything blurred together. Ben and Liza walking away, Ben's jumping to attention, it was all too fast. For a moment she wondered what Liza was up to… no, she shook off the thought. No, she wouldn't.

She turned, noticing an odd smell lingering in the air. What is that? Liza's shampoo? Yes, she recognized the delicate sweet whiff of spring flowers. But there was some other smell, a sour, grainy odor. What? Rouge shrugged, then found the roll of exposed film in her pocket. She was anxious to see what was there.

*

A bottle of bourbon sat on Liza's painting table, a tall, half-empty container of warm, amber liquid, glowing in the afternoon light. In front of it, like a multi-colored carpet, were swirls of oil paints dolloped onto the tabletop only a few days before, a handful of dirty brushes and a small palette knife pushed off to the side. An apt still life, Liza thought, sitting on her stool nearby. She chuckled to herself, took another slow, heating swig from the open bottle. "*Portrait of the Artist* is how I'd title it."

Though it was hot outside, it was cool in the studio. Comfortable now that Liza had begun to drink. Ah. Bourbon. She took another taste, a small sip to flush the insides of her mouth, savoring the resurrecting liquid. Could she begin another canvas? See what came out of this delicious, floating state. Maybe here, held at this level of lightness, her true measure would show itself. She put the top back on the bottle. No more. This was just enough, the perfect place to be.

She unscrewed the top. One more sip. That was enough. Ummm, these paintings weren't that bad. In fact, they might be quite good. Tessie would say so, Liza was certain of that. What about Ben? Drumming her fingers on the painting table, the image of Ben's adoring face flashed through her mind, the way his eyes gleamed when she talked about painting, anything about painting; her words garnered a sycophant's attention.

Yes, she thought, he will respond to these. But, first a shower, a change of clothes.

Hurrying later with him into the barn—thank God they were getting out of range of Rouge and that chatterbox camera—Liza actually found herself eager. She opened the door, took him by the arm and led him into the big room where, only an hour before, she had leaned four canvases against the walls. Large, colorful, energetic paintings against stark white walls.

Pausing in the doorway, she pushed him on ahead. He stopped at first, not knowing which to look at, in what order, then his eyes found the one she was hoping he'd find—the boldest of the series. Without a word, he tracked the natural progression around the room, stepping in to get a closer view. Liza smiled, leaned against the door and lit a cigarette. Ben took in the work for a long time before he responded.

"You've captured passion and nailed it to canvas," he uttered, the awed look in his eyes separating them into idol and fan. He kept his distance and continued his praise. "You're really good."

She would not let excitement expose her. She'd kept her gratitude to a measured grin as she moved toward the painting table to find her tin-can ashtray. Dropping in the spent end of her smoke, she opened the bourbon and lifted it up.

"How about a little drink to celebrate?"

Ben put his hands in his pockets and tipped back on his heels. "No. I should stay away from that stuff."

"C'mon." Liza was pulling two coffee cups out from the shelf under the table. "Just a little." Then with a laugh, she added, "You wouldn't watch a lady drinking by herself, would you?"

Ben shook his head, but Liza was already pouring drinks and did not care. "All right." His answer was tentative as it met a cup full of bourbon coming his way. "Maybe just one."

*

Rouge had cropped Ben's face and zoomed in on the eyes. Print after print watching his eyes. A quick exposure of the film onto paper, then, in the red of the safe light, swirling the white paper back and forth, back and forth until the eyes popped through, soaring out of the white.

She worked fanatically; she had been at it for hours. Image after image, hanging up to dry on the line strung across the room. She had become hooked on his eyes, mesmerized by the pair of them coming at her through the haze of red light, nearly zooming off the page, until one more wet print in hand, she found no space left to let it dry. The line was full. Where would she hang it? What is the time? It has to be late.

Stopping to search for an empty slot on the line, Rouge felt her fatigue. She probably wasn't even seeing straight anymore. Time to call it quits. She unpinned the first several prints that seemed dry enough now, enough anyway to take upstairs so she could inspect them over coffee in the morning.

Laying them on the counter as she poured herself some water, Rouge noticed the studio light was off. It was nearly eleven. Maybe Liza had actually gone to bed at a reasonable hour. Where was Ben? Rouge herself was somewhat dazed—all those chemicals—and, though tired, wanted to look through the photos one more time before going to bed.

The air outside was strangely still, not even a cricket to punctuate the dark. Only the ticking of the kitchen clock beating tersely. Rouge stared at the photographs, one at a time, holding them up in the bright overhead light. Ben's eyes were caught beholding Liza. Enlarged in one, she could even make out her mother's tiny reflection in his pupil. Ah, the eye bedazzled by a jewel. That was it! Rouge scanned the photos quickly again. There, enlarged and developed enough to etch in the deep, defining tones, Rouge could see enchantment in his eyes. The sparkle and strained desire. Right there. Clear in black and white.

Suddenly all the wayward hints came into focus. Ben's odd waves of ennui hovering in Liza's wake as she left the room, eagerly following Liza and Rouge around with his camera, his caution around Liza, his attentiveness, while he could be so cavalier with Rouge. Such a friend! This was why he didn't bat an eye at Rouge's change of face, highlighted with a little make-up—though Liza hadn't missed it. Rouge got it now. He had come because of Liza. Because he was infatuated with Liza. The first time and the second, as well. Rouge had been such a fool. She had been only a vehicle. The whole story stared right at her, there in his eyes.

Looking up, she noticed the light was still on in Ben's

room. What was he doing in there? She tiptoed up to the door to listen. Hearing nothing, she found herself going out the back to peek in through the window, not thinking now, just in motion. But the room was empty, the bed messily made. Where could he be? Not in the darkroom, she knew that.

And where was Liza? Rouge hurried up the stairs. Her mother's bedroom door was ajar; it was dark inside. Rouge stuck her head into the room tenuously shadowed by the light of a three-quarter moon. The bed was empty. Rouge's heart jumped to her throat and back. The studio!

Leaping lightly on toes, she made her way across the yard. Though she held her breath, she was certain her pounding heart heralded her approach. The door to the studio was closed. Taking her place a few feet away from the barricade of wood, Rouge stood squarely in front of it as she had done before as a little girl, outside Liza's door listening for the familiar grunts, loud, clumsy breathing, the rhythmic squeaking of the bed, the crescendo of horrifying noise on the other side to be finished, waiting for silence to follow so that Rouge could be sure she would have Liza back again.

Now Rouge stood drained of hope, the shell of herself gathering steam, mustering rage that streaked up her back like a sharp fingernail, until she was flooded with fury.

She opened the door and strode over to the mattress, to the disgusting bodies humping and flailing like pathetic animals, Ben's breathing growing louder and louder. "Wait a minute. Stop." It was Liza, grabbing him, pushing him away. He let off with a grunt. Liza sat up, pulling at fabric, trying to cover herself.

"Shit," she was yelling. "Get off. Someone's here."

Ben sat up.

For an instant, as it all became clear, no one said a word. Not Liza, not Rouge, certainly not Ben. They were frozen, the three of them, tortured shadows in the darkness.

Blood pulsed in Rouge's neck and the beat of it echoed through her body. Loud, angry surges of dark red fluid. At first, she thought of covering her neck with her hand, making a collar to hold it in. Instead, she opened her mouth and let the rage break through.

"Get out," she shouted.

Hands over her ears—for her voice nearly knocked her down—she could not stop yelling, "Get out, get out." Stumbling as she turned and ran across the room, out the door. "Get out, get out," across the driveway, into the house, up the stairs, her words resounding through the fields that surrounded the house, echoing across the valley in tempered tones, only the sound of her faint voice coming back in at her through the windows of her bedroom as she slammed her door shut.

SEVEN

Late Summer, Fall

P rone on her bed in an interminable rage, Rouge lay
for several hours as awake as she'd ever been. Earlier,
she had listened to the stumbling of feet coming out
of the barn, crunching on the dirt and the grass outside.
Then nothing.

It was quiet for a while, only the sounds of birds breaking
through the gradual lightening of dawn and clanging of
cow bells from across the road, O'Neil's cows off to pasture.
Rouge's body was a stone on her bed. Neither hot nor cold,
it simply pulsed with her breathing, her mind devoid of
direction, exhausted, as though every sense within her had
been flattened by a terrible storm. She could not bear the
sight of her room, its haunting familiarity, the smells of
summer, the approaching fall. At that moment, she could
not bear anything, too tired even to move.

The screen door downstairs opened, then closed, and
heavy footsteps echoed in from outside, moving toward Ben's
truck. Rouge heard the sound of a suitcase being flung in the
back, the truck door open, then pinch shut, the whining of
the engine straining to turn over, groaning, groaning until it
caught itself and sputtered into a tentative hum. The truck
crunched over tall grass at the far side of the driveway as it
moved backward, then pulled onto dirt and sputtered out

onto the road, a weary sound gaining speed as it moved into the distance, whispering its way into silence and what Rouge expected would be a pained journey home.

Rouge stayed put for another hour or two until she could stand it no longer. She would get herself up and get out the house. This damn house. She would go for a swim, crawl wet and clean into O'Neil's barn and sleep in the hay. No, she'd slip in through the basement of Shelly's house in town—her parents wouldn't mind her staying there until they returned. She'd keep it neat. No, the place was big and creepy. She would wait until Tess arrived and hide in the back of her car and drive back to Boston at the end of the summer and never come back. No, she'd go to the river and float on her back and not raise herself up until she had drifted into the sea.

An envelope bearing her name was propped up on the kitchen table. It was a note from Ben. Rouge stared at it. Then, as if by instinct, she lifted it up by the edge and carried it over to the wastebasket under the kitchen sink. She hated him maybe more than her mother. At least as much. What could he say to change that? Not that she cared, for she despised him more than she wanted it changed. Dangling the thing over the nearly full container, she opened her fingers and let the envelope drop.

"You poor, stupid fool." As she watched the letter slide down diagonally between leftover salad and coffee grounds, those words resounded through her. Stupid fool. She had meant Ben, of course, but, at that moment, seeing the last of his words stuck in garbage, she wasn't so sure which of them, Ben or her, deserved criticism. Or pity.

She went to the river. She floated and cried, got out of the water, twisted the excess out of her hair, lay on the bank until she was hot, then returned to the water. Floated and cried. The cicadas turned up the volume, a vortex of sound to hide the sobbing she was sure was wailing through the valley and alerting everyone in town. Poor, poor girl. Poor, silly girl.

Hours passed. The sun softened and began its slow slide down the sky as the surface of the water grew busy with insects. Behind her she could hear the noise of Tom and Dale O'Neil stripping down for an evening swim. If she left now, they would not run into one another, their hulky forms streaked with sweat and dust and splinters of hay bumping into her clean, drained body. She was not in the mood for contact with anyone.

The house was in shadows when she returned, the kitchen dark, though Liza's studio was lit. *Go ahead, lose yourself in work. Stay forever!* Rouge filled a glass with water and as she stood at the sink, gulping it down, she gazed at the open garbage can and noticed that Ben's envelope had absorbed oil from the leftover salad and was now translucent in one corner. She could almost make out some writing and bits of words. Reaching in to pull it out, she shook off the coffee grounds and blotted the paper dry. Carrying it with her, she went down to the darkroom to make sure everything was put away—the camera, the chemicals, the cover over the enlarger. Before she left, she hung the letter on the line all by itself, as though to dry, one small out-of-place paper in the otherwise orderly room.

Coming up the stairs into the kitchen, Rouge heard the studio door shut tight, Liza's footsteps coming from the barn.

"Shit," she muttered, and hurried to her room.

Liza was fired off the mattress by a surge of adrenaline, the echoes of Rouge's screams stinging her to the bone. A blanket had fallen to the floor. She grabbed it to wrap around her body, then turned to Ben who lay as she had pushed him, against the wall, stunned.

"You have to leave." She began to pace. "Now!"

"I'm going."

With that he rose, grabbed his clothes from the mess on the floor, dressed as fast as he could and hurried away.

She continued pacing as she listened to the sounds of his departure—the kitchen door open and shut, then the door to his truck and the whine of his engine trying to start, making her cringe each time it failed to catch and turn over. Until it finally did, and he maneuvered the truck out the driveway and onto the road.

"Damn, damn, damn," she yelled into the empty room. Spying the drained bottle of bourbon near her can of brushes, she grabbed it and heaved it against the wall above the bed. The bottle shattered as it made contact and left a brown stain on the pristine white wall.

"Never again!" Liza roared as she watched shards fall.

She continued to pace, lit a cigarette, smoked it to the end. Still nothing. No idea of what she would say to Rouge. She stood at the entrance to the barn, not a sound coming from the house. The blanket was heavy, but her clothes disgusted her. She yanked them from the floor and stuffed them into the trash. A shower first, the water hot and running full blast. Maybe that would pound some sense into her. Then some breakfast. Surely all this rage would have made Rouge hungry. She'll make blueberry pancakes, her favorite. Jesus, breakfast? What the hell was she thinking?

Liza hurried into the house, up the stairs, past the chilled silence of Rouge's room and into her own. Drawing the shades, she lay down on the bed. For a minute or two, she told herself, just a short rest while she figured out what to say. When she opened her eyes again, it was nearly noon. The events of the early morning hit her directly, as though she had snapped out of a nightmare. She threw on a robe and went to check on Rouge. Her door was ajar, and she was gone. The house was silent. A short reprieve.

Yet the afternoon was interminable. Still no Rouge. She could be anywhere—Shelly's? Were they even back yet?— probably working at Simpson's, maybe the bakery. Plenty of places for her to lose herself and stew. And make Liza stew. If it were any other time, she would have poured herself a drink. Now the idea of the easy escape made her bristle. Instead, she pulled weeds, lots of them, under the hot sun.

Still no Rouge come evening. Liza considered driving around town to try to find her, stopped only by her indecision about what to say. She was probably spending the night at Shelly's. Where else would she be? God knows what's being said.

Too wound up to sleep or read, Liza went to the studio to clean and put things back in order. Leaving the house dark, Liza flicked on all her studio lights and put Vivaldi on the record player. Music that soothed. Giants propped against the wall, her paintings glared at her, abstracted eyes of judgment, and her first impulse was to load a brush with black paint and heave it into the center of the one she liked best. How easily she could wipe this away. What stopped her?

She stood over her table and grabbed her hair. "Why am I doing this?" she wailed. "Do I still believe painting can save me?"

Such disgust. Yet it was better than despair, which she could feel circling around her. She must hold onto disgust. *Where the fuck are my smokes?* Probably in the kitchen. Stepping outside the barn, she noticed the kitchen light on. Rouge had come home. It's now or never, she told herself. Jaw clenched, she crossed the driveway but stopped outside the kitchen door to take a deep breath. The kitchen was empty. Rouge must be up in her room.

Her light was on. Liza knocked on the door. No answer.

"I know you're in there."

"Go away."

"We need to talk."

No response.

"Look, I'm sorry."

"I don't want to talk about it. Go away."

Liza turned to leave, but realizing how paltry her apology had sounded, tried again. "It was a careless accident. Really, we were just drunk. And stupid. I'm sorry."

Suddenly the door flung open. Apoplexy stared her in the face. "What's it to you? All you care about is yourself and your stupid painting! Fuck you, Liza!"

The door slammed so hard it nearly knocked Liza over.

What? I only care about myself? Do you even have a clue? I gave up almost everything for you.

Liza stormed into the room, catching Rouge off guard. She wanted to grab Rouge, to spin her around and face her square on, but chose to keep a distance. "Let me ask you something. What did you think would happen?"

"What do you mean?" Rouge's defiance began to melt.

"You know what I mean."

Rouge's face flushed and she looked away.

"For Christ's sake, Rouge, he's more than twice your age. And you're still a minor. What did you think?"

She was caving fast, a glint of tears in her eyes. But she was strong and quickly steadied herself and glared back at Liza. "You wouldn't understand."

"Oh, I think I would."

"Just leave me alone. Can you at least do that?" The two of them, stiff, intractable. Liza took a breath and softened.

"It's late. We'll talk in the morning. Get some sleep."

But they didn't. Liza did not fall asleep until dawn, and Rouge was long gone by the time she got up. Tess was due to arrive the following day. Liza needed to clean the house and get some shopping done. Should she call off the visit? What would she say? Such a mess she had made. Tess would be furious. But she could deal with that and maybe Tess could help smooth things over, get everything back on track. As she always fucking did.

Liza was restacking rolled canvases in the horse stall when she heard the car drive up the driveway, the shrill beep, beep of the horn, a familiar voice ringing outside, "Hello! Hello! Where is everyone?" Poor Tess, Liza thought, poor, enthusiastic Tess. What a storm she is about to meet.

"Liza! Rouge!" Liza threw the last of her canvases on top of the pile, about to greet Tess, when she heard a smack of the front screen door banging shut, Rouge's footsteps over the porch, hopping onto the grass—"Ah, there you are"—the cheeriness in Tess's voice draining as Rouge got closer

—"What on earth!"—the rumblings of muffled voices, all of it wafting around the side of the house and stopping Liza in her tracks. Let Rouge have a go at it first. Let's see what she says. Liza's clothes were dirty, bits of spiderwebs clung to the edges. She should clean up and change.

It was not long before Tess was knocking on her door, marching in, moving directly to the windows to open all the shades. As the last shade snapped open, Tess turned, crossed her arms, leaned against the wall, steeled. "What is going on?"

Liza kicked her discarded clothes into the closet. "What did Rouge say?"

"She asked if she could come live with me, for one thing."

"Jesus!" Liza hadn't considered that. Would it come to that? Her stomach sank.

"That she is tired of you ruining everything."

"Everything?" The notion rekindled her. "That's a little extreme. I made a big mistake. But I won't accept everything."

Tess rolled her eyes. Now it was Liza who turned inquisitor, her brow creasing. "What did she say?"

"That you fucked her teacher—her words. Then sent him away."

Liza felt herself slow down, the story needing to unravel, details required for any of it to make sense.

"Yes, we fucked. It wasn't planned, believe me. We had a few drinks in the studio. It just happened."

Tess's eyes sharpened like a hawk's. Her stance turned to stone. "Even numbed with bourbon—it was bourbon, I assume—you couldn't see what you were doing, the impact it would have?"

"Of course I did. But it happened so fast. And I didn't think she'd walk in on us."

"You didn't think she'd know?"

"Yes. No. I don't know." Liza scanned the room for her cigarettes. She could use a smoke. None was in sight. "Look," she said in resignation. This was not a conversation she could escape. "The whole thing had gotten out of control. She's only fifteen. I had to do something." Liza bent down to look under clothing strewn over the floor.

"You couldn't have just broken it up. Said something. Instead of all the drama."

Liza kicked the bureau. "I'm sure I could have. If I were a normal person. But clearly I am not!"

Tess chuckled an implied *Who is?*. "Thank God you're not, most of the time, anyway. Just sometimes I wonder about the choices you make, your lack of judgment."

Liza looked at her askance, annoyed at the patronizing. The problem with Tess was that she never did anything wrong. No mistakes to hone and deepen resolve, to carve out fuckin' character. Look at her standing there, so perfectly groomed, fresh in her crisp white shirt and floral skirt, an array of gold bracelets ringing her arms, her face made up just right. The perfect presentation. What was there, after all, to ruffle the surface, to invite contention, to feel the punch and jab of life? Tess never had affairs, though she had plenty of opportunity. Tess never let herself get out of control. Tess, with the connections, the manners, the right things always to say, the work—those portraits. How easy to sell portraits! Take the safe route, the one so nicely carved out for her. Such a safe, uneventful ride.

Sure, she didn't have children, something she had

wanted desperately. But it didn't happen and Matt had refused to adopt. A child would have changed things, made that smooth ride a bumpy nightmare, even for Tess.

Without that experience, without mistakes, who the hell was she to judge?

"Oh, shut up, Tess!"

"What?" Tess was aghast. "I'm not the one who fucked up here."

"No, no, we couldn't have that, could we?" Snide response, Liza knew. "Look, we both need to cool off. I'm going for a walk."

"Go then. We'll talk later."

Liza took off behind the barn and hit the bridle trail long ago etched through the woods by horseback riders. The path led to a small lake where she would often go to swim, Rouge preferring the river because she was scared that this deep opaque body of water harbored snakes. Or maybe an aqua monster. Such an imagination that girl had.

She walked briskly, with purpose, using motion to help calm down. Enough to think. How could things have gotten so out of control? It was her fault, completely. She should never have brought Ben back in the first place. Then again, if she hadn't, Rouge wouldn't have discovered photography. And look at her talent. It would have completely passed her by. Liza let out a guttural wail. "Why is life so complex!"

The lake was just up ahead. She'd strip down and go for a swim. But that felt like another distraction because clarity was breaking through the surface. Her world was coming apart and she was trapped in the chasm. Her daughter, almost a woman on the one side, Liza's stagnant career on the other. Her two selves split down the middle and she was paralyzed in between. How could she? Because she was frustrated, confused and angry. Because she was in pain. Liza heaved a stone in the water, then another. And began to cry.

When she returned, it was late afternoon, and she found Tess on the porch by herself reading. Liza sat at her feet. "Is Rouge here?"

"She's at work. She's taken a job at Simpson's."

"Good," Liza sighed. "I'm glad we're alone. I was an ass earlier, a selfish bitch."

Tess rested her book on her lap, about to respond but thought better of it.

"It's complicated," Liza continued. "I'm not going to back-pedal and go over what happened. Yeah, it was stupid and selfish and I don't know what. You can throw every negative word at it you like, the two of you. And I might have fucked things up irrevocably with Rouge."

"I'm sure you haven't," Tess began.

Liza held up her hand. "Time will tell. All I can do now is move forward. I'll try to clean up the mess with Rouge as much as I can. But I'm losing her, whatever happens."

"You're not losing her. You're her mother."

"I know, but she's grown up or nearly there, and it's all changing."

"Meaning?"

"Meaning we all have to move forward."

"So, what are you telling me?"

Liza looked at Tess with intent. "That the best thing I can do for Rouge, for me, is to get serious about my work."

Tess guffawed. "You've never stopped being serious about your work."

"That's not what I mean. Sure, I've always worked, but I gave up trying to do something with it long ago. I let a few rejections stop me. But goddamn it, Tess," Liza's voice was strong, "the work is good."

"The work is very good. You're right. You just need some sales and affirmations."

"I need to find a dealer."

Tess grinned, relieved. "I agree. It will do you a world of good to be recognized. Where will you start?"

"I still have names from Hank. I'll start there." Liza held out her hand to shake, a deal cemented. "I can do this," she said more softly, her attention drifting away. "And what about Rouge? You'll stay with her while I'm gone?"

Tess nodded. "Rouge is fine. She's got a job at Simpson's, says she needs to fill her time and get out the house. Don't worry. It's good for her. Unlike some of us," Tess added, though it was unnecessary, "she's a resourceful girl."

"Yes, thank God for that."

*

The crate of zucchini was heavier than Rouge thought and nearly knocked her down as she lifted it out of storage in the back refrigerator. "Careful," Mr. Simpson called out. "You shouldn't be lifting those heavy boxes anyway. Let Jerry get those."

"No, I can manage." Rouge hoisted the box up to waist level with her knee and carried it into the store to arrange the contents into orderly rows in the produce section. Mondays and Tuesdays, she helped out at the bakery. The rest of the week she spent at Simpson's store, sweeping, bagging, stocking shelves, realigning jars and cans after customers picked them up to read ingredients, then shoved them back any old way, sometimes carrying things with them all the way to the cash register before leaving the rejects on the floor. Mr. Simpson didn't need any more employees, but when Rouge explained she was saving money for college, he nodded and took her on.

As Rouge rounded the aisle to the produce section, the crate of zucchini propped tight against her hip, she heard a cough, then a giggle. It was Shelly, standing by the bread racks.

Rouge scowled. "What are you doing?"

Shelly pulled down her sunglasses to get an untinted look at Rouge. "Waiting for you. When are you off?"

"Another hour," Rouge whispered, turning her back to cut off the dialogue and stack the vegetables. "I'll meet you later. I can't talk now."

Casting a look toward Mr. Simpson busy with a customer behind the meat counter, Shelly sauntered past Rouge and whispered as she breezed by, "Meet me behind the barn and bring some smokes."

It was the third week in August. Recently back from her summer in Maine, Shelly had appeared a few days ago, refreshed by saltwater and deflowered by the local lifeguard on the 11th green at her grandmother's club. "God, it hurt so much. And, would you believe it! I actually bled." She had broadcast this news flopping down on Rouge's bed the day after her return. "He popped my cherry." She had giggled like an adolescent at the word 'cherry'. Her make-up was more pronounced than ever; thick black eyeliner above and below, her lids intersecting into a smooth point. She had taken to putting on false eyelashes, looking like she was preening to fuck every guy in the senior class at school, the older, more popular guys. How she got by her mother, Rouge hadn't a clue.

"But it was worth it. He is so cute. See, I have his picture. Take a look."

Rouge glanced at the snapshot—a boy really, standing by the lifeguard chair with his seductive grin, his chest inflated by an exaggerated inhalation that sucked the volume out of his stomach—then threw it back on the bed and shrugged. Blond hair, cute enough, but only that. How many girls had copies of this same photo? Probably everyone in town.

Shelly had leaned back on Rouge's pillow and fished out a pack of cigarettes from her pocket. "Watch this," she announced through her teeth, gripping the cigarette as she lit it. "Look what Robbie taught me how to do." Robbie the lifeguard. She sucked in a big breath of smoke, then slid her bottom lip forward just enough to inhale a shaft of smoke into her nose. Pausing for a moment, she blew the smoke out of her mouth. "It's called a French inhale. Neat, huh?"

Rouge was not impressed.

"So, what did you do while I was gone?"

"Nothing."

"Nothing at all?"

"No."

"You just sat around and did nothing at all."

"That's right."

"No photographs?"

"No photographs."

Shelly stood up and walked over to the bureau. She was looking for Rouge's camera, which was no longer there. After eyeing the bureau and the bookshelves, she spun around. "Why don't you get your camera and take some photographs to send to Robbie? Just so he won't forget me."

"Another time." Her answer was dismissive, but she didn't care.

Rouge had cocked her head and looked at Shelly, who stood in the center of the room, her hand on her hip, a roll of soft belly peeking out from the edge of her shirt. With her pink nails and dangly earrings and tight little shorts, she was all experience now. Rouge could have almost smelled her heat. You just wait, Rouge had wanted to warn her. You'll be flattened soon.

With the last of the vegetables neatly arranged in the produce section, Rouge had enough time to sweep the back storeroom. Then she could leave. Before she did, she bought some peanut butter, a loaf of bread and butter. There was no need of fruit, and Liza could get her own coffee. She and Tess were planning to shop the next day. Pausing at the counter while Mr. Simpson added up her purchase, Rouge dallied over the question, "Is this all?"

"Maybe you better throw in a pack of Lucky Strikes," she answered as nonchalantly as she could, adding, "just in case my mom is out."

Rouge was off from work the next day, and Tess found her alone that afternoon lying in the sun at the river's edge, her hair oozing droplets of water that ran down the side of her back, tickling with coolness. Tess's presence was announced by the soft crunching of grass under the flaps of her leather sandals, the ones with the little pink and white flowers sitting atop the gap between her big and second toes.

"There you are," Tess exclaimed, coming up beside her and sitting down. Rouge opened her eyes. Flashes of afternoon sunlight pierced through the leaves of the big tree overhead, momentarily blinding her. Tess's figure was gone. There was only the presence, the scent of perfume.

"It really is lovely here," Tess said.

Rouge was looking at her through fingers that she held up to shield her eyes from the sun. Her feet dangled in the water. From the corner of her eye, the river looked brown and still, meandering along like everything else in the heat, flat and torpid, the air thick with humidity, buzzing with bugs, hardly lovely at all. Except for the solitude. And the cool water on her toes.

"You've been mighty quiet these past few days." Tess shifted her weight, leaned back on her arms.

"There's not much to say." With her arms crossed under her head, turned sideways, Rouge spoke into the flesh of her shoulder, letting her voice mumble.

"Oh, come now. How long have I known you?"

Rouge didn't answer. Tess was patient. A clump of algae hit Rouge's toes. She raised her foot and opened her eyes to make sure it was only slime. As she did, she caught Tess's inquisitive eyes. Rouge loved Tess, longed for her, wishing more than anything that she were her mother. Tess would have met her at the bus after school. Tess would not have forgotten to pick her up at her friends'. Ever. Tess would know what not to say that was on her mind and save it for the privacy of home. Tess would never, never embarrass her or watch her from under cover of a sheet in a darkened room as she came in to leave some food on the bedside table or slip at the bottom of the stairs and pass out, too drunk to make it to her room. Tess would not seduce the man who stood between them, even if it was impossible. She would know her place and realize that, though Ben was just a friend, Rouge had wanted more, at least the fantasy of him, all to herself. The infatuation at least. Something that should always remain hers alone. Even that, Liza had managed to rip away.

"I don't want to talk about it," she finally answered to the question that hovered around her like a mosquito, buzzing in and out of her ears. Tess said nothing more, just lay back on the grass.

Finally, Tess got up. "Well, you're more stubborn than I am. I need to see about dinner. There'll be food when you're hungry." Tess started up the path. Then she paused, turned, and took a step back.

"This will sound trite, I know, but store it somewhere in your brain. Liza loves you more than anything else."

Rouge bristled and turned her head back the other way.

*

It was the end of August. The galleries in New York would be getting ready to open again. Time for Liza to leave. Using Hank's name as a referral, she had made appointments with three dealers. The car was packed with her drawings and small canvases, just in case she found someone who would take them. In the front seat was a portfolio of slides. She had asked Rouge to photograph the new work.

"No."

The curtness of her response startled both Tess and Liza. Though Rouge had done her best to stay away—to rush off early in the mornings to work, stay often overnight at Shelly's— surely she'd like a photographic job.

"I'll pay you," Liza offered.

"I don't have time. I'm too busy."

"Seriously?" Liza wanted to say more—You don't want to be hired as a photographer, you little bitch—but she held her thoughts. "Fine then." She'd get a photography student to do the work, as she usually did.

After dinner—Tess had insisted that Rouge be home— Liza interrupted the two of them sitting out on the porch in animated conversation, with a nod informing Tess she was ready for another try at reconciliation.

"It's my turn to do the dishes," Tess announced.

"I'll help," Rouge offered.

"No, you stay here. I can manage alone." Liza saw the look Tess gave Rouge, the look Rouge gave back, and she felt completely isolated. An intruder in her own home. Still, she needed to say things to Rouge before she left.

Once Tess had departed, Liza took a seat in the old rocker. Rouge had stiffened and Liza chaffed at her petulance. Damn her. This is hard enough. She took a few hard rocks in the chair, momentum to get her going, then blurted out her practiced confession.

"I'm sorry about what happened. It just happened. I was not thinking." Liza paused, not wanting to admit she had been drunk, waiting to see if Rouge would respond. But she said nothing, only perched her chin on crossed arms and stared at her mother. Unbearable, that look, no forgiveness in sight. Liza pushed herself up and took a step toward the door to go inside and find Tess. Before she did, she turned to say one last thing.

"You're not making this easy, but I am trying to change. The drinking is over, I promise you that. I will find a way to make this up to you." Then she was off.

Only Tess was there to see her drive away the next morning.

"Now you call us. I want to hear everything," Tess instructed. It was early morning. She had made a thermos of coffee and packed several blueberry muffins.

"I will," Liza promised as she hopped into the car, grateful to finally be leaving.

She arrived in the city to congestion and noise. It was early September and New York felt alive, its denizens rested after the sultry, slow summer, people moving with purpose this way and that. Traffic was thick, cars traveling impatiently, no time to pause, something might be missed. Liza focused on her driving as the life of the city enveloped her, pulling her along, accelerating her pace.

It was mid-afternoon when she arrived at her favorite hotel, a family-run business downtown off Broadway. After she'd checked in and got her room, there was still time to visit a museum, but she preferred to amble through the park and watch the birds. She would go to bed early, wake up refreshed, determined, and make her rounds.

It was clear blue and lovely as she stepped out the small, dark hotel, too nervous for anything but coffee, hopping onto the sidewalk, her portfolio under her arm. She had put on make-up, brushed her hair hard and tied it back, and she wore simple gold earrings, a black skirt and pale yellow blouse. As far as she could see, bodies scurried along the streets as towering buildings gleamed in the morning sun. The air was vibrant and she moved briskly along, choosing to walk the many blocks to the first of three galleries.

It took no time. She arrived before she knew it. Closing the door softly behind her, Liza was met by a palpable silence as though the place was deserted. A young woman was seated at the front desk but did not stir. Even as Liza approached, the receptionist did not look up until she was nearly an arm's length away.

"Is Richard Harrigan in?" Liza asked, trying to sound matter-of-fact, as though she were expected. The woman raised her head, presenting a stern face. Pretty, tightly groomed. Liza knew that face. Smiling, with a few drinks in it, it had peopled the Cedar Bar nearly a decade ago. The face of an art tart was how they were known, faces like that. Young things dreaming of rubbing bodies with celebrity artists—de Kooning, Pollock, Kline—being transformed into a muse.

Noticing Liza's portfolio, the girl's voice cracked the stagnant air. "Do you have an appointment?"

"Yes. Liza Baker. Ten am, I believe."

"Mr. Harrigan's been delayed. He asked if you'd leave some slides."

Liza glanced around the room. She did not like what was on the walls; overdone, sloppy abstractions filling one half of the gallery, the other half adorned with canvases draped in colored ropes. Turning back to the woman, Liza nodded. "I'll send you some."

"Fine."

The next dealer was more promising. At least he looked at her work. "It's very good," he said, though his voice lacked the requisite enthusiasm. "If you can leave your slides, I'll show them to my partner and we'll get back to you."

They wouldn't, of course. They never did.

Fuck them, she thought, as she hit the street. It was nearly half past eleven and, already, the street teamed with people heading off to lunch, bumping shoulders, knocking into her and throwing her off balance. Fuck them and their arrogant ways. *We'll get back to you.* They might as well just tell the truth—we're not interested in *you*.

She stopped to look at the piece of paper with the address of the last gallery written neatly at the bottom. Why bother? Why not just go have a drink? But she could see Tess and Rouge seated around the kitchen table, tapping their fingers, impatient for news. For good news. For progress.

The smell of street food wafted around her, smoke as well, making her long for a cigarette. One more gallery, then she would stop and take a break. One more. This takes time. And patience. Don't give up, she told herself.

She was luckier at the third. She could feel it walking through the vestibule, a tinge of assuredness nudging her in. The work on the walls was stunning, reminiscent of Barnett Newman's, though she did not recognize the artist's name. Stepping out from the back, an elderly man greeted her, clearly the dealer, George Compton—no assistant would dress in such a mishmash outfit: plaid tie, striped shirt pulled out on the side from fading corduroy pants. As he approached, he smiled. Liza smiled back.

"May I help you?" His voice was kind. His eyes went from her face to the portfolio then back to her face.

Liza held out her free hand. "Mr. Compton? We have an appointment."

He nodded. "Ah yes, Liza Baker, I'm always happy to see an artist recommended by Hank Bolton. Let's have a look."

After offering her coffee, he studied each slide on the light table, longer than her nerves could withstand, so she stepped into the showroom to have a smoke, pace the floor and inspect the application of paint on each canvas as she might with student work. But she was too nervous to view anything with a critical eye. Finally, the dealer emerged, carrying the portfolio.

"They're quite good, really." He spoke softly. "You're a strong painter. Clearly. But they're not quite right for our space. If you had come in a few years earlier, maybe," he added. He must have noticed all the color drain from her face.

It took all her energy to look him in the eye. "I understand."

"I wish I could think of someplace else to send you. Why don't you leave me your number and, if I come up with someone appropriate, I will give you a call."

"Sure," Liza answered, and scrawled her number on a pad at the desk.

He held out a hand. "Well, good luck now. You're a good painter. I wouldn't give up if I were you."

I wouldn't give up if I were you, she repeated under her breath, hurrying out of the gallery and onto the street, gripping her portfolio under her arm, trying to bolster herself against the void that was seeping in. What now? A drink was the immediate response. No, she had sworn to her daughter that she would not. She could call Tess to get more names. No, she needed something more immediate, something tangible to grip. She thought of Phil. He lived downtown in a big, ragged loft. She would go see Phil. Maybe he would be able to give her some help, make an effective introduction. Something.

*

"At least let me see some of your photographs."

Tess was standing against the sink, sipping tea while Rouge finished homework at the kitchen table. School had begun three days earlier. They had eaten dinner quickly, without much conversation, only perfunctory dialogue about the classes Rouge was taking in her sophomore year. For the entire time Tess had been here, she had avoided any mention of photography. Rouge was surprised that she would bring it up now.

"I don't know," she all but snapped.

Tess strode over to the table and leaned over her. "You would have known last summer. You wouldn't have been able to wait to show me your work."

"That was a year ago. Things have changed."

"Yes, from what I understand, you've gotten better."

Rouge finished writing and turned the page, blatantly ignoring Tess. The steam of tea rose between them. It took such effort for Rouge to stem these sensitive areas of discussion—photography, Ben, Liza. Particularly around Tess who sat, silently waiting. Who would embrace her any time Rouge was ready.

Instead, Tess reached over and shut the book hard. Rouge looked up. "I'm tired of this. When are you going to let your anger go?" Tess's voice was raised and the sound of it, the unfamiliarity, frightened her and slammed down the wall Rouge had struggled to maintain. She began to cry.

As she did, Tess lifted her from her chair and took her in her lap. Without resistance, Rouge folded her lanky body into the bulk of Tess who held her, patiently rocking her back and forth. As though all this time she had been waiting for the chance to hold a girl like a mother. In Tess's lap, with arms around her, Rouge let everything go. She cried and cried, thinking she would never stop.

But she did, finally. Exhausted, she barely managed to reach down for a shirt tail to wipe her face. Tess took a napkin off the table and held it up, and Rouge used that instead to dry her eyes and clean her nose, feeling better. Light. That relentless weight in her stomach, an iron fist of rage that had clamped down inside and punched fury through her, that, too, had diluted itself and let go. For the first time in weeks, she could breathe.

"What is her problem?" Rouge asked, as she moved off Tess's lap and back into her own chair, ready to talk. "Why does she do these things?"

Emitting a labored sigh, Tess ventured a reply. "I think she's very insecure, believe it or not. She does a lot of things out of desperation."

Rouge looked down at the tablecloth, woven out of thin threads of yellows, oranges and reds, finding the vertical lines of brown that formed the backbone of the fabric, something to focus on while she treaded in the confused, murky pool of her feelings, staying quiet as she followed the line of brown across the table.

Tess continued, knowing full well that 'desperation' needed dissection. "She suffers from depression, but you know that. And she's a perfectionist. You know that as well."

Rouge jumped in. "And she drinks. And she sleeps around. She breaks hearts and doesn't give a damn."

"Yes, I know. But that's all a cover. It's erratic behavior meant to distract."

"What do you mean?"

"I think she behaves the way she does to keep herself from completely caving in." Tess was grappling for a response. Rouge stared back, waiting for more. "It has to do with her insecurity, her depression."

Rouge sat up. "You want to know what I think?"

Tess nodded, please.

"I think she's competing with me. I think she sees something I want, and she wants it, too. She's like a spoiled kid that way."

"You mean Ben?"

At the first mention of Ben, Rouge blushed and wanted to back off. But it was too late. She might as well talk about it, because apparently Tess knew.

"Yes, Ben. She just had to seduce him, didn't she? She didn't even want him in the first place until he became my friend." Rouge stopped there. She couldn't admit to the crush, even to Tess.

"Maybe she *was* competing with you," Tess said. "I'm sure there's that element, just a little. But it's only one small part of it. Your relationship is way more complex than that. Look," she added, gripping Rouge's arm, "the important thing is Liza does love you."

Rouge felt Tess would not release her without an acknowledged shift in attitude. She inhaled deeply. "I know," she answered.

"Good," said Tess. Then she let her go.

Tess got up to make more tea. "Did he say anything to you?" Tess asked, this question taking Rouge by surprise.

271

"Who?"

"Ben."

"No. He left a letter."

"Well, did you read it?"

"No."

"It might help if you did."

"Why?"

The kettle whistled. Tess removed it from the flame. "Because people are complex. Liza is quite beautiful and seductive, you know. And he's a man, among other things."

"So?" Rouge was getting irritated again.

"So, maybe he has something worthwhile to say for himself."

"I doubt it."

"Only one way to know, isn't there?"

It was well past midnight when Rouge tiptoed out of her room, down the creaky stairs, into the kitchen, then into the basement. Tess's lamp had flicked off a while ago. Through her partially open door, Rouge had watched the faint glow in the hallway pop into darkness. Eyes open, she had lain in bed for over an hour, waiting for sleep even though she knew it would never come.

The darkroom was tidy, as though a relic in a museum—a reproduction of a famous photographer's studio. All the summer's work was stored in the big box of photographic paper they had used. One hundred sheets originally, out of which only thirty-four prints were kept, the others lost to the learning process. Rouge opened the lid and went through the prints, photograph by photograph, inspecting each before separating them into one of four piles—Ben alone, Rouge alone, Ben and Liza, Liza and Rouge. In the emptiness of the room and its subterranean temperature, Rouge felt one step removed in her warm body, as though she were an outsider, someone seeing them for the first time. If she could keep that distance and not relive each scene, it was easy for her to judge the image. This one is excellent, this one not so good, this handful here all right for now, but they would be discarded once something better came along. She knew immediately which ones Tess would like. Which one would be her favorite. From that distance, Rouge was sure of her favorite as well. There were two of them actually—the last image of Rouge and Liza, and a profile of Ben that highlighted the determined line of his nose, bumpy as though hand-drawn, and his angular chin.

Once separated, Rouge stacked the piles one on top of the other, returned them to the box. Then she unclipped Ben's letter from the line. The top corner was still stained with oil that clouded the lettering below the surface, as though the edges of words were drifting underwater. She looked at the oiled handwriting, the lines of her name on the front of the envelope. Inside would be an apology, sadness, no surprises she could imagine. There was nothing to hold her back. Still, she paused as she felt her pulse quicken, coldness prick her skin.

Tess's voice took over. *It might help you...* and Rouge turned over the envelope, slid her finger under the partially sealed flap and wiggled it open.

Rouge,
When you are second-rate, you settle into comfort, familiarity, you don't move too fast or too far. You keep

to what's expected, what is guaranteed to earn you a buck. More than anything, when you're second-rate, you are easily seduced by those who make believe you are great and pretend you matter. Even as you tell yourself it's a lie, you believe that they really care.

You won't understand this because you're beyond that. You're first-rate. You have a clear field in front of you. Don't you dare not leap into it.

I'm a loser. I don't deserve to be anywhere near your arena, though I'm honored to have been in your path.

Ben

Rouge hugged the letter to her chest. Her eyes teared. He was wrong. He had only been drunk, and Liza was seductive. He was so wrong. She would write him back and tell him... tell him what, that all was forgiven? No, that was too easy. That he wasn't second-rate? And her being first? Hah! Though she relished the compliment, reread it a few times, in fact, his judgments were wrong. If she were truthful, what she'd respond was this: *Of course you were attracted to Liza. Guys always are. It's just that I'd hoped you would have been different. I wanted you to be attracted to me.*

By the time she got back up to the kitchen, the darkness outside had softened. Light was beginning to show through. She glanced at the clock: *5:22.* Maybe she had an hour, a little more, to finish her project. Walking gingerly across the hall—Tess's room was right overhead—she slipped into

274

the living room, carefully inched away the sofa to expose the wall behind, opened the box and got to work.

She hung each series in a pie-shaped wedge, making quadrants that created a large circle of prints. At the center, its edges overlapping its neighbors, she tacked up the last photograph of Rouge with Liza—Ben's favorite, hers as well. Standing back to view the assembly, it seemed an odd collage of imagery, though intriguing. So many potential stories. Rouge crossed her arms over her chest. Her eyes stung in fatigue. She had to squint to see clearly as the lightness of early morning poured into the room. The mass of photographs was complex, disquieting if one didn't know the players, the real stories. Even if one did.

"I like it," she muttered to herself, then hurried upstairs to catch a little sleep before school.

*

Phil smelled of construction—he had been helping a friend renovate an apartment. A woman friend, it turned out, for when Liza gave him a hug, she detected perfume clinging to his skin, the sweet smell of love, or maybe just sex, faint under sweat and wood dust. Would she like a beer? That was all he had to drink, that and water. No, she wasn't thirsty. Maybe later. First, she wanted his opinion.

"Gee, I don't know, Liza," he said after going through her slides. His voice sounded tired. "They're good, don't get me wrong. You're a strong painter. Always were." He got up and opened a second bottle of beer. "You want one?" he asked again.

Liza shook her head. She could tell Phil she was no

longer drinking, but it might sound like she was going soft. The tone in his voice, the hesitation—she had expected more enthusiasm. Her own trepidation was flooding her, no room for a drink.

"So?" she nudged him.

"It's very competitive now. Especially for a woman. Sure, there's Frankenthaler and Hartigan. And Lee Krasner now that Pollock's dead. She's finally getting her due. But those are some aggressive women. They're tough." He sat back in his chair. "As are you. But they're here all the time and they have connections."

"You don't think being a student of Hofmann's would help?"

"There are tons of Hofmann students. But the bottom line is that abstract expressionism is old stuff right now. Come and gone." He put a hand on her shoulder. "Let's face it, Liza, unless you're somebody, no one gives a damn anymore."

His hand was too heavy. It was hard enough to hold herself up, even with all her weight pressing against the back of the chair.

She sighed, feeling defeated. "Shit, Phil, I don't know. I just don't know."

Phil grinned, though it was a sardonic one. "It's a helluva business being an artist. I wouldn't wish it on anyone, that's for sure."

He walked to the window, one of several in the space. The ceilings were high, the place barren except for a mattress and painting paraphernalia, a kitchen table and a small TV. With the windows open, the street noise played a Cage-like concert into the big, empty room. Sitting on the sill of an open window, Phil lit a cigar, took a few puffs. Liza was hot and tired.

Getting up, he wandered around, searching for an ashtray. "So," he said through a big exhale of smoke, "what are you really looking for, Liza?"

"What do you mean? I'm looking for a dealer, like I said."

"And then what?" he asked, putting both fists on the table, his cigar held tight in his teeth. Liza looked at him, perplexed. What the hell was he after? Phil removed the cigar from his teeth to continue. "You get a dealer, maybe, you're real lucky and he, or she, can sell some work. Then what? Because you know damn well, that changes nothing. Even if your work is successful. Even if you get a retrospective at the Whitney, nothing really changes."

Liza's quizzical look must have shocked him, for he turned strangely pale.

"You didn't hear?"

"Hear what?"

"When was the last time you talked to Hank?"

"About a year ago, when he was last here. Why? Did something happen?"

"Yeah," Phil said, looking down toward the floor. "He tried to kill himself." He paused, waiting for a response. But Liza could barely find her breath. He approached to wrap his arms around her, comfort arms, which she quickly pushed away, as though he would envelop her disbelief. She needed air.

"When? How? How did you find out?"

"Isabella called me. He doesn't want anyone to know. Naturally. Pills in his studio a week ago. You know he's been very depressed."

"Yes." Still stunned, Liza sat. And stared at her feet. All

that success come to this. How it starts as small waves of doubt, uncertain footing; *What am I doing? And why?* Slowly it spreads over you, a heavy coat of despair, until it pulls you under. No telling who will drown or who will swim back to the surface. "Yes," she answered again, though she refused to cry.

Liza chose to stay in New York one more night. The trip home seemed impossible. She slept hard, too hard to dream. To think about anything—thank God. But on the way home the next morning, as her knuckles clenched white onto the steering wheel to keep herself focused on the road ahead, Liza heard Phil's question replay itself over and over: "What are you looking for?"

Was he right? That even after sales and critical success, the emptiness would remain? Maybe success only made it worse. At least for Hank. But no, that couldn't be true, not for everyone. If it were, no one would paint.

She sighed. What then? What about her work? The answer was there. It had to be somewhere. If it weren't, she was truly deranged. Though she wondered. All these years, all this work, hundreds of canvases rolled up and stored in a stall. So appropriate, this place of exhibition. Ha! A crappy old abandoned horse stall. Not even an audience, just the indelible smell of shit. How perfect, Liza told herself then. A shell of a space, nothing inhabiting it. For what were the images really? Nothing beside color and brushstroke. Only an illusion, a trick of perception. Layers of colors to cover a flat white surface. Nothing more. It was never anything more than that. All these years, she had been driven to this—an illusion. A fucking illusion.

When she got home, she would pull every canvas out onto the driveway away from the trees. Pile them up, douse them with gasoline and set them on fire. And stand there watching them burn, for as long as it took for the snap, crackle of fire and heat to work its destruction as thick, black, oiled smoke coiled and sputtered and twisted itself free. It would be a beautiful sight, Liza imagined as she gripped the wheel. Such a release. Get rid of the mess, all of it. Just let it go.

Would that fill in her emptiness? she asked herself pointedly. The ashes of her inconsequential work. Would that give her the resolve to start again? What kind of substance is that?

She felt horribly depleted, driving with the windows down and the wind blowing in. Even the wind could blow through her, she was that brittle and barren. Just a container of ashes after all was said and done. Is that her attitude? What de Kooning saw so long ago, a glimpse into nothing. How exciting is that? Maybe that's what has been eluding her all these years. It was nothing more than a survival instinct to keep her from the truth. For, if she scraped down layer after layer and exposed herself completely, enough for the truth to be revealed, it would be only this, a big treasure chest opened to reveal... nothing.

Her hands were shaking; the car began to swerve. She had to pull over. Driving was impossible. Just up ahead was a big field, a place in the weeds to pull over. She hit the brakes and slowed onto the shoulder of the road. This was a back road, and she hadn't passed any traffic for miles. She could just sit for a while and get her bearings, if that was possible. She'd sit anyway; she felt too depressed to drive.

She should think about something positive. Rouge. Think about Rouge. Her steady, lovely face, her teenage body forming itself into maturity, standing tall in the field in front of their house, her attention captivated by something far away, an unknown adventure ahead. It was a beautiful sight. Eyes closed, Liza could see her clearly as though she were standing in the field just beside the car, so close, yet beyond Liza's reach. Even if Liza stretched herself as far as she could go, she could not touch her daughter now. There was too much distance. She was there and Liza was here and they were apart, two entities, separated completely.

There was a large tree up ahead near the road. Some crows came flapping over the car and landed in the uppermost branches, then began to cackle. Such a loud, agitating noise. Liza's head began to pound. As she drove, she had felt the infernal headache building, but now it had planted itself squarely in her skull. She had aspirin somewhere. In the glove box? She opened it and pulled out its contents. No, not there. In her purse. Emptying it onto the seat beside her, the mess landing chaotically, she had to fish around through cigarettes, pieces of paper, her wallet, pens, pencils, the stupid book she was reading, keys from the college, ah, there it is, the bottle of pills. She opened it and tapped a few into her palm and swallowed them dry.

Pills. How many did Hank take? What were they? Did he hope they'd let him just close his eyes and drift away, pain-free? What sadness he must have felt, all the more because he didn't deserve such misery, not with all his success. All that drinking didn't help, all that partying, guzzling booze until you couldn't stand, couldn't remember the fool you had made of yourself. So many artists—drunks, many of them. Were they trying to drown out sadness too, brace up their shaky foundations?

Sure, have a drink. Not standing upright yet? Have another. And another. Until you black out and forget.

Blackness. Just what does that hide? Liza remembered her father standing at the entrance to the greenhouse so many years ago, something in her memory recalling the interior as black. A portal into total darkness. She had let go of his hand and watched him enter and disappear—she could swear it swallowed him up as she stood there, unwilling to follow. Look, here comes Hank, walking right behind him. Poof, he disappeared too. The two of them, gone as she stood still, transfixed on the darkness, yet unable to move.

No, she thought. With clarity for the first time. I am not going to follow. I'm choosing a different life.

Liza imagined Rouge's voice then, faint, far away, calling her through time. Memories began flooding her. Rouge at eight fidgeting at the kitchen table while Liza drew a comb hurriedly through her hair, trying to braid it before the bus arrived. Rouge cringing at the hot washcloth needed to remove chocolate ice cream from her face. Legs wiggling in excitement, eyes aglow, as Liza concocted fantastic Halloween costumes. At twelve and thirteen, those moments of disgust at Liza's glaring oddity. How different she was from other parents. Remember when she even hated her name? "Why couldn't you have called me Mary or Sally, something the other kids wouldn't make fun of?" she had complained.

Smiling now—just the thought of her—it all made sense. Why she had chosen to have a child. What she was looking for all along. Why she couldn't ever find it through her painting. It was the maternal instinct she was after, the unconditional love that said, I will never leave you. No matter what, I will be there.

Just then, Liza thought of her mother, that image of her gentle, sweet face gazing out from the photograph. Liza imagined her walking away, abandoning her infant and husband behind her as she moved toward her death, leaving them, leaving her. Did she pause and look over her shoulder, one last smile, a wave at least, before she vanished? Liza tried to imagine the parting moment. Did she linger just a bit or did she just let go?

Suddenly a police car passed by, breaking her reverie, driving slowly a few feet ahead, then hitting the brakes—Liza watched the tail lights flash red—and backing up until he was just parallel to her. The cop reached over and rolled down his window. "Ma'am. You all right?"

Liza nodded and answered, "Yes."

"Are you sure? You're crying. You look pretty upset."

Liza put her hand to her cheeks, then felt the wet of her shirt. He was right. She had no idea. Quickly wiping her face with both hands, she shook her head slightly. "I'm okay, really. I'm fine now. Better."

The cop eyed her for a moment, then nodded emphatically. "Well, all right then, but drive carefully."

"I will."

*

Rounding the bend in the road on her bike, Rouge could see her house through the trees and make out Liza's station wagon parked in the back. She hit the brakes, dragging her shoes against the dirt surface to slow to a stop. She knew her mother would be back any day now, but until this moment, Liza's return was a concept only, an event held at bay by the pleasure of time alone with Tess. They had cleaned the house, discarding much of the junk that Liza perpetually saved, even the outdated jars of blueberry jam. They had shopped and filled the pantry. While Rouge was at school, Tess made new curtains for the front windows and started a dress. They had selected the pattern together. After dinner, they had walked to the river and sat on the banks until twilight. They had talked of her coming to Boston this year for Christmas. They had such fun. And now this, Rouge thought, stopped in the road, watching Tess come out the kitchen door, walk to the car, take something out, shove the car door closed with her hip. Rouge bit her bottom lip. Hard.

She was not ready for this. All that easy, uncomplicated time with Tess over. Like a perfect dream. If only she could go back to sleep and find it again. As if that ever happened, she thought. It usually slid into a nightmare or some eerie contortion of what she had dreamt earlier, the penalty for refusing to accept the advancing of time. Still, she hated that these few days were over. She could at least stand there in the middle of the road and have her feelings, privately. Time can't penalize her for stopping a few minutes. She wasn't going backward, after all. She was just trying to stay still, not move a muscle. Hold onto that space between past and present just a few seconds longer.

It was a clear, sunny fall day, everything buzzing and chirping as usual. The only anomaly was her standing so long in the road. The cows lifted their heads from the ground and gazed in her direction, chewing and chewing, their jaws working in circular motion, their bells ringing softly. They must think her a freak; look how they stare. Rouge stared back, hanging onto their huge brown eyes, the flaring of their nostrils, their tails busy after flies. Ignoring time, she waited, though she felt a countdown brewing. Five, four, three... Tess would see her in the window or Liza, eventually. Something or someone would break the safety of this moment.

And then? And then, she'd have to begin making the effort to keep her promise to Tess. How easy that had been when it was just she and Tess together, different now, a Herculean task that loomed before her. To remember Liza loves her and all the instructions inherent in that: you must condone her foibles, her mistakes. You must not be ashamed when she makes a fool of herself, when you overhear people talking in town, see raised eyebrows. You must hold your head high and defend her and be proud of her individuality, for she is definitely unique. You must be understanding and, most important, forgiving—because more than anything else, she loves you. And that counts for everything. Everything!

The cows dropped their heads and went back to ripping grass from the ground, sometimes clumps of dirt as well that swung around and around until they were finally chewed free. It was time. Feeling like a weathered wooden figure, she began wheeling herself home slowly, not pedaling, just pushing the ground with her feet as slowly as she could. Dreading the inevitable—Liza was back. Rouge felt sick.

But she had promised Tess. She'd have to make an effort. Leaning her bike against the back wall of the house, Rouge took a deep breath before entering the kitchen, as though she could blow all her negative feelings away, that hardness in her stomach. Liza and Tess were drinking tea,

Tess chattering to Liza, who stood against the refrigerator, arms crossed, leaning back. Seeing Rouge, Liza smiled, but she did not move.

"There you are." Tess twirled around, hearing the back door open. "Look who's back."

Rouge forced a grin, set her book bag down on the kitchen table and walked over to give Liza a hug. She forced every ounce of herself into that hug, holding her tight, remembering to keep holding, though she couldn't wait to spring back and let her go. "Welcome back," she added as she finally stepped away. "Did you have a productive trip?" Did she come across as stilted as she felt? Rouge tried to smile but she was sure her lips were only splitting into a painstaking smirk. Just stay neutral, she told herself, or you'll give everything away.

Liza was quiet, strangely reserved. Not enthusiastic nor flat, just neutral. Rouge couldn't read her. "Well, yes and no," she finally answered. "It was certainly helpful and I got a few leads."

Tess took over then. "She has a few possibilities. Things are looking up."

"That's good," Rouge answered, nodding her head, inching back to her book bag. "So, do you need any help with dinner? Unpacking the car?"

"No," Liza said. "We got everything. But thanks."

"Well, I've got work to do. I should get started."

"Just a minute," Tess spoke up, putting a hand on Rouge's shoulder to put an end to this charade—Tess must have read through her reticence. Rouge could feel the weight of Tess's awareness in her grip as she took the book bag from her and set it back on the table. "Before you rush on out of here, we have a few things to discuss. I have to go soon and I can't leave until the air is cleared."

"But?" Rouge looked at Tess, pleading.

"Sit."

Rouge sat as much as she was pushed down into the chair. Tess's eyes were on her like a spotlight, overpowering her completely. Rouge felt stripped and powerless beneath Tess's impatient glare, Liza's, too, as she leaned against the refrigerator. Had the two women decided to gang up on her? They must have, that easy camaraderie between them. It was always there, wasn't it? Now, too. Rouge knew they were going after her. But what was this interrogation? She was not to blame.

"What?" she blurted out from the prison of the chair.

Liza stepped up to the table. "Can we ever move past this? What more can I say except that I'm sorry? I'm sorry about Ben."

The thought of Ben stung Rouge then. It all seemed ridiculous, nothing she could argue for anyway. It was a stupid dream. She felt momentarily childish, but then angry. Ben was shoved completely out of the way.

"What about the others?" Rouge began to yell. "All the others, the men. You never care about the men. You don't care about anyone. Just your goddamn painting. Only your painting!"

Liza stepped toward her. "That's not true. Not true at all."

"You just sleep around, you don't care. Then you expect me to clean everything up. You always have."

Liza was speechless. Tess, too. Liza looked imploringly at Tess. Tess nodded to her.

"And what about my father?"

Again this question? They had gone over it so many times before.

"What about him?"

"You didn't even care about him. What if he wanted to know? What if he wanted to be included? Maybe he would have cared." Tears began streaming down Rouge's face. She hadn't even felt them coming on until they were there. Tess moved toward her, but Rouge stood as though to step away. She wanted so badly to say the thing that was stuck in the back of her throat. *Maybe he would have loved me.* But she couldn't. She couldn't relinquish those words. That hope. She couldn't bear to let it go. So she turned and rushed out the room and up the stairs.

"Let her go." She heard Tess's words as she reached the hallway upstairs. Then she slammed her door, fell down on her bed and cried.

It felt like hours until she was completely drained, though it was still light outside. Finally, she felt she could take a breath. Then another. And another, breathing again and again as though she were reviving herself. Getting over her resentment felt an insurmountable task. A wound now, an indelible internal scar, but she felt some relief.

There were footsteps then, below her room, Tess and Liza going into the living room, which was just below. Rouge remembered her photographs, still on the wall. She was surprisingly curious and leaned over the edge of the bed to get closer to the floor, feeling her head fill with blood as she strained to listen.

"Look what Rouge did." She could make out Tess's words,

but just barely. Tess had loved the work—loved it!—when she first saw it, said the installation of the images was brilliant.

Rouge couldn't hear Liza's response. All she caught was Tess saying something about dinner, then one pair of feet walking out.

After some time, she heard Tess's footsteps coming up the stairs, toward her room, then stop. There was a faint knock, then she pushed the door open, not waiting for a response. She came over to Rouge, pushed some hair away from her eyes.

"I made dinner if you'd like some."

Rouge felt ravenous. "I'll be down in a minute," she said.

Coming down the stairs to dinner, Rouge caught sight of Liza sitting in a chair in the living room, staring at the wall. Rouge could have sworn there was a tear running down one of her cheeks. She did not stop, but hurried into the kitchen. A few minutes later when Liza joined them, she did not look as if she had been crying. Quite the contrary. Her face was fresh, almost glowing. The air in the kitchen was now inviting, no remnant at all of the earlier confrontation lingering. Taking her chair, Liza put her hand on Rouge's arm and smiled.

"Incredible work. Just incredible."

Rouge could have melted right then and there, but Liza's touch kept her solid.

She smiled back, ever so slightly. Then nodded and began to eat. Tess had made meatloaf, her favorite.

*

"Let her go." Tess had put a hand on Liza's shoulder as the two of them watched Rouge rush out the room, Liza longing to speak, to answer her, to hold her in her sadness. Tess was right. This was Rouge's sadness and, no matter what Liza had to say, to feel for her even, it would always be Rouge's. Never hers. Rouge was wrong, Liza had wanted to tell her with absolute certainty, *I do care about others, mostly about you.* But in the wake of what Rouge had to say about her father, it seemed out of place and selfish. Maybe, if he had known, he would have loved her. Did Liza also rob her of that?

They stayed silent after she left, knowing there was nothing to add to what Rouge had painfully acknowledged. There'd be time to discuss it later. Instead, they'd talk about other things. As always, Tess found a more appropriate subject.

"I saw Rouge's work from the summer."

Liza looked sheepish. "Really?"

"Really. Come with me." Tess led Liza toward the living room. "Look at what Rouge did."

There on the wall were photographs everywhere, one giant circle of images hanging in overlapping quadrants— Ben alone, Rouge alone, Ben and Liza, Liza and Rouge. Photographs of moments she'd remembered, that incessant clicking of the camera as she sat on the porch talking with Ben or the two of them carrying groceries from the car. The ones she had seen that night on the table, portraits of Rouge, of Ben, the two of them such cohorts. Liza sickened momentarily at the sight of them, recalling that horrible moment that had prodded her actions. Remarkably telling, these pictures—Ben dreamy and unsatisfied; Rouge striking, lovely, growing without effort into her confidence. Liza paused at these portraits and marveled at what they revealed.

But then these others? That awkward interruption when he had caught Rouge and Liza together on the verge of an argument. How shocked she had been at the intrusion into this private moment with her daughter, exposed and caught on film. At first, she hated it, the anger and surprise and need for flight so obvious in her eyes, her twirling and rushing away, her desperation to escape that turned her into nothing but a blur. But Rouge stood there, almost unaffected. Strong, solid, enduring. That was the image that held her attention.

"Well, I have to get dinner going." Tess interrupted her reverie.

"Do you want some help?" Liza answered without looking away.

"No, I'm fine."

"I'll come help in a moment."

"No hurry." Then she was gone.

Thankfully. Though Liza had almost forgotten Tess's presence, she welcomed solitude in which to better study this installation, the sensitivity of Rouge's eye. Liza relished the way she had hung each photograph, the relationships between them alone and as a whole with Rouge at the center, the focal point holding everything together, creating harmony out of the disparate tension around her.

Such enormous talent this girl possessed! Liza welled up with pride, the warmth filling her up, up, until it spilled over the edge and ran softly down her cheeks. She thought she heard a sound behind her, but when she turned, no one was there. Then she heard Tess calling for dinner. Using her sleeves, Liza wiped her face dry, then rubbed her eyes back into a presentable appearance. Hearing Rouge's footsteps patter around the kitchen, Liza waited until she felt ready, then came to the table and took her seat between Rouge and Tess. Rouge could still be angry, it didn't matter. Liza was sure of herself and that was all she needed.

She put her hand on Rouge's arm and spoke quickly. "Incredible work. Just incredible." And Rouge let her hold on, one second, two seconds more than was necessary. Once Rouge smiled, Liza could release her and begin to eat.

Rouge retreated to her room after dinner. Her excuse was true—she did have a paper, a first draft to finish—and Tess began talking about the fall, the commission that awaited her, some executive's wife. She would be leaving the day after next. And later, after the two of them finally went to bed, Liza put aside her reading, tiptoed down to the living room, switched on the dim side table light and stood in front of the photographs once again. This time to study the one in the center and get a feel for the forms.

Rouge was looking toward the camera, sharply in focus while Liza blurred into oblivion off to the left side. Two models for humanity, she decided—the static and the dynamic, the strong and the weak, curiosity and fear. Daughter, mother. Such difference in the forms, yet such similarities, too.

As she stared at the photograph, Hofmann's lecture came back to her. She could still recall the sound of his Germanic voice, the words uttered emphatically: *Every subject has a characteristic basic form. The choice of basic form is dependent on the artist's feeling for his subject. His feeling develops from comparisons. Comparisons provide a perception of oppositions and relationships. Only through relationships and opposition can form be defined...*

Yes, Liza thought, tracing the forms with her fingers. That's it. Comparisons. That's the dynamic that has been missing from the work, the oppositions and relationships. How clear it is in this photograph. The clarification and purpose of form.

Liza longed to be in her studio, hoping there was an adequate supply of canvas there. Rushing out of the room— she did not even turn off the light—she hurried outside, across the backyard and into the barn. She would have stacked unused canvas in one of the horse stalls. There it was, a large roll suspended on a rack above the floor, the second roll she had bought last spring in a burst of optimism about the amount of work she'd planned to accomplish over summer. Thankfully, there was plenty left.

She carried the canvas into the studio and rolled it out on the floor. Six feet wide, she paced out another nine feet and cut it off there. Pouring gesso into a rolling pan, she covered the surface, then nailed it up to the wall to dry. It would not take long, a few hours maybe. In the meantime, she would make a few sketches.

The work from the summer was still propped up against the walls. It hadn't been touched since the night Ben saw it. Liza studied each painting and remembered her recent desire to relinquish agitated brushwork and let forms direct the composition. This early work had only begun the transition. She had yet to bring it to completion. Now she understood why. She knew what had been missing—confidence in her forms.

She squeezed out some paints onto her palette, black, whites and pale yellows, blues and reds. Then she cleaned four big brushes, set down her rag, scooped up a dollop of black in the largest brush and approached the canvas.

*

The sun was still high in the sky when Rouge left school, though the afternoon light was already changing, the air laced with coolness, the first hint of impending cold weather. Rouge wasn't ready for winter. She felt the same way each fall, the warmth of summer disappearing too quickly, the smells, the colors, the abundance of the natural world. And Tess leaving. She hated that. But Tess had promised to come back at the end of October to make applesauce and carve pumpkins. "We'll be monsters together," she had decreed before driving off, leaving Rouge standing in the driveway. Liza stayed back by the barn door, having taken a break from her painting to come out and say goodbye. She had returned to her studio by the time Rouge had turned around, Tess's car well out of sight.

That was three days ago. She rode home quickly. Rounding the sharp bend in the road that was the marker for their house coming up on the right, she realized she had forgotten to get paper for her presentation, facts about the Industrial Revolution in England that would be clipped into neat paragraphs and mounted around illustrations. She stopped and considered turning around. Maybe Liza would have paper. She had all those big drawing pads; surely she could spare a sheet or two. But Rouge was reluctant to intrude. Liza had been working almost non-stop for over five days—every free moment around her classes—and would not welcome the interruption. Possibly there was some paper out by the unused canvases and rolled up paintings in the barn.

The studio door was shut tight. Rouge moved about

carefully, inspecting the contents of the stalls. There were many rolled canvases, buckets, cans of turpentine and linseed oil, ladders and a variety of tools. Finally, she found large pads of paper slid in between several big paintings, two, three, six, eight, so many of them, Liza wouldn't mind if Rouge took a few sheets. She'd probably never notice.

Sliding out one pad, Rouge set it on the floor and flipped open the cover. She was shocked by what she saw. It was a drawing of her when she was, what, about eight? She had two long braids and was wearing overalls and was painting something on a doll's face she held up close to her own. The drawing was almost photographic, rich in detail and true to the image. Nothing abstract about it. She turned to the next page. It was another drawing, done about the same time, braids and all, this time Rouge pouting about something. The next, more braids, Rouge peeking through sunflowers. She remembered that game, hiding between the legs of sunflower giants. There she was asleep, those damn braids sticking out of her head like straw against the pillow. Rouge went through every drawing, then pulled out another pad, this one images of her at about five or six. Another pad was Rouge later, ten, maybe. She would have been in fifth grade from the look of her. Yes, she had a guinea pig then, and there he was.

It was dark outside. Rouge must have been at it for hours, pulling out every pad she could find, savoring each drawing as she leafed through her childhood, recalling the specific incident that provoked each pose. The details were labored and perfect—Liza was an incredible artist. The hours and hours she must have devoted to these. Rouge felt humbled. What dedication her mother had. She had preserved an entire childhood in drawings. Not photographs, nothing so instantaneous as that. No, these were works of serious endeavor and concentration. Works, she realized as she closed the last pad, that could only have been created out of love.

Rouge remembered then what Tess had said to her on the riverbank earlier, words that she couldn't stand to hear then. "Remember Liza loves you more than anything else." She hadn't believed it at the time, thinking that was simply one of Tess's optimistic exaggerations said to smooth things over, as Tess would typically do. But it was no exaggeration at all. The time that had gone into these drawings—there had to be more than a hundred of them. All that time Liza spent in the studio, the bulk of it had to have been used up doing these. All that time that Rouge disparaged her work, thought it obsessive and chaotic and wondered what the hell was going on. Why couldn't she paint things that mattered, that made her happy? Well, Liza had certainly surprised her with this body of work. And that she had been at it all along.

Replacing the last pad just as she had found it, Rouge went to the studio door and rapped softly. "Liza, can I come in?"

There was no answer; Rouge would have to speak up. She did and knocked a little more loudly. Still no reply, so she opened the door and stuck her head in. What she saw nearly bowled her over.

The entire back wall was covered with paintings— three huge panels, masses of lilac and black on each, faint areas of brushwork, beiges, whites and grays in between holding them together or maybe not, because the forms were beautifully defined, each against the other. The sheer magnitude of them alone was impressive, but the serenity of the work took Rouge's breath away.

Liza was sitting on a stool in the middle of the room, smoking, transfixed at the wall.

"So, what do you think?" she asked over her shoulder.

Rouge could barely find her voice. "I think, I think… they're amazing. Really, Liza, this is really… beautiful."

Liza smiled, took another hit off her cigarette and looked back at the wall. "Good," she finally said through an exhalation of smoke. "I'm glad you like it. Because it's for you. I'm calling it *Field for Rouge.*"

Tremors of excitement ran through Rouge. She thought she might crack into a million pieces, wanting so much to share everything with Liza all at once: the drawings, Ben, the photographs, the misguided feelings and attitudes and assumptions, all that was wrong, but more, all that was right. There was enough to break her apart, so to save herself, Rouge decided to say nothing. She'd savor it all first and reveal it, slowly, deliberately, when she was ready.

For now, she only smiled. Then added, "And where the hell are you going to hang it?"

Liza turned, gave her a wink, and responded with a shrug of her shoulders. "Haven't a clue."

*

Liza was working in the garden, clearing debris from vegetables whose time was over. It was early October, the nights grown too cool to sustain the bounty of summer, the zucchini and yellow squashes, beans, tomatoes, all finished for the year. Liza had been up early, clearing paths, her hands and knees clumped with dirt. The sun, now high in the sky, had finally baked away the chill of early morning. It must be about eleven, Liza thought, dumping the last of the tomato plants into the wheelbarrow. Rouge was still asleep. She's been working hard all week. Let her have her rest.

A car was coming up the road, driving slowly, as though its passengers were scouting early for fall leaves. By the time it reached their driveway, it was moving at a crawl. Liza looked up. Who could be coming? Had she made an appointment with a student? No, it's too early in the semester for critiques. Maybe someone was lost and stopping for directions. She got up off her knees to see.

The car—a yellow sporty thing—was turning in the driveway. There were two men, but she could not see them clearly through the windshield, just the bulk of them. A hand went up from the window of the passenger seat as though to wave. What? Liza wondered, stepping out of the garden and making her way to meet them as the car pulled up beside hers and came to a rest.

The window on the driver's side was down, and Liza saw a middle-aged man grinning at her. Glasses, slicked-back hair. Who the hell is he? Frowning at what she perceived to be an unwelcome intrusion, she wiped her hands on her pants, getting ready to send the pair on their way. As she did, the passenger door opened, a hand appeared on the roof, and Ben unfurled himself from the vehicle.

"Oh my God," Liza found herself muttering under her breath. "What are you doing here?" Stepping forward quickly, she tensed in recognition. "I wasn't expecting to see you. At least this soon."

He blushed and raised his eyebrows up, then down.

Their private conversation quickly over, he introduced the driver. "Hello, Liza. I have someone I want you to meet. This is Max Gruen. He's a dealer in the city and would like to see your work."

Max hopped out of his car and extended a hand. "Yes, Ben has told me you're quite the painter. I'm particularly interested in women artists. There's huge, untapped talent among women, and I'm eager to find it."

Liza was blushing now, embarrassed at her disheveled appearance after so many hours in the garden. She had heard of Gruen—he represented some impressive artists. She looked up at Rouge's window, her shades still drawn, then turned back, smiling at the dealer. "Well, I'm afraid I wasn't expecting anyone in my studio. It's rather a mess."

"So, you'll match nicely," Ben added, and all three of them laughed.

"Let me just clean up a bit. I'll be right back." Liza hurried inside and up the stairs.

"Rouge, Rouge." She was rapping hard on her door.

"What?" a sleepy voice answered, rife with teenage indignation. Liza stuck her head in. This was not news to shout down the hall in passing.

"I just want to warn you. Ben is here. He's brought a dealer."

"Damn." Rouge sat up, her hair tumbling around her. She pushed it out of her face, her eyes shutting against the abrupt awakening.

"I know," Liza answered her. They had not yet talked about Ben. Not directly anyway. It might be one of those subjects too touchy to ever handle, one that would forever remain unspoken. That might be easier. To let it drift away over time. Until it just became something distant, a speck in their emotional terrain, far enough away to render it powerless. But now he was here. So much for avoidance. "Whatever you want to do is fine with me. We can pretend you're not here. You could be at Shelly's or something."

Rouge was rubbing her face. "I don't know, Liza. Let me wake up first." She had meant to write him, to respond to his letter at least. There had been drafts started, many awkward attempts, but she hadn't been satisfied yet.

"Take your time. I'm going to show the dealer the new work. I won't say anything about you." Closing the door, she left to change.

The two men were walking around the property, out by the road, Ben pointing to O'Neil's fields across from them, when Liza approached. "I was just showing him where the river ran through the valley," he said as he turned, sensing her proximity.

"I can see why you live here," Max added. "It's certainly a beautiful place."

"It's that." Liza motioned with her head toward the studio. "I would ask you to wait while I cleaned the place up, but that could very well take all day."

Max laughed. "A clean artist's studio? A bit of an oxymoron, isn't it?"

"C'mon, then." Liza turned and led the way up the driveway, across the backyard, into the barn, then up to the door, which she opened quickly, before stepping aside to let the men through. The big painting, Rouge's painting, greeted them, its presence dominating the large white room.

Ben whistled. Max said nothing—though Liza swore she heard him take a sharp breath. He walked slowly to the center of the room and stood before the painting. Ben whispered into Liza's ear. "Wow. You've done it now. You've really done it."

His words were appreciated, but only that. Liza didn't need to hear them because she already knew. She had found her attitude, she had no doubt about it, even while she was painting. It was there guiding the work, her brushstrokes, the composition, not magic at all. Authority drove this painting, and she had felt it every bit of the way.

Liza was not really surprised either when Max finally turned to her, his face beaming. "This is magnificent. Absolutely magnificent. I haven't seen anything quite like it. Do you have others?"

While she showed him the paintings from the summer, she relayed stories from her days as a student in New York and how, without naming names, she was trying to break free of those influences. Ben sat on the stool and watched, his hands planted firmly on his knees. He was smiling; Liza did notice that, as well as his occasional glances out the window that faced the house. However, he didn't ask about Rouge, not a word. He just grinned and waited as Liza pulled out a few more paintings from the stalls.

"That's about it," she said, "at least of the current work."

"Well, I can't believe you haven't been snapped up yet. I would love to have you in the gallery. In fact, I want to give you a show."

"Really?" Liza gasped, turning to Ben beaming, then back to Max. "This is very good news."

When she looked back at Ben, she saw him staring toward the door. Rouge was standing in the threshold. How long had she been there?

"Did you hear?" Liza asked. She couldn't help blurting out her excitement.

"Yeah," Rouge nodded. "That's great. Really great news."

"Max, this is my daughter, Rouge. Rouge, Max Gruen."

The two stepped toward one another to shake hands. Max took hers warmly. "Yes, I've heard about you. Quite the photographer, I'm told."

Rouge flushed and let go of his hand. "Maybe." She turned toward Ben. "Hello, Ben, how are you?"

He was standing, not moving. His face stayed neutral, measured. "Good. How are you?"

Suddenly the air between them became stifling. Liza doubted Max sensed it, but she did. More than anything, she wanted to break them up, save her daughter from this discomfort. It was her mess. Why should her daughter have to suffer her mistake? Then she thought, wait, it's not that simple. Rouge has her own issues, independent of hers. It is not her place to interfere. This is Rouge's life, after all.

Max touched Liza's arm. "Do you want to show me earlier paintings?" he asked quietly, as though not wanting to speak above the silent dialogue going on between Rouge and Ben.

But it was Rouge who answered. "Why don't you. I was thinking of asking Ben if he'd like to take a walk."

"Yeah," Ben nodded, "Liza and Max have business to discuss anyway. A walk would be good."

Rouge preceded him out the studio. Side by side, they wandered silently down the driveway, across the road and toward the river. Almost without intent. Rouge hadn't thought that far ahead. She was too busy assembling what

301

was worth saying and discarding what was not. Feeling embarrassed, she was also surprisingly collected and this, more than uncertainty or even humiliation, was taking the lead. The field had been cut down in late August and the path through the grass was exposed now, clear all the way to the river.

"Have you been working much?" She looked down as she spoke, as though watching for shafts of dry grass that would jab into her bare feet.

"Yup, mostly shooting artists' work for dealers. It's the beginning of a new season. Things are busy now."

"That's good." She could tell he was embarrassed.

"And you? You've got school, of course. But have you had time to shoot?"

"Not really. I have a bitch of a history teacher. Tons of assignments already." They had reached the river and sat down on the bank, close but not touching. The river was low, though deep in a few places, yet there were many more rocks exposed, interrupting the easy flow.

Here, Rouge was at a loss. The niceties were easy. The rest, tough. What did she want to say?

But he began for her. "Look, Rouge, what happened. I'm really sorry. It was…" He picked up a stone and dropped it back and forth into his palms. She waited. What would he say? "Well, it was… I was…"

It all seemed too much of a knot, too big to ever untangle. They each knew their own strands, she realized, what they brought to the mess. It was highly personal and should remain private. No need for explanations. It had happened and was over.

She put her hand on his arm, then looked over at him,

making real eye contact for the first time. "It's okay, you don't need to explain. It's complicated for all of us. Let's just leave it at that."

Though his expression remained solemn, he was relieved. She could tell by the feel of his arm relaxing. Then he threw his stone into the river.

He was suddenly buoyant, looking her way. "You have to keep photographing. You have an extraordinary eye. I hope you don't lose touch with your talent."

Rouge grinned, one side of her mouth only, but her eyes were twinkling.

"Well, I signed up to take pictures for the yearbook."

"All right then. I won't have to worry about you," he said.

She laughed, then rose slowly and stood over him, lingering a moment, watching the river as it burbled along. Rouge was remembering his letter. She had memorized it, every word. In it, he had made no mention of Liza. Had he done that on purpose to spare Rouge's feelings? To keep them separate? Did he think Liza was first-rate too, or only second? That question kept coming up every time she repeated the letter to herself. It had bothered her, then; it disquieted her now. She could not help herself. She had to ask.

Turning toward him again, she asked, "What about Liza? How do you rate her, first or second?"

He bit his lower lip. "Liza?" There was wonder in his voice and caution, too. "Liza's pretty much in a league of her own. She's a hard one to judge." He picked up another stone.

Rouge put her hand on his shoulder. But just for a moment. "I'm going back. Are you coming?"

Ben threw the stone. "I'll be up in a minute. I want to soak up a little more of this bucolic scenery before I'm back in the world of cement and steel."

"I'll see you up there, then."

Liza left Max in the studio to go through some drawings. She needed a little fresh air to calm her exhilaration, maybe a smoke. Sitting on the porch, gazing over the valley, she spotted the heads of Rouge and Ben down by the river. They were talking. That was good. Then Rouge got up, but not urgently, and she stood over him, her head slightly cocked. Liza could not discern her mood from this distance. Rouge was putting her hand on Ben's shoulder. Some sort of affirmation, Liza hoped. They stayed this way a bit longer, until Rouge turned and started walking away.

She did not look up as she made her way along the path through O'Neil's field. She probably had no idea Liza was even on the porch, watching. She just kept her eyes focused on the ground, walking slowly, thoughtfully, making her way home.

Acknowledgements

The following works of nonfiction were invaluable while researching the New York artworld of the 1940s and 50s: *Joan Mitchell: Lady Painter* by Patricia Albers; *The Party's Over* by John Gruen; *Arshile Gorky: His Life and Works* by Hayden Herrera; *Jackson Pollock: An American Saga* by Steven Naifeh and Gregory Smith; and *de Kooning: An American Master* by Mark Stevens and Annalyn Swan. I'm indebted to William Boyd for his wonderful novel *Any Human Heart* from which I borrowed a favorite character, Logan Mountstuart, for a brief scene. I am also indebted to my many artist friends who gave me so much insight into the precarious arena of art-making.

Heartfelt thanks to Christine Lehner, Rosemary Ahern, Liza McKenzie and writer mentor extraordinaire Nancy Packer for their wisdom and discerning advice. Life, as well as writing, would have been so bland without the friendship and encouragement of James Bohnen, Melanie Fleischman, Carolyn Forsman, Jill Goodman, Amy Hemmert, Marianna Houston, Stacy Schiff, and Lisa Schmucki.

Alex and Jake showed me the true meaning of life.

Finally, I owe an incalculable debt to David Kimball Anderson. Without his prodding and enthusiasm this book could never have seen the light of day. Thank you for all you taught me about art, hard work, integrity and faith in one's abilities.

About the Author

Lis Bensley has written for *The New York Times, The International Herald Tribune, ArtNews, Elle Décor, Fine Cooking, and the Santa Fean.* She is author of *The Women's Health Cookbook* and *The Adventures of Milo and Flea. The Glimpse* is her first novel. She lives in northern California.